NORTH OF NOWHERE
SOUTH OF LOSS

**Other books by
Janette Turner Hospital**

Novels
The Ivory Swing
The Tiger in the Tiger Pit
Borderline
Charades
The Last Magician
Oyster
Due Preparations for the Plague

Short Stories
Dislocations
Isobars
Collected Stories

JANETTE TURNER HOSPITAL

NORTH OF NOWHERE
SOUTH OF LOSS

W. W. Norton & Company
New York   London

For information about permission to reproduce selections from this book,
write to Permissions, W. W. Norton & Company, Inc., 500 Fifth Avenue,
New York, NY 10110

Manufacturing by Quebecor Fairfield

Library of Congress Cataloging-in-Publication Data
Hospital, Janette Turner, 1942–
North of Nowhere, South of Loss / Janette Turner Hospital— 1st American
ed.

ISBN 0-393-05991-X (hardcover)

1. Australia—Social life and customs—Fiction. 2. Southern states—Social life
and customs—Fiction.
I. Title.
PR9619.3.H674N67 2004
823'.914—dc22

2004054723

W. W. Norton & Company, Inc., 500 Fifth Avenue, New York, N.Y. 10110
www.wwnorton.com

W. W. Norton & Company Ltd., Castle House,
75/76 Wells Street, London W1T 3QT

1 2 3 4 5 6 7 8 9 0

For Peter
1942–1998
In memoriam

CONTENTS

NORTH OF NOWHERE
SOUTH OF LOSS

THE OCEAN OF BRISBANE

His voice came out of the black space between the two projectors. When a slide slipped off the wall, dropping into nowhere, the tiered funnel of the lecture theatre was so dark that the darkness seemed to rub itself against her, furry, like the legs of spiders. She shivered. Then a bubble of light would come, a coloured diagram or a photograph would appear on the screen straight ahead but below her, and words would unfold themselves on the other screen, the one that was angled across a corner of the room, high up, and therefore eye-level with the tier where she sat. She would see him then for a moment, shadowy, a juggler of ideas, images, impenetrable words, remote control buttons, a magician waving his arms in the twilight cast by the screens.

I watched her watching him.

She was trying to explain him to herself.

I watched how she held onto her own body, arms hugged tightly, and how she kept shivering (it *looked* like shivering) in the sweltering airless room.

Don't worry, I wanted to whisper to her. I wanted to put my hand on her arm, soothing, but it would have alarmed her. Don't worry, I wanted to whisper. He's just as much a mystery to himself.

He spoke, and his words settled lightly onto the cantilevered screen in black block capitals, crowding, jostling like branches full of crows, she had always been frightened of crows, the way they swooped at you, dive-bombed, that time on the farm at Camp Mountain, long before Brisbane, she was still a child at Camp Mountain, the beaks slashing at her head (or maybe magpies, was it? had they been magpies?), they go for the eyes, *Always wear a hat*, teachers warned, *and if attacked, cover the eyes.*

ELECTRON MICROSCOPY, the screen said.

OF CRYSTALS.

And then in a fluttering rush: OF AN ALPHA-HELICAL COILED-COIL PROTEIN EXTRACTED FROM THE OOTHECA OF THE PRAYING MANTIS.

The black letters swooped at her and instinctively she covered her eyes. I watched the way her hands shook slightly (how would she speak to him? how had they *ever* really? and yet after all these years she had been hoping ... but what language could they possibly use?) and all the time, through her fingers, she was watching for crevices of hope, for something to grab onto, and *there* was something, *crystals*, yes, she recognised that, he used to have a set, those heavy headphones, telling them he could hear Indonesia, England, the cricket scores, winding the world into his room, swallowing it, he had this terrible hunger, this unnatural ... this kind of greed, she could never predict what ... and it was never big enough for him even then, his room, their house, their lives, Brisbane, the country, the world, he was like one of those alien children on the late late movies, growing into strangeness, his mind butting against the ceiling, webbed toes, a third eye, foreign to her from the beginning. She pressed a hand against her stomach and stared at it. Where had he come from?

"Coiled-coil," he was saying, from the dark space between the projectors. On the lower screen were intricate diagrams that looked like tangled chain-necklaces, or twisted ropes of sausages perhaps. "Solving the structures," he said. "Electron diffraction ... especially certain membrane-embedded protein strings resistant to X-ray imaging." A ghostly pointer picked out the braided strings, and she turned to look at me suddenly, so specifically, that I heard her thoughts, heard the click of association, or saw it, and felt for my plaits against my shoulders. It was like groping for an amputated limb, the coiled coils of childhood.

It seems only yesterday ... her look said.

The coiled coils of language, I thought, and knotted myself into the puzzle. I saw diagrams of shared and divergent lives braiding and unbraiding themselves. Alpha-helical, alphabetical, we both rode in an Alfa Romeo once, it belonged to someone his older brother knew, I think, someone from Sydney, the wind whipping through the coiled coils of our hair and we two thinking we were Christmas, swimming through Brisbane like fish. There was nothing to it in those days. We could walk on water. We thought we were the beginning and the end, the ant's pants, the ootheca of the praying mantis, no less.

O-ith-*ee*-ka,

    oh I *thee* thir,

        thaid the blind man

            though he couldn't thee at all.

What the hell did *ootheca* mean?

Bet you don't know, bet I do, don't, do, don't too, do so, don't, do. Those two, our mothers used to say, will argue till the cows come home. Fish out of water, other kids' mothers said, but we weren't, we were in our own element, we porpoised through books, we dived into argument, we rode our bikes into endless discussion and rainforest trails where we disappeared and swam in private time, no time, timeless rainforest rockpool debate time. We cavorted in the ocean of Brisbane, our own little pond.

I computed the odds against solving the structure of memory which dissolves and devolves and solves nothing.

Afterwards, waiting for him under the jacarandas, we fanned ourselves with the lecture handouts. From time to time, she smoothed hers out against her skirt and studied it with intense concentration, as though memorisation of the print might yield up a meaning. When she saw me looking, a kind of rash flared across her cheeks and she scrunched the handout into a fan again and whipped it back and forth. She said nervously, apologetically: "Me and his dad ..." Then she panicked about her grammar and bit her lip and began again. "His father and me ... *I*, I should say, I and his dad ... the Depression and the war and everything ... You know, Philippa, I'm sure Brian's told you, we only got to Grade 6."

"Oh heck," I said, "Brian's stuff is double-dutch to me too. To nearly everyone. To 99.9 per cent of the people in the world, I would say."

"Is it?"

"Oh God, yes. Brian lives in the stratosphere. He's really — oh, please don't, Mrs Leckie."

"I thought ..." She was fumbling in her handbag, sniffling. "I'm not very ... I thought it was just me. I don't want to embarrass him."

"You won't, you *won't*! How could you even think such a ..." There were people jostling us, and we had to step back, step aside, adjust ourselves. We eased our way to the outside edge of the crowd, beyond the cloisters, away from the hot blanket of bodies. "He's proud as punch that you're here. Look, he's just coming out now, he's looking around for you, see?" I waved madly and Brian made a sign of acknowledgment with his hand and went on talking to some colleague.

"You can't blame him," she said meekly. "It's just, sometimes we wished ... his dad wished ..." She mopped at her face with the Kleenex she had fished from her bag.

"It's dreadfully sticky, isn't it?" I could feel runnels of sweat making a slow tickling descent across my ribcage.

"I wished for his dad's sake." She studied her much creased fan again, its print smudging from sweat and oil. *Electron microscopy of crystals of an alpha-helical* ... "Me, actually, to tell you the truth, Philippa, I got to Grade 8 but I never let on. Not while his Dad was alive." A little smile passed between us, woman to woman — *Well, that's what we do, isn't it?* — and then she said wistfully, "His dad used to talk to him about the crystal set, he understood all that, they used them in the war, I think."

Delicately, with the thumb and index finger of both hands — handbag slung at crook of left elbow, lecture handout pressed under upper right arm — she took hold of the front of her bodice, just below the shoulders on each side, and lifted the polyester away from her body, raising it gently, lowering, raising, a quick light motion, ventilating herself. "*Your* dad, Philippa. That was a nasty bit of a turn. Is he all right?"

"Yes," I said, startled. "He's fine." I fanned myself vigorously, guiltily, because I had forgotten, completely forgotten, *like a fist squeezing his heart, he says,* an item in letters, *just a warning, the doctor says, Doctor Williams it was, you remember him, he says at our age you've got to expect* ... "How did you —?"

"Your mum, I think it was, told me ... yes, I saw her on the bus one day. Going into the city. We had a chat about you and Brian."

"Oh dear!"

"She had pictures of all the grandchildren in her purse, I couldn't get over it, little Philippa Townsend with those big teenagers. And all that snow, I just can't imagine. It's funny, isn't it, how we ...? To me, you're still that little girl swinging on the front gate talking to Brian after school. You don't look a day older, Philippa."

"Oh, don't I wish!" I was swamped by the smell of frangipani beside their front gate. It was so intense, I felt dizzy. Lightly, indifferently, I asked, "The frangipani still beside your gate?"

"Fancy you remembering! His dad planted that. His dad was very good with his hands."

"Yes, I remember. Your roses especially —"

"He was a quiet man, Ed, a very shy man, but he was a good man, no one realises how ... such a good ..." She began pleating her skirt in her fingers. "I suppose Brian told you about the nights, but it wasn't his fault, those awful nights, those terrible ..." She turned away. "I feel ..." she said, putting out a hand, casting about for some sort of support. "I don't feel too ..." Her hand drifted aimlessly through the wet air. "I think I have to sit down," she said.

"There's a bench, look." I led her towards it. "We don't have to go to the reception if you're not feeling well. I can drive you home."

"I don't know," she said uncertainly. She pulled at the damp frizz on her forehead, trying to cover a little more of the space above her eyebrows. The space seemed vast now. Her fingers explored it nervously, scuttling across what felt like an acreage of blotched skin. I shouldn't have had it permed so soon before, she thought wretchedly. This dress is wrong. I should have worn the green suit. I shouldn't have worn a hat. She said plaintively, "You were so clever, you and Brian. Such clever children." Her voice came from a long way back, from our high school years or even earlier, from the times of swinging on the gate. "*He'll go far*, teachers used to say," and her eyes stared into nothing, following the radiant but bewildering trajectory of Brian's life. She spoke as sleepwalkers speak: "*He'll go far*. They always told us that, I remember." She looked vaguely about. "I mustn't miss the tram, Philippa."

As though the action were somehow related to the catching of trams, she stretched her hands out in front of her and studied them, turning them over slowly, examining the palms, the backs, the palms again. Her hands must have offered up a message, because she gave a sudden sad little yelp of a laugh. "I'm being silly, aren't I? There's no trams anymore."

"Oh, I do that too," I said. "The trams still run in *my* Brisbane." I tapped my forehead with an index finger.

"You know who I ran into in the Commonwealth Bank one day? Last year it was, the big one, you know, in the city, on the corner of Adelaide Street? *Mrs Matthews!*"

"Mrs Matthews?"

"Richard's mum, you remember?"

"Oh, Richard," I said, dizzy with loss. It was so unsettling, this vertigo, hitting sudden pockets of freefall into the past.

"Richard went away too," she said. "They never see him. It

just seems like yesterday when Brian and Richard and you and the others ... and Julie ... and Elaine. It was terrible what happened to Elaine. I cried when I read it in the paper. It's not fair, it isn't fair." She picked up a leaf and began shredding it nervously and then dropped it. She ventilated herself again, holding the dress away from her skin, shaking it lightly. "Everyone's children went away."

"God, it's hot," I said. "The staff club will be air-conditioned though. For the reception. I wish they'd hurry it up."

"But you come back a lot, Philippa. I saw in the paper —"

"Oh yeah. Every year. Brisbane's got its hooks in me, I reckon. Look, he's coming at last, he's seen us. Oh damn."

We watched the student who had intercepted him: jeans and t-shirt, sandals.

"They all look scruffy," she said. It was an affront to her. Even the adults, the university people, the ones who would be at the reception, even they looked scruffy. Well, not scruffy exactly. But more or less as though they were dressed for an evening barbecue at the neighbours'. I shouldn't have worn the hat, she saw. I shouldn't have worn the corsage. But how could she have known? She had thought it would be like going to a wedding.

And he could have been a bridegroom coming towards us, easing away, trailing worshipful students like membrane-embedded alpha-helical streamers. He had the kind of bridegroomly self-consciousness and forced gaiety that goes with weddings.

"Dorrie!" he said loudly, full of energetic joviality, hugging her.

He had always called her that, from before he even started primary school. At five years of age: Dorrie and Ed. Never mother, father; certainly not mum and dad. It was as though even then

he knew something they didn't. And they had been too apprehensive, too apologetic, to protest. They had never even asked
why.

"Philippa."

"Good on ya, mate." We hugged, old puzzle parts locking
together. "You were bloody amazing. I'm speechless, I'm dazzled.
What the hell's an ootheca?"

"What's a *what*?"

"An oo-ith-*ee*-ka." I pronounced all four syllables carefully, the
way he had, the stress on the third, treating each sound like glass.
"The ootheca of the praying mantis."

"Jesus, Philippa!" Brian laughed. "Typical. Absolutely peripheral
to the lecture. Trust you to focus on a fucking *word*."

"What does it mean?"

"It's the ovum sac," he said.

"The *ovum* sac. Hmm. So the breakthrough was dependent
on female biology."

"Oh, fuck off." He made a fist and shadow-boxed, stopping
an eighth of an inch from my nose. "Listen, *Dorrie* ..." — turning
toward her. He had a message of great urgency and import.

"Brian," she rushed in eagerly, tripping over her nerves. "I
remember about the crystal set, you and your Dad, how you
used to hear foreign languages."

Brian frowned, at sea. He just stared at her, disoriented, and
then looked around nervously. ("You actually *blushed*, for God's
sake," I told him later. "As though anyone would give a damn,
even if they'd heard.")

"Now, Dorrie," he said gently. "There's this ghastly reception
that Philippa and I have to go to, it's a stupid boring thing, and
there's no sense in the world making you put up with ... So

listen, I'm going to call a cab for you, all right? And we'll come on later for dinner, just like you wanted. All right?"

"All right," she said, parrot-like, meekly, looking somewhere else. *And then afterwards there's a reception,* she'd told the saleswoman, seeing white linen and cake and champagne, and *I think this little one,* the saleswoman had said, adjusting a wisp of feather at her brow, *this little number will be perfect. Just the thing for mother of the famous man. Just the thing for the scientist's mum.*

It's because I wore a hat, she thought.

"Look," Brian said, raising his arm, waving. "Here's a Black and White." He hugged her again. "Take care of yourself now, Dorrie. Go and put your feet up on the verandah for a while. We'll see you later, okay?"

He said something to the driver, gave him money, and we both waved. We kept on waving till the taxi disappeared.

"Don't look at me like that, Philippa."

"Like what?"

"Just cut it out, okay?"

"Don't try and dump your guilt onto *me.*"

"She would have hated it. She's terrified of social stuff, always has been. They never went anywhere. I was being kind, if it's any of your business."

"Jesus, Brian. That was brutal. And so totally unnecessary. I would have kept her under my wing."

"She would have hated it," he insisted. "Anyway, I'm not even going myself. I'm off to the Regatta. Let's go."

"What? But it's in your *honour!*"

"I don't give a stuff and nor do they. No one'll even notice I'm not there. It's the free booze and free food they're after, that's all. C'mon, let's go. You got your car here?"

★   ★

"You think it's because I'm ashamed of her," Brian said moodily on the verandah at the Regatta. "But you're wrong. It's not that."

I sipped my beer and stared across Coronation Drive at the river. Two small pleasure craft, motorboats with bright anodised hulls, were whizzing upstream, and a great ugly industrial barge from Darra Cement was gliding down, shuddering a bit, moving its hips in a slow, slatternly wallow. The sight of it filled me with happiness. *Good on you, you game old duck*, I thought fondly, and raised my glass to it. "Probably the same rusty tub we used to see when we were riding the buses out to uni," I said.

"Probably," Brian said lugubriously, slumped over his beer. "Everything's stuck in a bloody time warp, it's like a *swamp*" — he waved his arms about to take in the verandah, the Regatta, the river, the whole city — "it's like a swamp that sucks everything under, swallows it, stifles it, and gives back noxious ..." His energy petered out and he slumped again. "There was this funny little man in the front row who used to sit in on lectures when I was in first year. Flat-earth freak, or something, he used to buttonhole people in the cloisters. We all used to duck when we saw him coming. Must be ninety now, if he's a day, and there he was in the very same seat. It gave me the shivers."

I squinted, and lined up the top of my glass with the white stripe on the broad backside of Darra Cement. "I saw in the paper that home-owners in Fig Tree Pocket and Jindalee and those newer suburbs are trying to get the dredging stopped. One of these days we'll come back and the river won't be brown anymore, it'll be crystal clear. I suppose that'll be a good thing, but it's funny how I get pissed off when anyone tampers with Brisbane behind my back. God, I love being back, don't you?"

"I hate it," Brian said. He'd thrown his jacket across a spare chair. Now he undid a couple of buttons on his shirt and rolled up his sleeves. "Look," he said with disgust, raising his arms one by one, inspecting the moons of stain at the armpits. "A bloody steam bath."

"That's what I love. This languid feeling of life underwater."

Between us and the river, the traffic rushed by in beetling lines but the noise was muffled, a droning damped-down buzz. Everything was fluid at the edges. Cars seemed to float slightly above the road and to move the way they do in old silent movies. Even the surface of Coronation Drive was unfixed, a band of shimmer. A drunk man was shambling along the bike path giving off mirages; I could see three of him. I could see the gigantic bamboo canes at the water's edge doubling, tripling, tippling themselves into the haze. I could see wavy curtains of air flapping lazily, easily, settling on us with sleep in their folds. "The only reason I don't come back to stay," I said drowsily, "is that if I did, I would never do another blessed thing for the rest of my life. I'd turn into a blissed-out vegetable."

"It makes me panic, being back," Brian said. "I feel as though I'm suffocating, *drowning*. I can't breathe. I can't get away fast enough. I get terrified I'll never get out again."

"Go back to Bleak City then," I said. "Stop whingeing. You sound like a prissy Melburnian."

"I am a Melburnian."

"Bullshit. You'll be buried here."

"Over my dead body. I can never quite believe I got out," he said. "I've forgotten the trick. How did I manage it?"

I shrugged, giving up on him, and let my eyes swim in Coronation Drive with the cars. An amazing old dorsal-finned shark of a Thunderbird, early sixties vintage, hove into view and I followed it with wonder. "Who was that friend of your brother's? The one with the Alfa Romeo. Remember that time we came burning out here and the cops —"

"You've got a mind like the bottom of a birdcage, Philippa," Brian said irritably. "All over the shop."

"Polyphasic," I offered primly. "Highly valued by some people in your field. I read an essay on it by Stephen Jay Gould. Or maybe it was Lewis Thomas. Multi-track minds, all tracks playing simultaneously. Whatever happened to him, I wonder?"

"To Stephen Jay Gould or Lewis Thomas?"

"Neither, dummy. To that friend of your brother's. How's your brother, by the way?"

"He's fine."

"Still in Adelaide?"

"Mm."

"Did *he* stay married?"

"Knock it off, Philippa."

"You stay in touch with her?"

"No."

"I'm sorry, Brian. I'm really sorry about all that. Are you, you know, *okay?*"

"Yeah, well." Brian shrugged. "It's easier this way. No high drama, no interruptions. I practically live at the lab."

"I read a glowing article about you in *Scientific American*. It was an old one, I picked it up in the waiting room at my dentist's."

Brian laughed. "There's achievement for you."

We lapsed into silence and drank another round of beer and stared at the river.

"Your mother said she ran into Richard's mum."

"Don't get started, Philippa," Brian warned.

"I miss them, I *miss* them. I miss our old gang. Don't you?"

"No."

"Liar."

"I never miss *anyone*," he said vehemently.

"Your mother said —"

"Okay, get it over with."

"Get what over with?"

"The lecture on how I treat Dorrie."

"I wasn't going to say a word," I protested. "But since you mention it, I don't understand why you feel embarrassed. You were actually *blushing*, for God's sake. As though anyone minds."

"You think I'm ashamed of her."

"Well?"

"It's not that. I'm not. I'm *protecting* her. I can't bear it when other kids smirk at her. At them. I can't *bear* it."

"Other *kids*?"

"There's a lot you don't know, Philippa."

"I don't know why you think they were any different from anyone else's parents."

He signalled for another jug, and we waited until it came, and then Brian filled both our glasses.

"They were," he said. "That's all."

"They weren't. I spent enough time at your place, for God's sake."

"God, I'm depressed," Brian said.

"I spent time at Richard's and Julie's and Elaine's. They weren't any different from anyone else's mum and dad." Brian said nothing. With his index finger, he played in a spill of beer. We were both, I knew, thinking of Elaine.

"Sorry," I said, "I shouldn't have ... That's something that happens when I come back. Every so often, you know, maybe once or twice a year, I still have nightmares about Elaine. But not when I'm back here. When I'm here, we all still seem to be around. In the air or something. I can feel us." I stared into my glass, down the long amber stretch of the past. "How long is it since you've been back, anyway?"

"Five years."

"That's your average? Once every five years?"

"It's not that I want to come that often," he said. "Necessity."

I laughed. Brian did not. "You're not usually this negative about Brisbane," I protested. "When was the last time I saw you? Two years ago, wasn't it? In Melbourne. No, wait. I forgot. London. June before last in London when you were there for that conference — Yes, and we got all nostalgic and tried to phone Julie, tried to track her down ... that was hilarious, remember? We got onto that party line somewhere south of Mt Isa."

"It's different when I'm somewhere else," Brian said. "I get depressed as hell when I'm back."

"Boy, you can say that again."

"Last time ever, that's a promise to me," he said. "Except for Dorrie's funeral."

"*God*, Brian." I had to fortify myself with Cooper's comfort. "You're getting *me* depressed. Anyway, speaking of your mother, we'd better get going. What time's she expecting us?"

"Oh shit." Brian folded his arms tightly across his stomach and pleated himself over them.

"What's the matter?"

"I can't go."

"What?"

"I can't go, Philippa. I can't go. I just can't. Can you call her for me? Make up some excuse?"

I stared at him.

"Look," he said. "I *meant* to. I thought I could manage it. But I can't. Tell her I'm tied up. You'll do it better than I could."

"What the hell is the matter with you?"

"Look, tell her —" He seemed to cast about wildly for possible bribes. "Tell her we'll take her out for lunch tomorrow, before my afternoon flight. I'm staying at the Hilton, we'll take her there."

"I won't do it. I'm not going to do your dirty work for you. This is *crazy*, Brian. It's cruel. You'll break her heart."

Brian stood abruptly, knocking over his chair and blundered inside to the pay phone near the bar. I watched him dial. "Listen, *Dorrie*," I heard him say, in his warm, charming, famous-public-person voice. "Look, something's come up, it's a terrible nuisance."

"You bloody fake!" I yelled. There were notes of rush and pressure in his voice, with an undertone of concern. It wasn't Brian at all. It was someone else speaking, someone I'd never even met, someone who couldn't hear a thing I was saying, someone who didn't even know I was there.

"They've got something arranged at uni," he said smoothly, unctuously. "I didn't know about it, and the thing is, I can't get out of it. I'll tell you what though. Philippa and I will take you out to lunch tomorrow. She'll pick you up at twelve o'clock, okay? and we'll all have lunch at the Hilton. Look, I've got to rush, I'm terribly sorry. Look after yourself, Dorrie. See you tomorrow, all right? Bye now."

"I'm going," I said as he lurched back. "I'm taking a cab right now to your mother's. I won't be part of this."

"Philippa, stay with me."

"I won't. It's just plain goddamn rude and boorish when she's got a meal prepared. At least *one* of us ... I'm just bloody not going to — *What?* What is it? What the hell *is* it?

He looked so stricken that there was nothing to be said.

"All right," I conceded, resigned. "Where do you want to go?"

"Come back to the Hilton with me. I don't want to be alone. I have to get blind stinking drunk."

In the cab I said: "How come I feel more wracked with guilt than you do?"

He laughed. "You actually think I'm not wracked with guilt?"

"Oh, I know why I am," I said. "It's because I'm a mother too." If my son did this to me, I thought, I'd bleed grief. My whole life would turn into a bruise.

"There's a lot you don't know," Brian said. "I can't talk about it unless I'm blind stinking drunk."

We didn't go to his room. It wasn't like that. We have never been lovers, never will be, never could be, and not because it isn't there, that volatile aura, the fizz and spit of sexual possibility. I vaguely remember that as we got drunker we held each other. I seem to remember us both sobbing at some stage of the night. It wasn't brother/sister either, not an incest taboo. No. We were once part of a multiform being, a many-celled organism that played in the childhood sea, that swam in the ocean of Brisbane, an alpha-helical membrane-embedded coiled-coil of an *us*-thing. We were not Other to each other or them, we were already

Significantly *Us*, and we wept for our missing parts. We drank to our damaged, our lost, our dead.

When drink got us down to the ocean floor, I think Brian said: "It's the *house*. I really believe that if I went there, I wouldn't be able to breathe. I'd never get out of it alive."

And I think I asked: "What did your mother mean about the nights? *Those awful nights*, she said."

And the second I said it, a memory I didn't remember I had shifted itself and began to rise like a great slow black-finned sea-slug, an extinct creature, far earlier than icthyosaurus, earlier than the earliest ancestor of the manta ray. It flapped the gigantic black sails of its fins and shock waves hit the cage of my skull and I was swimming back to Brian's front gate, I was waiting for him there, fragrant currents of frangipani were swirling round, and these monstrously eerie sounds, this guttural screaming and sobbing, came pouring out through the verandah louvres in a black rush that whirlpooled around me, that sucked, that pulled … I clung to the gate, giddy with terror.

Then Brian came out of the house with his schoolbag slung over his shoulder and he pushed the gate open and pushed his way through and walked so fast that I had to run to catch up. "What is it?" I asked, my heart yammering at the back of my teeth.

"What's *what*?" Brian demanded.

"That noise." I stopped, but Brian kept walking. "That noise!" I yelled, and Brian stopped and turned round and I pointed, because you could almost see those awful sounds curdling around us. Brian walked back and stood in front of me and looked me levelly in the eyes and cocked his head to one side. He gave the impression of listening attentively, of politely straining his ears, but of hearing nothing.

"What noise?" he asked.

He was so convincing that the sound sank beneath the floor of my memory for forty years, even though, two blocks later, he said dismissively, "It's nothing. It's Ed. He does it all the time. It's from the war."

And forty years later, swimming up through a reef of stubbies and empty Scotch bottles, he said: "He never left New Guinea really. He never got away. And it was *catching*. After a while, Dorrie used to have Ed's nightmares, I think."

"Oh Brian."

"Sometimes the neighbours would call the police. The only place they felt safe was the house. They never went *anywhere*."

"I never had any inkling."

"Because I protected them. I was magic. I designed a sort of ozone layer of insulation in my mind, you couldn't see through it, or hear, and I used to wrap them up in it, the house, and my dad, and my mum."

My dad and my mum. It would be something I could give her the next day, something to put with the corsage.

It was a long time after I rang the doorbell before anyone came. And when she came, she didn't open the door. She just stood there on the verandah peering out between the old wooden louvres. She looked like a rabbit stunned by headlights.

"It's me, Mrs Leckie. Philippa."

"Philippa?" she said vaguely, searching back through her memory for a clue. She opened the door and looked out uncertainly, like a sleepwalker. She was still in her housecoat and slippers.

She squinted and studied me. "*Philippa!*" she said. "Good gracious. Are these for me? Oh, they're lovely. Lovely. Just a tic, and I'll put them in water. Come on in, Philippa, and make yourself at home."

It was eerie all right, one little step across a threshold, one giant freefall to the past. There was the old HMV radio, big as a small refrigerator, with its blistered wood front. There were two framed photographs on it, items from the nearer past, tiny deviations on the room as I knew it. One was of Brian's wedding, the other of his brother's. I picked up the frame of Brian's and studied it. I hadn't been at his wedding. We'd all got married in the cell-dividing years of the us-thing. I'd been overseas, though my mother had sent a newspaper clipping. I was trying to tell from the photograph if Brian had been happy. Was he thinking: *Now I've escaped?*

"I don't understand about marriages these days," she said, coming up behind me with the vase. She set the flowers on top of the radio. "I always thought Brian would marry you, Philippa."

"That would have been some scrap," I said. "We were always arguing, remember?"

"You would argue till the cows came home," she smiled. "I always thought you'd get married."

I set the frame down again, and she picked it up. "They didn't have any children," she said sadly. "Barry either. I don't have any grandchildren at all." She returned Brian and his bride to the top of the radio. "I wish they'd known him before the war, that's all. Before it happened. I just wish ... But if wishes could be roses, Ed used to say, or maybe it was the other way round. Would you like to see them, Philippa?"

I scrambled along the trail of her thought. "Oh," I said. "Yes,

I would. I noticed them from the gate. And your frangipani's enormous, it's going to swallow up the house."

"Ed planted that," she said. "He was always good with his hands, he had a green thumb. I have to get the boy down the road to mow the lawn for me now. Watch out for that bit of mud, Philippa, there were some cats got in. These ones," she said, "Ed planted when the boys were born, one for each. This one was for Brian."

It was a tea rose, a rich ivory. Champagne-coloured, perhaps. Off white, I would probably say to him in some future joust. His mother hovered over it like a quick bird, darting, plucking off dead petals, curled leaves, a tiny beetle, a grasshopper, an ant.

"You've kept them up beautifully," I said.

"And I call this one Ed, I've planted a cutting on his grave."

There was something about the way she bent over it, something about her gaunt crooked arms and the frail air of entreaty, that made me think of a praying mantis. Maybe she heard my thought, or maybe the grasshopper she pinched between finger and thumb reminded her. "He said something about a praying mantis," she said. "You asked him about it, Philippa. What was that thing?"

"The ootheca."

"Funny word, isn't it?" She pulled her housecoat around her and tightened the sash. "He won't be there for lunch, will he?"

I bit my lip. "He had to take an early flight," I said. It was and it wasn't a lie. We both knew it. "He had to be back in Melbourne."

She concentrated on the roses, bending her stick limbs over them, a slight geometric arrangement of supplication. "Anyway," she said. "I don't like going out. We never did, Ed and me." She straightened up and turned away from me, walking toward the gate. "I hope you won't mind, Philippa, if I don't ..." At the gate, she reached up and picked a frangipani and gave it to me. "Could you tell him," she said, "that I've still got his crystal set? It's in his room. I thought he might, you know ... I thought one day he might ..."

I held the creamy flower against my cheek. It's excessive, I thought angrily, the smell of frangipani, the smell of Brisbane. I had to hold onto the gate. There was surf around my ears, I was caught in an undertow. When I could get my voice to come swimming back, I'd tell her about the safety layer that Brian kept around his mum and his dad.

NORTH OF NOWHERE

They are curious people, Americans, Beth thinks, though it is easy to like them. They consider it natural to be liked, so natural that you can feel the suck of their expectations when they push open the door to the reception room and come in off the esplanade. Their walk is different too; loose, somehow; as though they have teflon joints. Smile propulsion, Dr Foley whispers, giving her a quick wink, and Beth presses her lips together, embarrassed, because it's true: they do seem to float on goodwill, the way hydrofoil ferries glide out to the coral cays on cushions of air. Friendliness spills out of them and splashes you. Beth likes this, but it makes her slightly uneasy too. It is difficult to believe in such unremitting good cheer.

Of all the curious things about Americans, however, the very oddest is this: they wear their teeth the way Aussie diggers wear medals on Anzac Day. They flash them, they polish them, they will talk about them at the drop of a hat.

"Got this baby after a college football game," Lance Harris says, pointing to a crown on the second bicuspid, upper left. Lance is here courtesy of Jetabout Adventure Tours and a dental mishap on the Outer Reef. "Got a cheekful of quarterback cleats, cracked right to the gum, I couldn't talk for a week. It was, let me see, my junior year, Mississippi State, those rednecks. Hell of a close fight, but we beat 'em, all that matters, right? Keeps on giving me heck, but hey, worth every orthodontist's dollar, I say."

Beth never understands the half of it, but in any case, what can you make of people who talk about their teeth? She just smiles and nods, handing Dr Foley instruments, vacuuming spit. American spit is cleaner than Australian spit, that's another interesting difference. Less nicotine, she thinks. No beer in their diets. But Scotch is yellowish too, wouldn't that ...? and certainly the boats that go beyond Michaelmas Cay for marlin are as full of Johnnie Walker as of American tourists with dreams. Champagne too. She's seen them onloading crates at the wharf. She imagines Lance's wife, camcorder in hand, schlurping up into her videotape Lance's blue marlin and his crisp summer cottons and the splash of yellow champagne and the dazzling teeth, whiter than bleached coral. How do they get them so white? Here I go, she thinks, rolling up her eyes for nobody's benefit but her own. Here I go, *thinking* about teeth. What a subject.

She wonders, just the same, about amber spit and clear spit. Is it a national trait?

"Australians don't floss," Lance mumbles, clamp in mouth, through a break in the roadwork on his molars.

Beth's hand flies to her lips. Has she done it again, blurted thought into the room? Possibly. She's been jumpy, that's why; ever since the dreams began again, the dreams of Giddie turning up. Or maybe she just imagined Lance spoke. Maybe she gave him the words. Her head is so cluttered with dialogue that bits of it leak out if she isn't careful.

"It astonishes me, the lack of dental hygiene hereabouts," Lance says. "We notice it with the hotel maids and the tourist guides, you know. As a dentist, it must break your heart."

"Oh, we manage," Dr Foley says. He lets the drill rise on its slick retractable cord and winks at Beth from behind his white sleeve. She lowers her eyes, expressionless, moving the vacuum hose, schlooping up the clear American words.

"You see this one?" Lance mumbles, pointing to an incisor. "Thought I'd lost this baby once, I could barely ..." but the polished steel scraper gently pushes his consonants aside and only a stream of long shapeless untranslatable vowels grunt their way into the vacuum tube.

If we put all the tooth stories end to end, Beth thinks, we could have a twelve volume set. Oral history, Dr Foley calls it, laughing and laughing in his curious silent way at the end of a day, the last patient gone. Every American incisor and canine has its chronicle, lovingly kept, he maintains, laughing again. Many things amuse him. Beth can't quite figure him out. She loves the curious things he says, the way he says them. She loves his voice. It's the way people sound when they first come north from Brisbane or Sydney. He seems to her like someone who became a dentist by accident.

As he cranks down the chair, he murmurs: "The Annals of Dentition, we're keeping a chapter for you, Lance."

"I'm mightily obliged to you, Doctor, mightily obliged. Fitting me in at such short notice." Lance shakes the dentist's hand energetically. "And to you too, young lady." He peers at the badge on Beth's uniform. "Beth," he reads. "Well, Miss Elizabeth, I'm grateful to you, ma'am. I surely am."

"It's not Elizabeth," she says. "It's short for Bethesda."

"And a very fine city Bethesda is, yes ma'am, State of Maryland.

I've been there once or twice. Now how did you come by a name like that?"

"The tooth fairy brought it," Beth says.

Dr Foley's eyebrows swoop up like exuberant gulls, then settle, solemn. Lance laughs and, a little warily, pats Beth on the shoulder.

"Well, Lance," the dentist says in his professional voice. "Fight the good fight. Floss on. Mrs Wilkinson will handle the billing arrangements for you." He ushers the American out, closes the door, and leans against it. "Don't miss our thrilling first volume," he says to Beth, madly flexing his acrobatic brows. His tone has gone plummy, mock epic, and she can hear his silent laughter pressed down underneath. "Wars of the Molars. Send just $19.95 and a small shipping and handling charge to Esplanade Dental Clinic, Cairns —"

"Ssh," she giggles. "He'll hear."

"No worries. Now if Mrs *Wilkinson* hears me —"

"She might make you stand in the corner."

"You're a funny little thing," he says, leaning against the door, watching her, as though he's finally reached a judgment now that she's been working a month. "How old are you?"

"Eighteen," she says, defensive. "It's on my application."

"Oh, I never pay attention." He brushes forms aside with one hand. "I go by the eyes in the interview." Beth feels something tight and sudden in her chest, with heat branching out from it, spreading. "You can *see* intelligence. And I look for a certain liveliness. You haven't been in Cairns long, I seem to remember."

"No."

"Just finished high school, I've forgotten where."

"Mossman."

"Hmm. Mossman. No jobs in Mossman, I suppose."

"No," she admits. "Everyone comes down to Cairns."

"Does your father cut cane?"

He might have winded her.

"Well," he says quickly, into the silence, "none of my —"

"My father *raises* Cain," she says tartly.

His eyebrows dart up again, amused, and spontaneously he reaches up to touch her cheek. It's a fleeting innocent gesture, the sort of thing a pleased schoolteacher might do, but Beth can hardly bear it. She turns to the steriliser and readies the instruments, inserting them one by one with tongs. "Sorry," he says. "It's not funny at all, I suppose. And none of my business."

She shrugs.

"I didn't realise Beth was short for Bethesda," he says.

"It's from the Bible. Mum gave us Bible names."

"It's rather stylish."

"Thanks."

"I'm pleased with your work, you know."

"Thank you." She fills the room with a shush of steam.

"Listen," he says, "after I close the surgery, I always stop for a drink or two at the Pink Flamingo before I go home. You want to join me?"

"Uh ..." She feels dizzy with panic. Anyway, impossible. She'd miss dinner. "Uh, no thanks, I can't. Dinner's at six. We're not allowed to miss." She keeps her back to him, fussing with the temperature setting.

"Not *allowed*?"

"At the hostel."

"Oh, I see," he says doubtfully. "Well, I'll drop you home then."

God, that's the last thing she wants. "No. No, really, that'd be silly. It's way out of your way, and the bus goes right past."

"You're a funny little thing, Bethesda," he says, but she's reaching into the steriliser with the tongs, her face full of steam.

"Girls," Matron says from the head of the table. "Let us give thanks."

Beth imagines the flap flap flap of those messages which will not be spoken winging upwards from Matron's scrunched-shut eyes. Thank you, O Lord, for mournful meals. Thank you for discipline, our moral starch, so desirable in the building of character. Thank you for stiff upper lips. Thank you for the absence of irritating laughter and chatter at the table of St Margaret's Hostel for Country Girls. Thank you that these twenty young women, sent to Cairns from Woop-Woop and from God Knows Where, provide me with a reasonable income through government grants; in the name of derelict fathers, violent sons, unholy spirits, amen; and also through the urgings of social workers and absurdly hopeful outback schools. Thank you that these green and gov-ernment-sponsored girls, all of them between the dangerous and sinward-leaning ages of sixteen and twenty-four, are safely back under my watchful eye and curfew, another day of no scandal, no police inquiries, no trouble, thanks be to God.

"We are grateful, O Lord," Matron says, "for your abiding goodness to us, and for this meal. Amen."

And the twenty young women lift grateful knives and forks. Beth, hungry, keeps her eyes lowered and catalogues sounds. That is finicky Peggy, that metal scrape of the fork imposing grids and priorities. Peggy eats potato first, meat second, carrots last. Between a soft lump of overcooked what? — turnip, probably — and some gristle, Beth notes the muffled *flpp flpp* of gravy stirred into cumulus mashed clouds, that is Liz, who has been sent down from the Tablelands to finish school at Cairns High. Liz's father is a tobacco picker somewhere near Mareeba, and Liz, for a range of black market fees, can supply roll-your-owns of head-spinning strength. That ghastly open-mouth chomping is Sue, barely civilised, who has only been here a week, dragged in by a district nurse who left her in matron's office. Where's this bedraggled kitten from then? matron asked, holding it at arm's length. From Cooktown, the district nurse said. Flown down to us. You wouldn't believe what we deal with up there. North of nowhere, believe me. In every sense.

"Inbreeding," Peggy sends the whisper along. "Like rabbits. Like cane toads, north of the Daintree. If this one's not a sample, Bob's your uncle. Whad'ya reckon?"

What does Beth reckon, between a nub of carrot and a gluey clump of something best not thought about? She reckons that this, whisper whisper, is the sound of matron's own stockinged thighs as Matron exits, kitchen-bound.

"Oh Christ, look at Sue," Peggy hisses. "Gonna cry in her stew."

A sibilant murmur circles the table like a breeze flattening grass — *Sook, sook, sook, sook!* — barely audible, crescendo, decrescendo, four-four time, nobody starts it, nobody stops. Stop it! Beth pleads inwardly. Malice, a dew of it, hangs in the air. *Sue wants her Daddy.* Nudge, nudge. *Maybe she does it with her brother.*

"Leave her alone," Beth says.

Peggy makes a sign with her finger. "Well, fuck you, Miss Tooth Fairy Queen."

"Girls," Matron says. "Jam pudding and custard for those who leave clean plates."

⋆   ⋆

January presses hotly and heavily on the wide verandah. Beth, in cotton shortie nightie and nothing else, lies on the damp sheet and stares through the mosquito net at a tarantula. How do they squat on the ceiling like that? If it falls, it will fall on Peggy's net. *Please fall*, Beth instructs it. She beams her thoughts along the road of moonlight that runs straight from the louvres to the eight hairy legs.

Night after night, the tarantula will show up in exactly the same spot, but is gone by day. There's another. It has been camped below the louvres, opposite Corey's bed, for six nights. Then suddenly both of them will pick new stations. Or maybe they change shifts. Maybe there are hordes of tarantulas waiting their turn in the crawlspace below the verandahs? What do they see from the ceiling? Ten bunks on the east verandah, ten on the west. Do they sidle in through the glass louvres that enclose the verandahs? The louvres are always slanted open to entice sea breezes. Is that how the spiders get in? And where do they hide by day?

No one worries about them. Or perhaps, Beth thinks, no one *admits* to worrying about them, though everyone takes note of where they are before the lights go out. As long as she can still see, by squinting, the filaments of spiky hair on the spider's legs, Beth can stop the tide from coming in. She can keep back the wave that has her name on it.

Beyond the spider, beyond the louvres, she can see the tired palms that bead the beaches together, filing south and south and south to Brisbane, reaching frond by frond by a trillion fronds north to Cape York. She can hear the Pacific licking

its way across the mangrove swamps and mud flats, though the
tide is far out. God, it's hot! She reaches to her right and yanks
at the mosquito net, tucked under the mattress, and lifts it to let
in some air. Uhh ... bite! Bite, bite, bite. God, they're fast little
blighters, noisy too, that high-pitched hum, it could drive you
crazy in five minutes flat. She hastily tucks the net in again and
swats at the stings. Greedy bloated little buggers. By moonlight,
she examines the splats of blood on forearm and thigh.

"Who's making all the fucking noise?" complains someone,
drowsy.

"Can mosquitoes spread AIDS?" Beth asks.

"Ahh, shuddup 'n go to sleep, why don't ya?"

But if dentists can ...? Beth wonders. She is fighting sleep, she
is fighting the wave coming in.

She fans her limp body with her cotton nightie, lifting it away
from herself, flapping air up to the wet crease beneath her breasts.
There is no comfort. The tide is coming in now.

Every night the tide comes in. It seems to well up from her
ankles. She feels this leaden heaviness in her calves, her thighs,
her belly, her chest, it just keeps rising and rising, this terrible
sadness, this sobbing, it can't be stopped, it bubbles up into her
throat, it is going to choke her, drown her, she has to stuff the
sheet in her mouth to shut it up.

Then she goes under the wave and sleeps.

Black water. Down and down and down.

Beneath the black water, beneath the wave, in a turquoise
place, the pink flamingos swim. Their breath is fragrant, like
frangipani, and when Beth vacuums the bright pink ribbons of
their spit, *pouff*, tables appear, and waitresses in halter tops and
gold lamé shorts. This way, the waitresses say, and Beth follows,

though the sandy path between the tables twists and turns. There are detours around branching coral, opal blue. Here and there, clamshells lurk with gaping jaws. At every intersection, the bright angelfish dart and confuse.

"Where is he?" Beth calls, and the waitresses turn back, and beckon, and wink. "Is he waiting for me? Is he still here?"

The waitresses smile. "He is always just out of reach," they murmur. "See? Can you see?" The waitresses point. And there he is beyond a forest of seaweed, fiery red. He sips a piña colada that wears a little purple paper parasol like a hat, but when she fights her way through the thicket of seaweed, he's disappeared.

"Terribly sorry," the waitresses say, winking, "but he'll be right back. Dental emergency. Floss on, he says, and he'll join you as soon as he can. He really really likes your work. He really likes you, you know."

And all the waitresses line up and link arms and kick up their legs in a can-can dance. He really really really really likes you, they sing, but they roll their eyes to show it's just a sick joke and then she sees that the waitresses are Peggy and Liz and Corey and Matron herself and she throws the piña colada at them and they disappear.

But their laughter stays behind them like the guffaw of a Cheshire cat. *Sook, sook, sook*, it splutters, hissing about Beth's ears. *We can hear you crying in your sleep.*

No, Beth protests. *Never!* Never ever.

Nevermore, the waitresses sing, offstage. *He's gone for good.*

No, Beth argues. *That isn't true.*

And see, he's coming back, he is, she can't mistake his coat, there it is, yes, white against the brilliant coral, starch against sea-hair flame, but she won't turn her head, she's not going to make a fool of herself, she pretends not to see. She wants to be surprised. She wants to feel a light touch on her cheek and then she will turn and then ...

And then? And then?

The dream falters. The water turns opaque with thrashing sand. Shark, perhaps? The pink flamingos avert their eyes. There is something they know, it's no use pretending, the suck of the sobbing wave is pulling across the dimpled ocean floor. But still he taps her lightly on the arm. "It's all right," he says. "You're such a funny little thing, Bethesda."

And so she turns. But it isn't him, it's Giddie.

"Oh Giddie," she says, resigned. "I might have known."

"G'day, Beth." It's his lopsided grin, all right, and his bear hug, which haven't changed. It's the same old dance. Will you, won't you, will you, won't you? the waitresses sing. We're back again, he's back again, all together now, the old refrain. "C'mon," Giddie says, pulling her, and the waitresses twirl. Will you, won't you, will you, won't you, *won't* you join the dance? "C'mon," Giddie says, and now they're swimsliding down and around, it's a spindrift sundance ragtime jig, it's the same old tune going nowhere. Shark time, dark time, lip of hell; they are going, going, gone. "*C'mon,*" he says, and it's the edge of nothing, the funnel, the whirlpool, he's gone over, he's pulling her down.

"No!" she screams, struggling. "No! Let me go, Gideon, let me go!"

But he won't let her go and she's falling, plummeting, there's no bottom to this, it's forever and ever, amen, though she makes a last convulsive grab at the watery sides — *Gid-ee-oooooon!* — and crash lands on her bed.

She gulps air, trembling, the sheet stuffed into her mouth.

Heedless, the sobbing wave rushes on, noisy, shaming, a disgusting snuffling whimpering sound, the sound of a sook.

No, wait. Wait. It's not Beth's wave. It's not Beth.

She listens.

Sue, she thinks.

She must warn Sue: keep the sheet in your mouth. They don't forgive, they're like the fish on the reef. Remember this: the smell of injury brings on a feeding frenzy. They go for blood. You have to keep the sheet in your mouth.

"What are you reading?" he asks, and Beth startles violently. "Hey," he says. "Sorry. What a jumpy little thing you are, Bethesda." He sits down beside her on the sea wall, the hum of the esplanade traffic behind them, the tide lapping the wall below their feet. "Is this all you ever do in your lunch hour? Read?"

She says primly: "I'm watching the tide going out."

He grins, then offers: "I've offended you. Would you like me to leave?"

"No," she says, too quickly. Then, indifferently: "If you want. It doesn't matter." She tucks the book into her bag and sets it on the wall between them. "It's me, I was rude." She is angry, not with him, but with herself, for the thing that happens in her throat when he says her full name that way. "You gave me a scare. I didn't think anyone could see me here." She gestures toward the pandanus clump behind them, the knobbed trunks and spiky leaves rising from a great concrete planter with a brass plate on its rim: *Rotary Club, Cairns District*. She trails her finger over the engraved letters and says, inconsequentially, "I used to have to be a waitress at the Rotary dinners in Mossman." She rolls her eyes. "Grown-up men, honestly. They sing the stupidest songs."

"Oh God, I know. They tried to get me to join. One dinner was enough. They were raffling a frozen chicken and throwing it round the room. Playing catch."

"In Mossman," she says, "they had this mock-wedding. Fund-raising for a playground or something. You should've seen the bride." She shakes her head, incredulous. "Mario Carlucci. His father's a cane farmer but Mario's in the ANZ bank, he's the manager already, everyone says his father got it for him because the Carluccis have the biggest account. Anyway, Mario, he's about six-two, and they made this special dress, satin and pearls, with you know ..." She gestures with her hands.

"Large mammary inserts," he says drily.

She laughs. "Yeah." She looks at him sideways. "You seem like you should be an English teacher, not a dentist."

"What!" he says in mock outrage, his brows working furiously. "Fie on thee! Out, out, damned spot, you're fired."

"You're funny."

"You're pretty funny yourself, Bethesda." He smiles and she swings her eyes away, nervous. She focuses on the Green Island ferry, in the distance, nosing in toward the wharves.

"Look, Beth," he says, "I don't want to pry, but I've been making a few inquiries, and from what I hear, that hostel is pretty awful. I wondered if you'd like me to —"

"It's okay," she says. "I don't mind it."

"And another thing. I've been looking at your application and your references again. God knows, I don't want to lose you at the clinic, but you got a Commonwealth Scholarship, for heaven's sake. Why didn't you take it?"

The ferry is bumping against the pylons now. Men will be wheeling the gangplanks into place. More tourists — people who are free to go anywhere they want, free even to go home again — will disembark and others will board.

"All right," he says quietly. "I just want you to know, if you need any help ... I'm worried about you, that's all."

"No one needs to worry about me," she says politely, swinging her legs back over the sea wall in an arc, away from him. "But Mrs Wilkinson will worry about *you* if we don't get back."

Every Thursday afternoon, last thing, he gives Mrs Wilkinson and Beth their pay envelopes, and every Thursday she saunters along the esplanade, pretending to browse, in the opposite direction from her bus stop until she's about three or four blocks from the clinic. Then she crosses over and makes for her spot on the sea wall behind the pandanus palms. She takes the pay envelope out of her bag and opens it. Four crisp fifty-dollar bills, brand new, straight from the bank every time, a miracle that makes her hands shake. She puts them back in the envelope, back in her bag, and takes her bank book out. Its balances, marching forward line by line, entry by entry, shimmer. Already she can see the way the page will look tomorrow morning at the teller's window. She kisses the open book, slips it back in her bag, and hugs the bag to her chest. She can feel a warm buzz against her ribcage.

On Thursday evenings, she feels as though she could walk across the water to the marina. She feels as though she would only need to lift her arms and she would rise, float, up to the decks of the big catamaran, the one that goes to the Outer Reef. And out there on Michaelmas Cay where the seabirds are, where they rise in vast snowy clouds, she would feel the lift of the slipstream, the cushion of air beneath, the upward swoop of it, climbing, climbing, *We are climbing Jacob's ladder* ...

She is singing the old hymn triumphantly inside her head, or maybe belting it out loud — why not? — because here she is, Sunday night in Mossman again, after the minister and his wife have taken her in. Here's the small Sunday night congregation, the ceiling fans turning sluggishly, moths thick around the altar lights, everyone fanning themselves with hymnbooks, singing their hearts out, *Every rung goes higher, higher*, her mother loving every minute of it, one of her mother's favourite hymns, her mother turning and smiling ... Oh no, wait, this isn't right, she's mixing things up, she shouldn't have thought of this. Wrong track.

She swings her legs over the sea wall and crosses the road and runs all the way to the bus stop, her feet thud thud thudding on the pavement, too noisy for thought. Three people waiting, that's good, and she recognises the woman in the pink cotton dress who always catches her bus. She throws herself into bright conversation. "Thought I'd missed it," she says. "We had this little kid this afternoon, an extraction, and it turned out he was a bleeder, you have no idea what a —"

"You *would've* missed it, love," the woman says, "except it's running late. I think I see it coming now."

"You should've heard this kid's mother," Beth babbles. "Poor Dr Foley, I thought she was going to —"

"G'day, Beth." She hears the voice behind her and comes to a dead stop. She hears the voice but she doesn't believe it. Old hymns, her mum, now this. Someone taps her on the shoulder. "G'day, Beth." If I don't turn, she thinks, he'll go away. He isn't really there, he's inside my head.

The bus is pulling into the curb, and she stares straight forward and gets on. She pays, walks halfway back, and sits down. Someone is following her down the aisle, someone sits down beside her, someone in jeans and white T-shirt and denim jacket, but she won't look, she stares out the window. Her own reflection stares back at her, resigned.

"G'day, Beth. I reckon you're pretty mad with me, hey?"

She sighs heavily. "How'd you find me, Gideon?"

"Well, you know, I went to Mossman first, natch. And that's how I found out about Mum. Geez, Beth. You should've let me know."

"And how was I supposed to do that, Giddie?" — given that she hasn't seen him for about two years — "How was I supposed to know where you were?"

"I dunno," he says irritably. "There's ways. For one, you could've told Johnny Coke. It would've got to me. There's links all the way from here to Melbourne, you know. I mean, this is where they bring half the stuff in, for Chrissake, it stands to reason. And the rest of it *grows* up the Daintree. *Think* about it, Beth. You've always got your head in the bloody clouds."

She stares out the window, appalled at her own ignorance. She thinks of all these people, hundreds of them, thousands of them maybe, all hooked, all hooked up to each other, a vast network of arteries and veins and capillaries all bleeding each into each.

"Anyway, the minister says he got you fixed up in this hostel in Cairns, and at the hostel this arvo some grouchy old biddy tells me where you work. So. I plan to be waiting for ya when ya knock off, hugs and kisses, surprise surprise, only nobody's there. Then wham-bam you come racing past me out of nowhere. You mad at me, Beth?"

"Yeah," she says. "No. I don't know." She punches the seat in front of her. "You stole the money out of Mum's biscuit tin. How could you *do* that to her, Giddie?"

"I didn't *steal* it," he says, offended. "*Geez*, Beth! I would've paid her back. Geez!" He swivels to look at her better. "You look pretty good. I hardly recognised you, lipstick and all, and your hair like that. Aren't you gonna give me a hug? Yeah ... Hey, that's more like it."

She's smiling in spite of herself. "Mum always said you could wrap the devil round your little finger, Giddie."

"Yeah," he grins. "She did, didn't she? I went to her grave, Beth, the minister told me where it was. Picked some flowers, an' that."

She can't speak, and puts her head fleetingly on his shoulder, then straightens up and looks out the window again. There's nothing to see but herself, and beyond that the curl of a breaker coming in, a great fizz of crest turning into foam, a monster wave. She has to get home first, she has to get to the hostel before the wave breaks, she has to lock herself into the loo. "Hey," she says brightly, turning. "So where've you been all this time?"

"Oh, up and down the coast, you know. Brisbane mostly, but."

"*Brisbane*. You visit Dad?"

"You gotta be kidding," he says. "Anyway, I think he's out again. One of me mates got a few weeks in Boggo Road for possession, and he heard Dad got out on good behaviour. That's a laugh, eh? Went out west, Charleville or somewhere, *shearing* is what I heard, can you believe? *Dad*?" He laughs.

"Remember that time he took us fishing on the Daintree?" Beth asks. "You were ten, I think, and I was seven, yes, that's right. I remember because I had Mrs Kennedy that year, Grade 3, and I wrote a story about it and she read it out to the class and kids told you and you were mad as hell with me. You'd had something on your line and it was pulling like crazy and you wouldn't let go and you went right over the boat. I was screaming because I thought the crocs would get you."

Gideon frowns. "I don't remember that," he says. "You made that up, Beth. You're always making stuff up."

She's incensed. "Dad yanked you back in the boat and walloped you. And you were so mad, you sneaked out that night and stayed at Wally Rover's place just to give Dad a scare. So he'd think you'd run away."

But it's no use. He can't remember a thing. Gideon's memory is like a little heap of expensive white powder. He bends over it and breathes, and *pouff*, there's nothing but fog.

She stares at her face in the black window. I remember enough for both of us, she thinks.

"I'll tell you something I do remember," he says suddenly. "Remember that time Mum made us matching shorts out of *curtains* and we had to wear them to school?"

"Yeah, I remember. We wanted to die." She smiles and slides her arm through his. "I miss you, Giddie."

"Yeah, me too. Listen, Beth, it's great that you've got this job. You couldn't lend me a bit of dosh, could ya? Just enough to get me back to Brissy on the train. I'll pay you back."

She holds herself very still, then she withdraws her arm. "Sure," she says. "I suppose. How much?"

"Well, I dunno. Fifty should do it."

She opens her bag and takes out the envelope. "I'm saving up, Giddie," she says. "I'm going to go to Brisbane, go to uni and stuff, and be a teacher."

NORTH OF NOWHERE   41

"Wow," he says, but he's looking at the crisp new bills. "You're doing all right."

"I bank nearly all of it," she says. She hands him one of the bills, her eyes following it as though it were a child leaving home. She can feel this pain, this kind of bleating stab, at the edge of one eye. *Knife*, that's what it feels like. Switchblade. When he reaches for the money, palm up, she sees the tracks on his forearm, a dot matrix map. "Oh Giddie," she says in a desperate rush, and it's like finding blessed safe words to hold all the blood. "I hope you use clean needles." The words feel bottomless. They hold the sadness neatly and nothing spills out.

"What? Oh, yeah, well mostly. Whenever I can."

She puts the envelope back into her bag and sets it down between them. The black window stares at her, explaining nothing. Gideon begins to fidget in his seat. His ankles, jazz dancers, jiggle violently against hers. The black window says: *Fix it then, Mr Fixit Man*. Beth mouths at the window: *Don't*. Not that it matters. Not that it matters to her.

At the Blue Marlin Shopping Centre, a couple of blocks before her stop, Giddie bounces up like a rocket. "Hey, this is where I get off. Great seeing you, Beth. Take care of yourself." He leans down and gives her a kiss on the cheek. He's blinking furiously and his eyes, clear a few minutes ago, are bloodshot.

"Yeah," she says. "You too. Take care of yourself, Giddie." She hangs onto him but he pulls irritably away.

"*C'mon*, Beth, I'll miss me stop."

She watches his jerky progress to the front of the bus, down the steps, out. She presses her nose to the window to wave, but when the bus moves he's already sprinting across the parking lot, a blur. Unfixed. It isn't until she gets to her own stop that she realises he's taken her bag. She remembers now the way he held his left arm, pressed against his denim jacket, as he stumbled down the bus.

She can feel the wave coming in. It's tidal, a king tide. She stares at the tarantula, the sheet stuffed into her mouth. King tide. There's a watery halo around the tarantula's legs. Sobs are leaking into the room.

She sits up, panicked. So much of the sheet is balled up in her mouth she's afraid she will gag. But it's Sue again, the next bed to hers. *Damn, I warned her,* Beth thinks, exasperated.

She lifts her mosquito net, slides out, tiptoes to Sue's bed, lifts the net and leans in. She puts her lips against Sue's ear. "For God's sake, stuff the sheet in your mouth," she whispers savagely. Her own anxiety is acute. Sue has her hands up over her face, the way Beth's mother used to when her father was drunk. It is always the worst worst thing. "*Stop it*," she hisses, furious, grabbing Sue's wrists. "You're *asking* for it, damn it."

Then she realises Sue's asleep. Sue is flinching and bucking and moaning and crying in her sleep.

Oh God, she thinks. Any second now, someone's going to wake and hear this shit. Show blood and you're dead, that's the rule. Her mind is racing.

Okay, she thinks. Nothing else for it. Swift and efficient, she slides into Sue's bed, jabs the mosquito net back under the mattress, grabs the girl in her arms, and muffles Sue's face between her breasts. "It's all right," she murmurs. "Shh, it's okay, it's okay, everything's going to be all right." Sue's snuffling sobbing breath is warm against her. With her left hand, she strokes Sue's hair.

"Go to sleep now," she murmurs. "Go to sleep. It's all right, baby, it's okay."

Sue's body shifts slightly, softening, rearranging itself, moving up against Beth's like an infant curling into its mother. Her breathing turns quiet. Beth goes on stroking Sue's hair with one hand, and stuffs the other into her own mouth. At the fleshy place where her thumb joins the palm of her hand, she bites down so hard she tastes blood.

FOR MR VOSS OR OCCUPANT

"Foreclosures," Mr Watson was in the habit of saying, "are a steal."

Further wise thoughts would follow: a foreclosure was manna from heaven, a sweetheart deal, a buyer's dream. He did not, however, run through the litany for this particular client, the young mother whose pubescent daughter had refused to get out of the car, the young *single* mother it would appear, *hubba, hubba* maybe he'd try his luck — God, if people knew how much quick hot fucking took place in empty rooms behind For Sale signs! — but no, on second thought, he smelled trouble right off the bat. A bit off, he reckoned; a bit out of it, the way academic types always were. A bit pinko, for sure, the stink of Sydney (Balmain, even Newtown maybe) coming off her like Four-X pong off a pub, a real wolverine in sheep's clothing, weird clothing, they were all Commies down there, dykes, women's libbers, worse. Put your thing in the wrong place with her kind, chop chop and goodbye. One way or another, she was bound to get herself into strife in Brisbane, and serve her right.

Still, a sale was a sale. For the political and moral sensibilities of a live prospect, he had nothing but respect.

A "distress sale", he called it delicately, evasively, though not a single distressing thought entered Laura White's head when she saw the house. Not at first. It was as though she had willed desire into solid form.

"Oh," she said. "I grew up in a house with wide verandahs." Stricken almost, mesmerised, soft rot of the railing and lattice against her back, she leaned into childhood. "Everyone used to close them in for sleepouts. To think there's still a house ... and so close to the city. I can't believe my luck."

Nor could Mr Watson. Not a modern piece of plumbing in sight, stove out of a bloody museum, but she was hooked before she walked through the door. Piece of cake. (Though the daughter sitting out there in the blue Mazda might be a question mark. He could hear pistol-cracks of rock music like rude punctuation.)

"And the roof!" the mother sighed.

"Yeah, well. Gonna have to put in a few quid. I got a friend can give you a good deal on clay tiles."

"Oh no," she said. She got quite choked up at the thought of hearing rain on corrugated iron again. Command performances: January cyclones, cloudbursts, thunderbolts, you lay in bed and the universe did its quadraphonic full-frontal subtropical act. "And the garden!"

Garden? Bit of a jungle if you wanted Mr Watson's private opinion, but who was he to complain?

"All this space and right in the city," she marvelled.

"Yeah, well!" Mr Watson said. "The Gap, you know. Very desirable, very pricey these days." She wasn't the usual type for The Gap. Volvo country, Saab city, it was yuppie turf, they went for it like lemmings. They got turned on by the idea of being half an hour from their stockbroker's one way, half an hour from the rainforest the other, but they liked family rooms and built-in bars and swimming pools to go with it. You had to be fly to unload a place like this in a location like The Gap. A double lot too, what a waste. If it weren't for the bloody zoning laws, a developer would snap it up in two shakes. "That's why the price is once in a lifetime," he said fervently.

"I'll take it."

"What?" She threw him off completely, breaking the rules like that, not even trying to haggle. It made him uneasy. It was like seeing someone naked in public, it put you at a disadvantage somehow. From sheer habit he said belligerently, "Nobody in their right mind quibbles about an asking price like this."

"No," she said, startled. "I'm not quibbling."

"Hafta be crazy." He couldn't quite get hold of the reins, couldn't stop his mouth from galloping along a track it knew too well.

Her lust for the place was too obvious, she thought. Unfashionable, this intense desire to come home; unfashionable to express it even in Brisbane these days. She walked along the front verandah, trailing her hand along its railing, getting acquainted, sighing over the lattice, burying her head in the jasmine that was matted around the posts. She had the feeling that she had to justify something, pass a test, *explain.* "I've been poring over the papers for weeks. Traipsing all over, looking and comparing. Why *is* the price so low?"

"Oh, as to that." He was back on familiar turf, he knew exactly where he was with sweet suspicion. "Not a thing wrong with the place. Solid gold, believe me. Not a thing wrong that a bit of cutting and pruning won't fix." He laughed. "Not to mention a modern appliance or two, eh? though there's people *paying* me to find them old stoves and pull-chain toilets, there's people phoning from *Melbourne* for places like —"

"Yes, I know. That's why I'm curious."

"Distress sale," he said with voluptuous sorrow. "Old codger lived here all his life." He intimated a pensioner's woes: fixed income, land revaluations, rising rates, the remortgaging trap. "Familiar story, eh? And then the interest rates the last straw. Terribly sad." Shit, he was going to blow it. *Overdoing it, Sonny Jim.* She was looking at a point beyond his left shoulder so intently that he turned around, spooked, half expecting to see the old bloke he'd just invented.

"Who's that man?" she asked.

"What? Where? Oh ..." There was a man across the road, in shadow, who stared at the two of them on the slightly sagging verandah. "Neighbour, I suppose. Bloke from across the road." Very likely, Mr Watson thought, some bloke who objected to a hippie moving in, well maybe not a hippie exactly, but not a Volvo owner either, and you would have to call her a hippie *type* with that mane of brown curls and that strange arrangement of black tights under a longish gauzy skirt and those very long earrings apparently made out of bike chains and that black stretch top. Not unattractive, if you went for that sort of thing which Mr Watson didn't, well maybe on occasion if you could slip in and out without complications, but you hardly ever could with her type.

"The thing is," he said smoothly, "the old man told me himself it was really beyond him now. He told me: 'Just sell it to someone who loves it, that's all I ask.' " He saw her uncertainty and her desire for the house, he followed the quick dart of her eyes across the road to the silent watcher, back to the verandah and the jasmine, across the road again. "Those were his very words," Mr Watson said. "His very words. Sell it to someone who loves it."

"But what about him? What will he do?"

"Ah," Mr Watson said modestly. "Well, actually ..."

"Is that him over there?"

"Of course it's not him. I told you, the owner's *old*, much older, a pensioner. As a matter of fact ..." He became expansive, his chest rising to fill the lift of his imagination. He spoke of going beyond and above the call of, etcetera, he evoked hearts of gold and a nursing home and knowing the right people and jumping waiting lists — "Contacts, you know, another client, you scratch my back I'll scratch yours kind of thing" — and, in short, taking care of everything exactly as the old man had wished.

"Well," Laura said. "I'll take it, then. I know Jilly will love it."

"You won't regret it, Mrs White," Mr Watson beamed; and then boisterously, recklessly: "It's a *steal*. Believe me, a real steal."

Jilly hated it, but was resigned. "Honestly, Mum! You'd think we were freaks or something, the way people stare around here. And there's not another kid for miles around who's over the age of ten."

"Think of all the babysitting money you can earn."

"Squalling brats every Saturday night? *Yuck!*" Jilly pined moodily for the fast pack of thirteen-year-olds she'd run with in Sydney. "Brisbane is the pits," she said.

Laura grinned. "Yeah, I know. That's what I thought when I was your age. It grows on you though."

Jilly rolled up her eyes. "Spare me," she said.

You learn a lot about a man from the garden he creates, Laura thought. You could fall in love with the creator of a garden. There was half an acre — well, it was hectares now, but she'd never learned to think metric — it was large anyway for a city lot but what enchanted her was the way the former owner had made it seem infinite. She knew how it was done in a garden; technically, she knew; but there still seemed to be sleight of hand or magic involved. She knew it was done with boundaries — high walls or lush plantings — that blocked out a sense of external scale and drew the eye upward; and she knew that within the enclosed space, a clever gardener never used rectangular beds but created outdoor "rooms" with different moods and personalities, rooms that flowed naturally from one to another like nooks along a rainforest path. Everything was curves, sinuous loops, unexpected little circular oases of lawn that slithered into S-bend banks of passionfruit or massed orchids.

There was a place where she loved to sit. It was not large, but it seemed so, a grotto-like space that imparted a sense of absolute seclusion and tranquillity. Around a small pond rose a curve of bamboo on one side, a bank of tree ferns matted with climbers on the other, so that only water and green enclosure and sky could be seen. Birds called and their calls bounced about, odd and haunting, among the hollow bamboo canes. The slightest breeze made the canes click softly against one another: *klik klik*. The house, the street, the neighbours might have been miles away. If it weren't for the wooden bench and the watcher, Laura could have believed herself deep in the rainforest.

The watcher. He nestled into grasses at the muddy edge of the pond, leaning out like Narcissus towards the waterlilies. How could she account for him in a Brisbane suburb? A gargoyle that might have been filched from some French cathedral, he stared at his own mordant reflection with a wicked grin. Or was it a grimace? The mouth of someone being tortured, perhaps? Instantly she nicknamed him Caliban.

But where had Caliban come from? He weighed a ton. She tried, but there was no lifting him. Cast iron, she thought. But imagine a Brisbane pensioner with such tastes, and where would he have had the casting done? A vision came to her of the old man caged in his nursing home: how he must grieve for his garden. The gargoyle eyes, bulging like a fly's, watched her from the gnarled head. *Intruder*, the eyes accused.

A house is suffused with the presence of its former owner, Laura thought. For a time, one felt like a trespasser. She must write to the displaced gardener, thank him, tell him what a sorcerer he was. *Dear Mr Prospero ...*

"I think it's creepy," Jilly said sulkily. What was she supposed to do with herself in Brisbane, watch the waterlilies grow? "And there's a man who drives past and stares at me when I'm waiting at the bus stop for school. It gives me the creeps."

"It's just because we're new here, that's all."

"Well, no one stares at you in Sydney just because you're new. And this is the only house in the whole street without a pool."

"We've got the most beautiful pool in Brisbane."

"That muddy puddle," Jilly sniffed scornfully.

"It's so peaceful, don't you find it peaceful here?"

"Who wants *peaceful*? I want excitement, Mum."

Laura said carefully, neutrally: "Would you rather go back and live with your father in Sydney?"

"I dunno," Jilly kicked at the gargoyle and screwed up her face. "Anyway, Dad's not in Sydney, he's back in New York right now. His secretary said."

"Oh."

"I could go if I want. Dad'd send a ticket."

"Yes, I suppose." The bamboo canes clicked softly, the gargoyle leered. Laura stared at the eyes reflected in the water. *Full fathom five your father lies ...* She managed to keep her voice even. "Is that what you'd like to do?"

"I dunno. S'pose I'll give it a bit longer before I make up my mind."

"Thanks, Jilly." Laura hugged her, but Jilly stiffened and drew back.

Two letters arrived. One was junk mail, a garden catalogue addressed to Mr Voss or Occupant. The other, for Laurence Voss, was a letter.

Laura phoned the real estate firm and asked for Mr Watson. "What can I do yer for?" he boomed cheerily. "Pruned the jungle back yet?"

"I love it the way it is, Mr Watson. I'm calling to ask for Mr Voss's forwarding address."

"Whose?"

"You know, the former owner. Mr Voss."

"Oh, *Mr Voss.* Right. Of course."

"It's a curious coincidence, isn't it?" Laura said.

"How'd you mean?"

"Well, Patrick White. Voss and Laura. You know."

Mr Watson didn't know. "Sorry. Don't follow you."

"Patrick White's novel *Voss*? Voss and Laura are the main characters, they have this strange sort of *connection*, a fusion almost —"

"Never read it," Mr Watson said briskly.

"Well anyway, what's Mr Voss's forwarding address?"

"Wouldn't have a clue, luv. The bank was already the owner, you know. I acted for the bank."

"Yes, I know. But you said you got him into a nursing home."

"What? Oh right, *right*. *That* Mr Voss. Look, I got someone in the office at the moment. Call my secretary back in half an hour, will ya? She'll give you the nursing home address."

Laura called back. It turned out that there had been some problem or other, and Mr Voss had changed his mind about the home. Neither the nursing home nor the real estate company had a forwarding address. Mr Watson was sorry, his secretary said. She suggested Laura contact the Westpac Bank. Laura did. The bank had no forwarding address. No one knew what had happened to Mr Voss, the mortgage manager said. He'd vanished into thin air.

Though there was no return address on the letter to Laurence Voss, Laura marked it "Return to Sender. Forwarding address unknown" and dropped it into a mailbox. Let the post office open it, send it to the dead letter office, whatever they did.

No more personal correspondence arrived, but every week or so junk mail came. To Mr Voss or Occupant, to Laurence Voss, sometimes to L. J. Voss. It was very classy junk mail: glossy garden catalogues, magazines for orchid fanciers, kits for gazebos and teak garden benches, mail-order kits for grandfather clocks and harpsichords, brochures for leather-bound sets of Tolstoy and Goethe. You could tell a lot about a man from the mailing lists he was on, Laura thought. You could feel great fondness for a man of such elegant tastes.

She filed all the catalogues in a carton in her study, but kept one or two on her bedside table to browse through at night. Once, she was startled and excited to turn a page and find a photograph of Caliban with identical bulging eyes and knowing smirk. You could have him delivered. He had a companion piece, a sylph-like cast-iron sprite with wings, a stooped figure who could be placed in such a way that he appeared to be drinking from a cupped hand. *Ariel*, she thought with delight, and decided to order him. She would put him on the opposite side of the pond: Beauty and the Beast, so to speak.

She used the catalogue order form as it was, imprinted with the name of Mr Laurence Voss and his address — which was also hers — at Settlement Road, The Gap. She filled in her own credit card number.

She felt she had stepped into the envelope of Mr Voss's life. She felt they were kindred spirits. She felt his presence most strongly by the pond.

"The Spicers said he was weird," Jilly said. She babysat fairly often for the neighbours, who had a real pool. "They hardly ever laid eyes on him, but they were glad when he went. The police had to come, Mrs Spicer said."

"The police?"

"Yeah. He wouldn't leave when the bank foreclosed."

"I don't blame him," Laura sighed. "After you've spent your life building the perfect garden. Poor old man."

"He wasn't all that old," Jilly said. "Same as Mr Spicer, they reckon. And he only came a few years ago and planted all that fast-growing bamboo and stuff. Pretty suspicious, they reckon. Like what was he hiding? He was kinda spooky, Mrs Spicer said, a real loner. The kids called him the bogeyman."

"Suburbanites don't understand the desire for solitude," Laura said. "They probably think I'm a bit weird too."

"Yeah, well," Jilly shrugged. "I told Mrs Spicer you were on sabbatical, writing a book. She said that's different."

"How kind," Laura said drily.

"She asked me what your book's about, and I said Patrick White and literature and stuff. I couldn't remember exactly."

"It's a study of authors who become reclusive. Patrick White, Emily Dickinson, J. D. Salinger, Thomas Pynchon. The way they create solitary characters and personae and then disappear into their fictions."

Jilly mimed a theatrical yawn. "Oh wow," she said.

"Or maybe it's the other way round. Maybe the characters swallow up the author. You know, move in and take over. With both White and Pynchon, you get a sense in the later novels of *invasion*, and there's a line in Dickinson —"

Jilly groaned. "I wish I had a *normal* mother. You know, who plays tennis and stuff, and has people round for barbecues."

"We'll have a barbecue," Laura offered guiltily, quickly.

All the neighbours came to the barbecue, and all Jilly's friends from The Gap high school. Also a man whom nobody knew. The man nobody knew looked vaguely familiar to most of the neighbours, but everyone assumed he came with somebody else. Laura wasn't aware of him till Jilly pointed him out: "Mum," she said urgently. "That's the man who stares at me at the bus stop."

Laura was disturbed. She'd seen him before somewhere, but she couldn't think where. "Does he do it every day?" she asked Jilly.

"*Almost* every day. He drives past in this red Toyota. Sometimes he drives round and round the block and stares when he goes past, and sometimes he just parks and stares. He gives me the creeps."

"Men who stare are usually harmless," Laura said with a lightness she did not feel. "That's all they do. *Stare.*"

("Don't think I won't be watching," her ex-husband had promised after the custody case. "Don't think you'll get away with this."

But anyone angry made that kind of threat. It meant nothing.)

"Who's that man?" she asked a woman she'd got to know in the supermarket, a woman who was wiping hamburger from a toddler's face.

"Oh, I see him in the library all the time," the woman said. "I think he's a friend of the Spicers. Very shy, but rather nice. Gives the kids iceblocks and lollies."

The man seemed shyly friendly, or perhaps cordially aloof, like someone dragged to a party by friends too soon after a divorce or a death in the family. He moved from group to group, he smiled, he chatted, he was charming, he kept moving. Laura heard someone say, "I didn't catch your name," and he laughed quietly as though this were a particularly clever joke and moved on. She watched him gradually work his way further from the fringes of the crowd until he disappeared behind the bamboo.

Perhaps he was someone her ex-husband had hired. But then again, perhaps he was just a friend of the Spicers.

She slipped away to the pond.

The man was sitting cross-legged beside Caliban, with his hand on the gargoyle's head, staring into the water. Laura looked at his reflection and thought he had the saddest eyes she'd ever seen. It's *his* garden, she thought with sudden certainty. He's grieving for it.

Oblivious to Laura's presence, the man began stroking Caliban's head in a blind, desolate way, a gesture both intimate and ... what? *Hungry.*

Stricken, Laura said: "I ordered Ariel to go with him. Do you like him?" and the man started violently, as wild-eyed as Caliban himself. Laura felt momentarily frightened. She could not tell if the look was hostile, or haunted, or simply that of a man much disoriented by loss. Then he smiled, and Laura thought with a shiver that his smile was a little like that of her former husband, who could move from charm to threat to charm again without warning.

Caliban's reflection grinned at her from the water. *A real steal,* he smirked. She thought uncomfortably: it *is* a kind of theft, a foreclosure.

"I know how you must feel," she said apologetically. The man's eyes unnerved her. She spoke to his reflection, which watched hers. "Look, if you want to come and sit here sometimes ... well, that's okay. I'll understand." She felt as though she were placating some capricious force, and couldn't tell if she spoke from compassion or fear.

"Mrs Spicer," she said, when the flow of the party had reabsorbed her, "that man over there, just coming up from the pond. Is he Mr Voss?"

Mrs Spicer was startled. "Good God," she said. "I shouldn't think so." She studied him intently. "To tell you the truth, it's hard to say. We practically never saw him. I don't believe we ever once saw him face to face." She squinted, and tipped her head to one side. "It *could* be ... but no, I don't think so. That man's a friend of the Taylors, I think. I've seen him round. Mr Voss was stockier, heavier than that. Just the same, I wouldn't take chances. I'd notify the police."

"The *police*?" Laura said apprehensively. "Why the police?"

"Well, confidentially," Mrs Spicer lowered her voice. "I didn't want to alarm Jilly with the whole story. But I play tennis with Milly Layton whose husband's a cop. Voss was suspected of murder, you know."

"*Murder*?"

"The story is that his wife ran off with another man. He got custody of their daughter, and that was the situation when they moved in here, Voss and his kid. She used to babysit for us, as a matter of fact, when Kev was a baby. Lovely girl. Just about Jilly's age. Could never get a word out of her about her dad or mum, though I poked around. Discreetly, you know. Then one day she just disappeared. His story was that the wife had kidnapped her, but the police weren't so sure. They couldn't find any trace of the wife or daughter, and for a while they had a theory he'd murdered them both. Came and dug up the pond because they thought he might have buried them in the mud."

It seemed to Laura that she could feel the meaning of the gargoyle's leer seeping into her body like cold water. "But they never found anything," Mrs Spicer said lightly, "so charges were dropped. Voss went a bit berserk, Milly says. They had to cart him off. All I know is, the police cars came and went, came and went, I don't know how many times. Then the For Sale sign went up. It was there for *months* you know. They couldn't sell it. Word spread, people had a bad feeling about the place. Quite frankly, I say where there's smoke, there's fire. You've got to wonder what someone was hiding behind all that jungle. I expect you'll be having it cut back."

"Oh, well, I grew up in a house like this out past Samford, you see. Right in the rainforest. I like it this way. Mrs Spicer, Jilly says that man drives past when she's at the bus stop and stares."

"Really?" Mrs Spicer studied him more intently. "You've got to wonder about some of the Taylors' friends. Bloody peeping Toms, it's disgusting. Listen," she said, "I'd inform the police. You can't be too careful when you've got a daughter." She looked obliquely at Laura. "Especially when you're managing on your own. Not easy, I'm sure, being a single mother."

"No," Laura said.

"Jilly says you're doing a book on Patrick White's *Voss*. Funny, isn't it? The name, I mean. The coincidence."

"It *is* a bit weird," Laura acknowledged.

"Read *Voss* in high school. Based on Leichhardt, wasn't he?"

"More or less, yes."

"All those explorers were raving lunatics," Mrs Spicer said. "Well ..." She squinted across the lawn. "No, I'm sure that's not Mr Voss, he's too shrunken and pale for Mr Voss, but you must call the police. We don't want pervs in The Gap, it's a family place. Ask for Milly Layton's husband. As a matter of fact, I'll give Milly a tinkle myself."

"Mrs White," Sergeant Layton said. "Staring is not a criminal offence. I'm not saying there aren't loonies around, but if we followed up every phone call we get from a frightened woman, we'd never do anything else, d'ya see what I mean?"

"Yes," Laura said. "It's just that ... I thought it wouldn't hurt to have it on the record, you know, in case anything ... He drives a red Toyota, my daughter says."

"Mrs White." The sergeant spoke in the patient tones of one whose daily task involved fending off — wearily, kindly — hordes of neurotic women. "I have a daughter myself. I worry myself sick about her safety. Know what I do? Tell her never to accept rides from strange men. It's that simple. Train them to be sensible, know where they are, give them a curfew: that's all any parent can do."

But look, she wanted to say. I think I may have done something stupid. I told this man he could come and sit by my pond. I could see he was hurt you see. I could see he was in pain. But that wouldn't necessarily mean he wouldn't do harm, would it? And now I'm worried that he'll read something into my offer, I'm frightened that ...

But how could she expose such foolish behaviour to the police? *Women ask for it, you know. They're all masochists at heart, they're like children really.*

She said: "Well, you see, I thought he might be Mr Voss, the former owner. My neighbour says not, and I suppose she would know, but I don't feel completely certain, and your wife told my neighbour that Mr Voss —"

Sergeant Layton laughed. "My wife," he said fondly. "Listen, Mrs White. For number one: women embroider things, bless their souls. And for number two: I don't tell Milly everything. And for number three: we never had anything solid on Voss, he was a routine suspect, that's all. And as a matter of fact, we got the bodies and the killer on that one. Started off as a kidnap, all right, but then it seems the ex-wife's fancy boyfriend tampered with the kid — excuse my language, Mrs White, it's a dirty world. Anyway, the ex-wife threw a tantrum (jealous or maternal, we don't know which) and the boyfriend went off his rocker and killed them both. We caught up with him west of Port Augusta, found the bodies in the boot of his car. And for final: your Mr Voss cracked up, poor bugger. Stands to reason, dunnit? With his wife running off, then *pouf*, his kid disappearing, then the bodies."

And with the police accusing him of murder, Laura thought.

"Your Mr Voss is in the loony bin, poor bugger, so you can set your mind at rest on that score, Mrs White. He's not the bloke who's staring at your kid. Set a curfew, and tell her never to accept rides from strange men. All a parent can do."

"Yes, you're right of course, Sergeant Layton," she said.

Jilly woke with a start. It was the middle of the night, quiet as death, so what had disturbed her? The French doors were open on to the verandah and a wisp of breeze barely nudged the humid air. Damp hot silence settled onto damp sheets. So why, Jilly asked herself, every nerve taut and her heart thumping like a rock band's drum, why do I feel like I'm being watched? Then she saw the man beside her dresser, standing in shadow.

She screamed.

Fast as thought, he left on silent cat feet, and when Laura came running there was no sign, not a single telltale sign save Jilly's fear.

"It was that man," Jilly sobbed. "That creepy man was in my room."

"God, Jilly!" Laura switched on the floodlights for verandah and back porch. She watched the light pick out the curve of lawn that ended in the bamboo. Nothing beyond the bamboo could be seen. "He's gone now," she said as calmly as she could. "There's no one anywhere near the verandah." She bolted the French doors and all the windows and pulled down every blind in the house and they huddled together on Laura's bed in the sticky still heat. "It's okay," she said, stroking her daughter's hair. "It's okay. I'm afraid this is my fault, Jilly. I thought he was Mr Voss, you see. I told him he could come and sit in the garden. It was incredibly stupid." Jilly was trembling like a live bird held under a cat's tender paw. Laura said, to calm her: "I do think he's probably harmless. I think he's just a very sad man, you know. They say that's all voyeurs do, they just *look*."

"Call the police," Jilly begged, still shaking.

"Yes," Laura said. "Yes, of course."

Laura called the police. We'll send a squad car, the night dispatcher promised. And in due course — it seemed a very long time to Jilly and Laura — a squad car arrived. There were heavy footfalls on the verandah, and lines of torchlight raking the yard, and then a constable came to the door.

"No sign of an intruder, ma'am," he said. "Uh, our records indicate you've got peeping Tom worries. Understand this is a second report?"

"It was the same man," Laura explained. "The one who's been staring at my daughter at the bus stop."

"Yeah, well, generally harmless, these blokes. Let us know if anything happens." Then he dropped his voice, confidentially. "Teenage girls, you know, ma'am, very, uh, vivid imaginations." He dropped his voice still further and whispered: "Hormones." Then he smiled. "Still, keep us informed."

"Thank you, officer. I will." Laura kept her anger tamped down. "Thank you for coming so quickly." The sarcasm was lost on him, however.

"Any time," he said cheerily. "Give the kid a hot cup of tea and settle her down. She'll be right."

"Bloody police," she fumed to Jilly.

"Bloody useless police," Jilly said.

"Yeah," Laura grinned, cooling down a little. "Bloody hopeless cops."

They did make tea. It felt good, Laura thought, to have your teenage daughter leaning against your shoulder, cuddling into your arms the way she did when you rocked her through tooth-cutting nights long ago. They sat on the bed with the blinds down, and a candle burning, and talked all night.

"Mum," Jilly asked somewhere near dawn. "Do you think Dad misses me?"

"Of course he does. How could he not?"

"I mean, really *misses* me? Or, you know, just feels he should? Or just wants to bug you."

Laura's hand paused for a moment, then resumed its stroking of Jilly's hair. "How do you mean, bug me?"

Jilly sighed. "Well, I phone his office, you know, sometimes, when I'm lonely. Reverse charge, from pay phones. I didn't want to upset you. Do you mind?"

"It's natural, Jilly. He's your dad."

"His secretary says Dad and Caroline want me to visit them in New York. She says there's a Qantas ticket waiting in Sydney any time I go and pick it up."

"I see."

"But how come I only ever get to talk to his secretary? How come he never calls *me*? How come he never writes?"

"I don't know, Jilly."

"D'you think he *really* wants to see me?"

"I'm sure he does."

"It's a one-way ticket." Jilly pleated the sheet between her fingers. "D'you think he'll try to keep me there, Mum?"

"That's a tough one, Jilly." Laura sighed. "Your father's rather used to getting his own way, and to being able to buy anything he wants. Which isn't to say he doesn't love you. I know he does. You'll have to decide what you want to do."

"Mum, I hardly have any friends at school. They think I'm weird. And I'm scared of that man in the red Toyota. Why's he following me? Why's he always watching? I'm even scared of the house now. I'm not even gonna feel safe in my own room." She snuggled into Laura's arms. "If I promise to come back from New York, will you mind if I go?"

It's a steal, Laura thought. Her whole body felt like lead, but what could she say? The fears you could feel for a child were bottomless. They could fill the world. Suppose Jilly stayed and the man whom nobody knew ...? She'd never forgive herself. "I'll miss you horribly," she said. "But maybe it's best for now." Either way, she didn't think she'd feel any safer.

It was done within days. Laura drove Jilly to the Blue Coach terminal for the deluxe bus to Sydney. Her father's secretary was to meet her at the other end the next morning, take her to a hotel, put her on the plane for New York. It had all been arranged by Jilly's father. "Please don't stay around, Mum," she said. "We'll just get weepy if you do, and I hate goodbyes. I'll be embarrassed for the whole trip."

"It's not the kind of thing people mind, Jilly," Laura said. "Crying at goodbyes." She wanted to say: I don't feel safe when you're out of my sight. I want to drive you to Sydney. I want to sit beside you on the bus, see you safely on to the plane. I want to make certain your father meets you at the airport, I don't want any New York taxidrivers whisking you off to God knows where. I want to wrap you up in cotton wool.

"Yuck, I *hate* crying, I hate goodbyes," Jilly insisted. "I'm nearly *fourteen*, Mum. I can look after myself, you know."

"Yeah, I know."

"I'll phone you from New York, I promise."

"From New York!" Laura cried in alarm. "Phone me from Sydney, okay? Reverse the charges. Phone as often as you like. Phone me when the bus gets in, and phone me from the airport, okay?"

"*Mum!*" Jilly protested. Sometimes, she thought, parents needed so much protecting, it was exhausting. But at the sight of her mother's face, she relented. "Yeah, all right." She gave Laura a quick brusque hug. "But don't make such a big deal of it, okay?"

"Okay." Laura watched her daughter, with nothing more than a duffel bag slung over one shoulder, wave brightly and disappear into the terminal. She saw the line in her mind's eye. *Laura watched her daughter disappear.*

She got into her blue Mazda in the parking lot and sat and listened to the radio for fifteen minutes, then she drove round the block and parked discreetly down the street where she could watch the coach leave the depot. She couldn't see a thing through the darkened windows, but she pictured Jilly sitting halfway back, resolutely not crying.

It was a hot, blindingly bright subtropical day, but it felt bleak and chilly to Laura. She drove home and sat morosely by the pond.

Caliban's grin seemed full of menace to her now. The bamboo sounded like the click of knitting women who gossiped and pointed the finger and counted heads.

★   ★

In her dream, Laura was sitting at the back of the bus, and for some reason she couldn't move or make her voice carry. She could see Jilly sitting near a window halfway down, and she could see the back of the head of the man sitting next to her. What really frightened her, however, was the gargoyle driving the bus.

Down the hairpin turns of the Pacific Highway, they hurtled at alarming speeds. Caliban laughed like a maniac. At times, where the scree fell away sharply from road to ocean, the bus lurched on the soft shoulder, and shuddered, and barely righted itself. "Slow down!" Laura screamed, but other passengers turned back and shook their heads at her, annoyed, as though she were a child throwing tantrums. She was weak with relief when the bus stopped at Gosford for petrol — until she saw the man next to Jilly stand up. She recognised him. Jilly stood up too. "Jilly, no!" Laura shouted. But her daughter got off the bus with the man whom nobody knew. They both got into a red Toyota. Laura strained and shouted but could make no headway. It was as though she were buried up to the neck in sand.

She woke with a thudding heart and sodden sheets.

Six in the morning. She made coffee and paced. The bus wasn't due into Sydney till 10 a.m., which was light years off. All those stops: half an hour in Tweed Heads, an hour in Newcastle, half an hour in Gosford. If only she had asked Jilly to call from each stop. The distance to office hours seemed infinite. An image kept coming to her: the intimate way the man at the barbecue had stroked Caliban's head.

On the stroke of nine, Laura telephoned Sergeant Layton.

"When you said Mr Voss was in an asylum," she asked him, "did you mean Goodna?"

Well, actually, Sergeant Layton explained, he personally had had nothing to do with the loony-bin end of things. It was something he'd heard about from the police psychiatrist's department. He assumed they meant Goodna. He could find out if she wished.

Yes, she wished.

Meanwhile, impatient, Laura telephoned Goodna herself. That was not the kind of information they could give out, the registrar told her. Unless she was a doctor or the police.

Nine-thirty, only half an hour till the bus got in; plus give Jilly time to collect her bag, meet the secretary, make an excuse to go to the restroom, find a phone.

Ten. Soon now, soon.

Eleven. Oh, what could be keeping her? Maybe the bus was late, maybe there'd been a highway crash like that one near Newcastle last year. Laura phoned the bus company. The bus had arrived in Sydney on time at 10 a.m. No ma'am, they didn't give out passenger information over the phone.

Hadn't she told Jilly to phone her immediately? But Jilly had thought that was silly. Jilly would phone from the airport. Laura didn't even know what time the plane left, since she didn't know what the ticket arrangements were. Maybe there wasn't time. Maybe Jilly had had to rush from bus to check-in.

Laura called Qantas. The flight to New York via Los Angeles left at 4 p.m. Jilly would have lots of time then, after check-in, to make a call. Could Qantas confirm that a Ms Jilly White was a passenger? No, Qantas didn't give out that kind of information over the phone.

Midday, Laura couldn't stand it. She felt ill. She'd have to swallow her pride and phone her former husband's secretary. No, wait. If there'd been a problem, the secretary would have phoned. Laura would wait. If she hadn't had a call by 4 p.m., *then* she'd phone.

At 1.45 p.m. the phone rang and Laura leapt on it. "Jilly?"

"Uh, Sergeant Layton, ma'am."

"Oh," she said disoriented. "Oh yes, was it Goodna?"

"What? Oh, you mean about Voss. Uh, well, I've got someone working on that for you, but, um, actually, I'm not calling about that, Mrs White. I'm calling about your daughter."

Laura went weak at the knees. "Yes?" she said faintly.

"Can you tell me exactly where she is, exactly?"

"She's in Sydney, she'll probably be on her way to the airport by now. I'm terribly worried, as a matter of fact, that she hasn't phoned yet."

"Mind if I come round, Mrs White? I have to ask a few questions, that's all."

"Sure," Laura said faintly. She leaned against the wall and slid down it slowly and sat on the floor till the door bell rang.

"The thing is," Sergeant Layton said. "Your husband's sec-retary —"

"*Former* husband," Laura said sharply.

Tell me, tell me, her nerves screamed. *What's happened to Jilly?*

"Yes, excuse me. Your former husband's secretary said your daughter never got off the bus —" Laura heard the rest as from a great distance — "so she called your former husband in New York. Seems like he has a few friends in powerful places. Suddenly I have half the big brass in New South Wales breathing down my neck." He shook his head as though clearing it of Sydney frenzy. "Never known anything escalate so fast in my life. Probably all a mountain out of a molehill. Hope so, anyway." In the long run, he implied, easy-going Brisbane common sense could be expected to prevail.

"The thing is, your former husband does have legal access for holidays, and he's, ah, laying charges, it appears. He's accusing you of abduction. Hiding her, so she wouldn't be able —"

"But for God's sake, where *is* she?" Laura cried, surfacing from shock. "If she wasn't on the bus, where *is* she?"

Sergeant Layton sighed deeply. There was nothing so ugly as custody battles, nothing so savage as marital revenge, nothing so skilful as the acting he'd seen on both sides. "Are you counter-charging your former husband with kidnapping, Mrs White?"

"What?" For a second, Laura's eyes flashed with hope, but she shook her head dully. "No," she said. "There'd be no point. She was on her way to him anyway. He knew he could easily keep her there, if that's what he wanted."

"Let's get back to the bus terminal," Sergeant Layton said. "You put her on the bus, and you watched it leave. What time was that?"

"I didn't actually put her on the bus," Laura said wretchedly. "She didn't want me to come inside the terminal. I saw the bus leave at 3 p.m., but I didn't actually put her on it."

"You cannot swear to the fact that she was on the bus?"

"She was on it, well she *must* have been on it … No, I suppose I can't actually swear …"

Sergeant Layton said sternly: "You drop a thirteen-year-old kid off at a bus terminal full of riffraff and God-knows-who and let her fend for herself? That's not gonna look too good in court, is it?"

"No," Laura said in a small voice. She could see that it would not. Neurotic and overpossessive, or negligent: those were the choices. It seemed to her that whatever mothers did was wrong. She found herself guilty on every count.

Sergeant Layton turned gruff: "Listen," he said. "Husbands and wives think they know each other, but they don't. Parents think they know kids. Ten to one, she never got on the bus. Or she got off at Tweed Heads and bolted. No." He held up a hand to ward off her shocked interruption. "I know you *know* she wouldn't do that. But it happens all the time, just the same. Happens in nice middle-class suburbs like The Gap. Have you any idea how many runaways we track down every week? Sometimes they want to give their parents a scare. And sometimes they just want to go off for a while and think, get away from the push and pull. Nine times out of ten, they turn up with their tails between their legs when the money runs out."

"Please find her," Laura said.

"We got a full scale search on, Mrs White. But we also got an ex-husband laying charges. And we got another funny little thing here that came up on the computer trace."

He fumbled in his pocket and handed her a police printout. She read it blankly.

Re: Laurence J. Voss. Credit card search indicates that subject is currently living at Settlement Road, The Gap, in Brisbane, under assumed name of Laura White.

"Amazing, those electronic-search brains," Sergeant Layton said, watching her closely. "Pretty hard to fool them. They're like an octopus, they suck in dental visits, credit card purchases, phone calls, mail-order lists, you can't rent a video without they keep tabs on you and then match things up."

She couldn't tell if she was being asked to take the printout seriously or not. "So Mr Voss is a woman and I'm him," she said drily.

"They're not laughing at CIB," he said. "Sort of link-up that rings bells on a police computer."

"I can't believe this." She could feel something indecent, black laughter maybe, gathering like steam about to blow. "I ordered something from one of his mail-order catalogues. I left the order form in his name, and wrote in my credit card number."

"And why did you use his name?"

"I don't know. No particular reason. It was already set up that way, and the delivery address was the same. It was just less trouble, that's all."

"Maybe," he said. "Or maybe you wanted to confuse the issue. Maybe you wanted to draw attention away from yourself. Maybe you want us to think Mr Voss abducted your daughter. You seemed very keen for people to believe he was at your party. I'm just telling you how it looks."

How it looks, she thought blankly. How does it look? When he left, she went and sat by the pond but she couldn't bear Caliban's smile. *Was* it a smile? What was it? Was anything the way it looked?

Laura had never known time to pass so slowly. She sat on the verandah and stared at the jasmine. Mrs Spicer came with little cakes and pikelets and sympathy. There must have been strong reasons of course, Mrs Spicer said, with a soft click click of her tongue. There must have been strong reasons why Jilly wanted to visit her father, and why her father was so hasty, click click, click click, and why Jilly told that story about the man in the red Toyota. Click click, she said. Click click.

"Yes," Laura said vaguely.

Mrs Spicer told Milly Layton that you had to wonder about a woman who was so secretive, and who kept to herself so much. "She never pruned a thing in that garden," Mrs Spicer said. "You have to wonder why."

"You have to wonder," her former husband said icily, over the phone from New York. "You have to wonder what goes on in your mind, Laura. Quite frankly, Caroline and I think this is something you've cooked up between the two of you, though I hold Jilly blameless. Brainwashing's a dirty piece of work. I think this Voss is a figment of your imagination, a red herring. I think you wanted to get at me."

Laura searched her memory to see if he could be right. Had they cooked something up? Hadn't she, secretly, really wanted to keep Jilly from him? How did it look? She couldn't feel confident about any of her motives. Her memory of the sequence of things had gone slack, like butter left out in the Brisbane heat. She felt her cheeks and chin and mouth with her fingertips, in trepidation, for fear Caliban's obscene leer was lurking beneath her skin. She was afraid she might have done fearful things she could not remember.

"But if I'm wrong," her ex-husband said, "If something's really happened to her, I hold you fully responsible."

That seemed to Laura fair, and no more than the charge she laid against herself.

Sergeant Layton came back. "Our investigative branch has come up with something on Voss," he said, "that lends weight to your side of the story."

Yes, it was Goodna where Voss had been committed, but for quite a short time. In the wake of the murders of his wife and daughter, he'd been suffering from shock. "Post-traumatic stress disorder," the psychiatrist called it. No history of instability before that. Used to be a horticulturalist of some standing, used to lecture at the Queensland University of Technology. Sedation and counselling till the worst of the shock wore off, that was the treatment. Fairly straightforward really, then he'd been discharged. There'd be long-term effects of grief and anger and disorientation, which would gradually lessen. And possibly there'd be times when a trigger incident would make him re-experience the trauma. This could be intense, as vivid as the actual event.

"Happens to war vets all the time," Sergeant Layton said. "Shell shock, we used to call it. Now they got this fancy name for it. Basically, though, Voss would be all right. And he was getting regular counselling as an outpatient, no worries there. And here was the crucial thing: he was haunting the scene of the trauma like a ghost, his psychiatrist knew all about that, it was par for the course. He's your man in the red Toyota all right. Takes some of the suspicion off you."

"Sergeant Layton, it's *Jilly* I'm worried sick about. Would he do anything to Jilly? I mean, when you talk about trigger incidents, what ...?"

"Ah, on that score, not a thing to worry about. Stuffing's taken right out of him, poor bugger. Worst he'd do would be cry in Jilly's lap. Great relief, eh?"

"Yes," Laura said. She told herself she felt relieved.

"Atta girl!" he laughed. "Ten to one she'll turn up of her own accord."

A police van pulled up outside Laura's house and two constables came to the door.

"Laura White?" one of them asked.

"Yes?"

"We have to ask you to come with us, Mrs White. We have an order for your re-committal."

"My what?" Wheels spun in Laura's head: *it's to do with Voss, he's flipped again, he's done something.* "I think there's been a mistake," she said. "Don't you want Mr Laurence Voss?"

The officer looked uncertain. His partner said in a low quick voice: "When you've done this as many times as I have, you'll know. They always claim it's a mistake. Then they get violent."

"Look," Laura said, getting angry. "This is a mistake. I've never been committed once, so how could I be *re*-committed? It's the former owner, Mr Voss, you're after. Call your own Sergeant Layton from my phone, and you'll find out."

"Tell you what, ma'am." The officers had her arms now, and were treating her with the kind of wary patronising gentleness reserved for the dangerously mad. "We'll call Sergeant Layton after you come with us, how's that?"

Laura sat in the cage in the back of the van and told herself: I must not dissipate my strength in rage. I must stay calm. This will all be sorted out very quickly.

It was sorted out, of course, though not quite as quickly as Laura had hoped. Sergeant Layton himself, wreathed in apologies and shame, came to pick her up at Goodna.

"Thing is," Sergeant Layton said, "the psychiatrist suddenly realised this was happening a week ago, it's not that uncommon. Well, it *is* uncommon, but not after very severe trauma. The boyfriend that ran off with Voss's wife, see, the boyfriend killer … well, the very thought was unbearable. *Unbearable.* So the mind switches places. Mind's a funny clever bugger in its way. He's, uh, we think he believes he's the killer. He's *become* the boyfriend, you see?"

Laura saw. Abused kids become abusers, there were children in Auschwitz who had worshipped their guards. She'd read about this.

"Psychiatrist signed the forms a week ago." Sergeant Layton sighed. "Government bureaucracies, damn them. The right-hand memo never knows what the left is doing till it's too bloody late. And then the flaming police computers step in." He pulled up in front of her house and said gruffly: "The implications aren't good, I'm afraid."

"No," she said. "I see that."

The one thing she had to hold on to was that Jilly would never accept a ride from a stranger in a red Toyota. She was certain of that.

She couldn't sit by the pond. The place seemed to her humid with evil. And she understood, now, the meaning of Caliban's leer. It was the laugh of someone who had looked at horror, because horror was a jokester, no questioning that. And this was the grimmest joke in horror's bag: that the innocent and the damaged were capable of fearful crimes.

The serpent swallows its tail, she thought. The victim eats the man with the knife.

She couldn't bear to stay in the house. She drove about aimlessly, restlessly, in her blue Mazda. She remembered the day she'd bought the house, the day Jilly had sat outside in the street in the same blue car, listening to the radio, while Mr Voss watched them both.

She remembered the day she'd stood with him by the pond and watched his reflection watching hers, just the two of them. Four, counting statues. Eight, if you counted reflections.

What is evil? she wondered. How does it look?

On the seventh day, a baggage loader for the Blue Coach company admitted something under police interrogation. He confessed that on the day Jilly disappeared, a man waiting in a car out the back in the loading bay had given him ten dollars. He was to go inside and tell the young woman with the grey and yellow duffel bag that her mother was waiting in the car with something she'd forgotten.

The baggage loader had been suspicious. "Her *mother?*" he'd said pointedly.

The man had lifted up a parcel. "Yes, her mother. She forgot this. Her mother sent me racing into town with it. Tell her to come out to the loading bay."

When the girl came out, the baggage loader pointed to the car. No, it wasn't a red Toyota; it was a blue Mazda. He noted that the man was no longer in it, but the parcel was on the seat. "That's it," he told her. "That's what you forgot."

He saw the girl open the door on the passenger side and reach for the parcel, but after that he hadn't paid attention. He'd gone back to loading baggage on the bus.

★   ★

Laura felt as though she were on a very long journey into nowhere. She had a sense of desert waste and blowing sand and bleached bone. When, as though in a nightmare, Sergeant Layton appeared again at her door, she thought he might have been a mirage.

"I'm sorry," he said. Pieces of words blew about, scuds of sand, *blue Mazda, Jilly's body, in the boot,* but she couldn't put them together. Sergeant Layton went on talking like a face in a silent film, "Same model as yours, different plates. Not much comfort, but he blew his own brains out afterwards ..." Laura couldn't hear a thing. There was such a roaring in her head, such searing pain, it felt as though her skull was blowing out.

UNPERFORMED EXPERIMENTS
HAVE NO RESULTS

You could say it began with the man in the canoe rather than with the dream, though I can no longer be certain of the sequence of events. It is possible, after all, that the letter arrived before either the dream or that frail and curious vessel, though I do not think so. I used to be without doubts on this matter. Chronology used not to be even a question. But since the disappearance, trying to catch hold of any kind of certainty has been like catching hold of water.

Sometimes, when a tradesman or a parcel delivery man comes to the door, I have to restrain myself, by a fierce act of the will, from grabbing him by the lapels or by the denim coverall straps and demanding: "What do accidents mean, do you think? Do you have an opinion? Are you a gambling man? Have you ever been spooked by coincidence?" The truth is, I have become obsessed with the patterns of chance — the neatness of them, the provocation such neatness gives — but chance is a subject that very much resists scrutiny, and the more I ponder random conjunctions of events, the more intensely I try to focus my memory, the hazier things become. You cannot, as the physicists keep telling us, engage in the act of close observation without changing the thing observed. Of course I resort to such analogies because it is Brian who is dying.

Nevertheless, though it may or may not be the first cause, I will start with that afternoon on my dock and with the man in the canoe. It was a late summer afternoon and very humid, and the forecast — for thunder storms — was sufficient to keep most boats in marinas. There were white-caps on the lake and the river. When I looked east, I could see the pines on the tip of Howe Island bending like crippled old men in the wind. Westward, past the Spectacles, past Milton Island, I thought I could just see one of the ferries, veiled in great fans of spray, crossing the neck of the lake. Wolfe Island, directly opposite, was invisible, or almost so, behind a billowing indigo cloud that threw the whole head of the river into twilight, although it was only about four o'clock in the afternoon.

I was right at the end of my dock, and I had a book propped on my knees, but the wind kept buffeting my light aluminium deck chair to such an extent that I began to wonder if it was aerodynamically possible to be lifted up on a gust and dumped into the water. I kept looking up over the page, partly to assess my chances of staying dry, but mostly to enjoy the extravagant theatre of wind and water. And then, startled, I thought I saw a canoe emerging from the bateau channel between Howe Island and the shore.

I'm imagining things, I decided, rubbing my eyes. Who would be so foolhardy on such a day? Or so strong, for that matter. Here, the currents are swift and ruthless. Every summer, bits and pieces of our ageing dock disappear, and end up, no doubt, somewhere around Montreal; every winter the pack ice brings us splintered paddles and fragments of boats bearing registration marks from Toronto, Niagara, and even, once, from Thunder Bay. I shaded my eyes and squinted. Nothing there. Wait ... Yes, there it was again, a canoe, definitely, with a solitary paddler, heading upriver against all this mad seaward-running energy.

It is by no means impossible to paddle upriver — I have done it myself — but even without a headwind it is very hard work and is rarely tried solo. Astonished, I kept my eyes on the paddler. He must have muscles like steel ropes, I thought. His chances of capsizing seemed extraordinarily high. Clearly, he was someone who liked danger, someone who was excited by risk, perhaps even someone who got a certain kick out of pain, or at any rate, out of enduring it. But for how long, I wondered, could his arms take so much punishment?

Do not undertake anything unless you desire to continue it; for example, do not begin to paddle unless you are inclined to continue paddling. Take from the start the place in the canoe that you wish to keep.

Old advice, three centuries old, but still sound: that was Jean de Brébeuf, writing home to Paris with tips "for the Fathers of our society who shall be sent to the Hurons". I always think of them, those French Jesuits, *voyageurs*, when I see a canoe pitching itself against the current. I think of them often, as a matter of fact, since I moved out here onto the river. I frequently browse through their *Relations*, those lively, detailed, sometimes despairing reports to their superiors. Paris, Rome: it must have seemed as uncertain as prayer, dispatching words by ship.

The *Relation for 1649* to the Very Reverend Father Vincent Caraffa, General of the Society of Jesus, at Rome: *I have received, very*

Reverend Paternity, your letter dated 20 January 1647. If you wrote us last year, 1648, we have not yet received that letter …

The *Relation for 1637: You must be prompt in embarking and disembarking; and tuck up your gowns so that they will not get wet, and so that you will not carry either water or sand into the canoe. To be properly dressed, you must have your feet and legs bare: while crossing the rapids, you can wear your shoes, and, in the long portages, even your leggings.*

I imagine them with their blistered European hands and their cassocks hoisted up around their thighs, paddling full pelt up their *Great River St Lawrence* (they wrote of it with such affectionate possessiveness, with such respect for its stern powers), dipping their paddles toward their deaths, skimming past these very rocks that buttress (and will eventually smash) my dock, heading west with their mad cargo of idealism, dedication, and wrong-headedness.

You must try and eat at daybreak unless you can take your meal with you in the canoe; for the day is very long, if you have to pass it without eating. The Barbarians eat only at Sunrise and Sunset, when they are on their journeys.

I could see the flash of the paddle now, knifing into the water, keeping to the right side, pulling closer to shore. His arms are giving out, I thought. He is going to try to beach on this stretch. Now that the canoe was close enough, I could see that it was neither fibreglass nor aluminium, but birchbark. It wasn't until the next day that I was struck by the oddness of this, and by the fact that I had never seen a bark canoe before, except in photographs and museums. At the time it seemed quite unsurprising, or at least, not significant. I merely noted it, wondering exactly where the canoeist would reach shore, and if he would manage this before capsizing.

And then, gradually, it became clear to me that the paddler had no intention of trying to land. He's crazy, I thought. Shoulders hunched forward, head slightly down, eyes on the prow of his craft, he was bent on defying the current and continuing upriver, parallel to shore and now only about thirty feet out. It seemed incredible. He was all manic energy and obstinacy, and I fancied I could hear the pure high humming note of his will above the general bluster of the wind. His strength, which seemed supernatural, was oddly infectious. It was as though infusions of energy were pumping themselves into my body, as though the paddler's adrenalin was an atmosphere that I inhaled. I couldn't take my eyes off him. *Go, go, go*, I urged, weirdly excited.

It is odd how certain body shapes, certain ways of moving the body, are retained like templates on the memory. So we recognise a voice, a face — we take this as unremarkable — but so also a gesture or a way of walking can be recalled. I could still see only the outline of the figure (though I'd assumed from the start the paddler was male), and he was wearing a hooded windbreaker so that he (or even she) could have been anyone. And yet, watching the way the shoulders hunched forward, the way the arms dug into the water, the sharp thought came to me: *This reminds me of someone. Who is it? Who? Who?*

It was maddening. It was like meeting someone at a party and knowing you have met that person before somewhere, but being unable to summon up a name or a context. This sort of incomplete recollection can drive you crazy. The canoe was drawing level with my dock now and I wished I'd brought my binoculars down. The plunge and lift and dip of the shoulder blades, oh, it was at the tip of my mind, who did that movement remind me of? Now the canoe was level with the end of my dock, but the hooded head kept its eyes resolutely on the prow and the water, the paddle flashed.

Oh please look up, I willed.

And he did.

"Good god!" I cried out, thunderstruck. "*Brian!*"

Brian — no, of course not Brian, I was aware almost instantaneously that it couldn't possibly be Brian, who was either in Australia or Japan — not Brian, then, but the man in the canoe simply sat there, resting his paddle and staring at me, startled, which naturally meant that he scudded back downstream very swiftly. He dug the paddle furiously into the water, dip, dip, dip, until he drew level again, closer this time. He rested his paddle and stared. I felt, as the current again bucked him backwards, that I had to do something potent and instant to stop time unwinding itself, but I could neither speak nor move, the resemblance to Brian was so eerie. I was experiencing something like vertigo, and a pain like angina in my chest. Shock, I suppose.

I was dimly aware that my book had fallen into the water and that I was on my hands and knees on the dock. I watched the canoe draw level a third time, and the paddler and I stared at each other (he was very pale, and there seemed, now, to be no expression at all on his face), and then he, Brian, I mean the man in the birchbark canoe, turned away and lowered his head, and resumed paddling more fiercely than ever.

I watched until he disappeared from sight, which seemed to take hours. I have no idea how long I stayed on my hands and knees. I know that when I tried to climb the steep steps up our cliff, my legs felt like jelly and kept shaking so badly I had to stop and rest several times.

People climbing mountains and cliffs hyperventilate, this is common knowledge. They see things. Visitations alight on them.

Between the fiftieth step and the fifty-first, the past distended itself like a balloon and I climbed into it. I could feel its soft sealed walls.

Trapped, I thought. And simultaneously, pleasurably: *home*. I could smell the rainforest, smell Queensland, feel the moist air of the rich subtropics. *I am here again. Home.*

Brian is a few feet ahead of me, both of us drenched, both feeling for handholds and footholds, both of us (I realise it now) equally scared, but too proud to admit it.

(This would have been our last year in high school, and this was something we did every year, spend a day in our bit of rainforest — we thought of it that way — on the outskirts of Brisbane, climbing the waterfall. But our last year in high school was the year of the floods. I think we both gulped a little when we saw the falls, but neither would ever have been the first to back out. We were both given to constant high anxiety, and both temperamentally incapable of backing away from our fears.)

So. Every handhold slips, every foothold is algae-slick. My fingers keep giving way. My heart thumps — thud, thud, thud — against its cage. Delirium, the salt flavour of panic: I can taste them. Just inches above my eyes, I see the tendon in Brian's ankle. If I were to touch it, it would snap. I tilt my head back and see his shoulder blades, corded tight, lift like wings, pause, settle, lift again. He reaches and pulls, reaches and pulls, he is a machine of bodily will. The energy field of his determination

— pulses of it, like a kind of white light, bouncing off him — brush against me, charging the air. This keeps me going.

At the top of the falls, we collapse. We lie on the flat wet rocks. We do not speak. Our clothes give off curls of steam that drift up into the canopy, and creepers trail down to meet them. We float into sleep, or perhaps it is merely a long sensuous silence that is sweeter than sleep. I dream of flying. I have languid wings. I can feel updrafts of warm air, like pillows, against my breast feathers.

"Mmm," I murmur drowsily at last, "I love this heat. I could lie here forever. How come the water's so cold, when it's so hot here on the rocks?"

"I'm not even going to answer that, Philippa," Brian says lazily. "It's such a dumb question."

"Piss off," I say. I inch forward on my stomach and peer over the lip of the falls. I can't believe we have climbed them. I watch the solid column of water smash itself on the rocks below. I feel queasy. I can see four years of high school shredding themselves, all the particles parting, nothing ever the same again. "Where do you reckon we'll be five years from now?" I ask him. I have to shout. My voice falls down into the rift and loses itself in spray.

Brian crawls across and joins me. Side by side, we stare down ravines and years, high school, adolescence, childhood, we've climbed out of them all. There is just university ahead, and then the unmapped future.

"Where will we end up, d'you reckon?"

"Not here," Brian shouts. "We won't be in Brisbane."

"But even if we aren't, we'll come back. Let's do this every year for the rest of our lives."

"Not me," Brian says. "After uni, I'm never coming back."

The shouting takes too much energy, and we crawl back to the relative hush of the flat rocks ringed with ferns.

"So where will you be?"

"I don't know. Cambridge. Japan, maybe. There's some interesting research going on in Tokyo. Wherever's best for the kind of physics I'm interested in."

"What if you don't get into Cambridge?" I ask, although I know it's another dumb question. It's like asking: what if you don't get to the top of the falls?

Brian doesn't bother to answer.

"I'll probably still be here," I say.

"No you won't."

"You're such a bloody know-it-all, Brian."

"I know you and me."

"You think you do."

"Philippa," he says irritably, with finality. "I know us well enough to know we won't stay in Brisbane. You'll end up somewhere extreme, Africa, Canada, somewhere crazy."

"You're nuts," I say. "Anyway, wise guy, wherever I am, you can bet I'm going to stay close to water."

"Yes," he says. "We'll both stay near water."

In the dream, I am at the end of my dock, reading, when I notice the most curious light over Wolfe Island. The whole island seems burnished with gold leaf, and there is an extraordinary clarity to things, to individual trees, for instance, as though each detail has been outlined with a fine-tipped black brush. I can see vines, orchids, staghorn ferns against the tree trunks. I can see that Wolfe Island has gone tropical, that it is thick with rainforest, that lorikeets and kingfishers are flashing their colours on the St Lawrence banks.

Then I note that there is a suspension bridge, the catwalk kind, with wooden planks and drop sides, the kind sometimes strung a hundred and fifty feet up in the rainforest canopy to allow tourists to see the aerial garden running riot up there. This bridge starts at the end of my dock and crosses the river to Wolfe Island, but it is submerged.

What catches my eye first are the ropes tied to the end of my dock, just below water level. I lie flat on my stomach and peer down. I can see the arc of the bridge, little seaweed gardens swaying on its planks, curving down and away from me.

There is someone lying on his back on the bridge, or rather floating with it, just above the planks, just below the rope siderails. It is Brian. His eyes are open but unseeing, his skin has the pallor of a drowned man, algae spreads up from his ankles, tiny shell colonies are crusting themselves at all his joints. Seaweed ferns move with him and around him. He looks like Ophelia. *There with fantastic garlands did she come ...*

"Alas, then," I say to him, "are you drowned?"

"Drowned, drowned," he says.

No one would be too surprised by the fact of my dream. First I see a man in a canoe who reminds me of someone I know, and that very night I dream of Brian. A canoeist in a storm is at risk; I dream of death. There is a simple logic to this sequence of events; anyone would subscribe to it.

Nevertheless, I woke in a state of panic. I woke with the certainty that something was wrong. I hadn't seen Brian for, I had to count back ... well over a year, it must have been. It was always hit or miss with Brian. Luckily, childhood friends had a slightly better chance of making contact with him than ex-lovers or his ex-wife, but no one alive could compete with the sharp scent of a new hypothesis. I used to picture him literally *living* in his research lab, Melbourne or Tokyo, either city it was the same. I used to imagine a railway bed tucked under the computer desk. The last time we met for dinner in Melbourne he said, sometime after midnight: "My god, the time! I've got to get back to the lab."

"You sleep there?" I asked sardonically.

"Quite often," he said.

On principle, Brian never answered his phone. He kept it unplugged (both in his lab, and at the home address he rarely used) except for when he was calling out. I knew this. Nevertheless I called, Melbourne and Tokyo, both; and of course got no answer.

I sent faxes and got no response.

I called the secretary at his research institute in Melbourne. "Professor Leckie is in Tokyo," she said, "but no one has seen him for weeks. We still get his e-mail though, so he's all right."

E-mail! I never remembered to check mine, I used it so rarely. I plugged in the modem on my computer, keyed in my password, got into the system, and opened my "mailbox" on screen.

There was only one message, undated.

Philippa: I'm going away and wanted to say goodbye. Remember the falls! Those were the good old days, weren't they, when nothing could stop us? I often think of you. Of us back then. Pity we can't go backwards. Take care. Brian.

I sent a message back instantly.

Brian, I typed onto my screen. *Had a disturbing dream about you last night. Are you okay? I miss you. Take care. Philippa.*

★   ★

Back then, on the day of the message on my screen, the order was still beyond question for me. First the man in the canoe, then the dream, then the message. I began to be less confident of this sequence after the letter from my mother in Brisbane. Not immediately, of course. But a few weeks after the letter, I had to make a point of reminding myself that the terrible thunderstorm weather had begun in late August, that my mother's letter was postmarked September, and that I could not anchor (by any external proof) either my dream or my e-mail to a date.

I bumped into Brian's mother in the city last week, my mother wrote. *She says something's the matter with Brian, some nervous-system disorder. I think she said, something quite dreadful, there was some Latin-sounding word but I can't remember. She said she flew down to visit him in the Royal Melbourne, and he looked like a skeleton, he'd lost so much weight. He's not taking it well, she said. He's never been able to tolerate any kind of interference with his work, not even his marriage, as you know. She's terribly worried. He refused treatment and checked himself out and flew to Tokyo, can you believe that? You know he used to phone her once a week from wherever he was? Well, he's stopped doing it. She's quite depressed and quite frightened. I thought maybe you could get him to phone her, poor dear. Or maybe you'd like to write to her yourself? She must be awfully lonely since Mr Leckie died. We thought perhaps we should invite her for Christmas, but it's hard to tell whether she'd enjoy this or not. Maybe you should write to her, Philippa. You know her much better than we do.*

Every day I would begin a letter in my mind.

Dear Mrs Leckie: Remember when Brian and I used to go on rainforest treks and get home hours later than we planned? You used to

worry yourself sick, and my parents too. But we always did show up,
remember? Brian's just off on another trek, he's lost track of time, that's
all ...

No. Begin again.

Dear Mrs Leckie: Brian's gone on a journey, as we always knew he
would, from which (both you and I have a hunch about this) he might
not return. He carries everything he needs inside his head, and always
has. In his own way, he misses us. I promise I'll visit when I'm in
Brisbane next year. How is your frangipani tree? Remember when Brian
and I ...?

I never sent these unwritten letters.

I began to ask myself whether I'd imagined the man in the
canoe. Or whether I'd dreamed him. Or whether I'd dreamed
the e-mail message which had vanished into electronic ether
without a trace.

For my night-time reading, I followed records of lost trails.
The *Relation of 1673,* for example, written by Father Claude
Dablon: *He had long premeditated this undertaking, influenced by a*
most ardent desire to extend the kingdom of knowledge ... he has the
Courage to dread nothing where everything is to be Feared ... and if,
having passed through a thousand dangers, he had not unfortunately
been wrecked in the very harbour, his Canoe having been upset below
sault St Louys, near Montreal ...

In Brisbane (two years ago? three?) on the verandah of the
Regatta Hotel, a mere stone's throw from the university, a jug
of beer between us, Brian said: "D'you ever get panic attacks that
you'll burn up all your energy before you get there?"

"Get where?" I asked.

"I shouldn't even answer that, Philippa. God, you can be an-
noying," Brian said. "Get to where you wanted to go."

I couldn't concentrate. I stared across Coronation Drive at the Brisbane River. I could never quite believe that the present had inched forward from the past. "Look at those barges," I said. "I bet they haven't replaced them since we were students. They're decrepit, it's a miracle they're still afloat. I could swear even the graffiti hasn't changed."

"It hasn't," Brian said. "We come back younger because we're in orbit, that's all. Brisbane gets older, we get younger. A clock on a spaceship moves slower than clocks on earth, don't you know that, Philippa? If we went on a journey to Alpha Centauri, a few light-years out, a few back, we'd come back younger than our great-great-granchildren. Got that? And we've moved light-years from Brisbane, haven't we? So it figures. The trouble with you arty types is you don't know your relativity ABCs."

Dear Mrs Leckie, I could write. *Brian's in orbit. He's simply lost track of time, it's all relative. We could go backwards, and swing on your front gate again. We could unclimb the waterfall. We could go back through the looking-glass and watch the future before it came.*

I sent out daily e-mail messages to Brian's number. *Past calling the future*, I signalled. *Brisbane calling Far Traveller. Please send back bulletins. I miss you. P.*

I tried to goad him into verbal duelling: *Which clocktime are you travelling on? Please report light-year deviation from Greenwich Mean.*

Every day I checked my "box". There was nothing.

I called Brian's secretary in Melbourne again. "When you said you were still getting his e-mail," I asked, "how often did you mean? And where is it coming from?"

"You never know where e-mail is coming from," his secretary

said. "Actually, we haven't had any for several weeks, but that's not so unusual for him. Once he went silent for months. When he gets obsessed with a new theory ..."

"How long has he been ill?" I ask.

"I didn't know he was ill," she said. "But it doesn't surprise me. We're always half expecting all our researchers to drop dead from heart attacks. They're all so driven."

I think of the last time I saw him, in Melbourne. "Why don't you slow down a bit?" I asked. "How many more prizes do you have to win, for god's sake?"

"Prizes!" He was full of contempt. "It's got nothing to do with prizes. Honestly, Philippa, you exasperate me sometimes."

"What's it got to do with then?"

"It's got to do with getting where I want to go." I could hear our beer glasses rattling a little on the table. I think it was his heartbeat bumping things. He couldn't keep still. His fingers drummed a tattoo, his feet tapped to a manic tune. "I'm running out of time," he said. I would have to describe the expression on his face at that moment as one of anguish.

"You frighten me sometimes, Brian. Sometimes, it's exhausting just being with you."

Brian laughed. "Look who's talking."

"Compared to you, I'm a drifter. Wouldn't it be, you know, more *efficient*, if you just, even just a little, slowed down?"

"When I slow down," he said, "you'll know I'm dead."

Between the soup and the main course of a dinner party, my mind elsewhere, I heard these words: *that birchbark canoe that washed up* ... and *police inquiries* ...

I had a peppermill in my hand at the time, and I ground it

slowly over my salad. I took careful note of the sharp pleasing contrast made by cracked peppercorn against green leaf. I looked discreetly around the table. Who had spoken the words? Had they been spoken?

I could hear Brian say irritably: "Honestly, Philippa, you never *verify* things. You live inside this vague world of your mind, you make things up, and then you believe they're real."

"But so do you. You make up a theory, and then you set out to prove it's real."

"*There's* the crucial difference," he says. "My hypotheses are verifiable, one way or the other. I chase details, I nail them down. I won't stop until my theory is either proved or *dis*proved. If I can't do either, I have to discard it."

"Same with me," I say. "I put riddles on one side, and come back to them. I do realise the birchbark canoe could have been a figment of my mind and my bedtime reading. I'm checking around. What's the difference?"

"I'm not even going to answer that question," Brian says.

"But don't you ever come back to your discards?"

"Of course I do. Some problem sets have been passed on for generations. The trick is, you have to approach from a new angle every time. Half the battle is how you frame the question. Un-performed experiments have no results."

"Exactly," I say.

And over the candles on a dinner table at the other end of the world, I hazarded cautiously, flippantly: "Did someone just say something about a birchbark canoe, or did I imagine it?"

Seven pairs of eyes stared at me.

"Sometimes, Philippa," my husband joked, "I swear you put

one part of your mind on automatic pilot, and the other part is god knows where."

"It's true," I said disarmingly. "So did I hear something about a birchbark canoe, or didn't I?"

"The one washed up on the ferry dock," one of the guests said. She waved a ringed hand and smiled, courteously tolerant. ("Bit of a flake, isn't she?" I could imagine her saying to someone later. "Where *does* she get to, between the crackers and the cheese?") "The one the police are making inquiries about. I was just telling everyone that I'd had to go down to the station and make a statement. And John did too, didn't you, John? Didn't you see him? Yes, I thought so, I was talking to Milly on the phone. So that makes two of us. I mean, who saw the canoe when there was someone in it. Paddling."

"I saw him several times, as a matter of fact," John said. "Came within ten feet of my boat once, when I was fishing. I waved — well, it's customary — but he didn't wave back. Funny, I only ever saw him paddling upriver. Beautiful canoe."

"The Burketts," someone else said, "the ones who live on Howe Island, you know? — they said there was a hunter camped there most of July and August. No one knew where he was from, and no one was very happy about it, but that's who it must have been. I mean, they said he had a birchbark canoe and it's not as though you see them every day.

"And then he just up and disappeared. The Burketts gave the police a full description and they're putting out a trace, you know, for next of kin."

"I expect they'll find the body eventually," John said. "I wouldn't mind buying the canoe, she was a real beauty. I suppose she'll go up on police auction sooner or later."

"Won't they have to hang onto it as evidence until the body is found?" someone asked.

"I expect so," John said. "Yes, I expect so. Still, sooner or later. The police boats are out dragging every day."

"I hope they don't find him," I said.

Everyone looked at me.

Sooner or later, I think, evidence of one kind or another will cast itself up: a dream, a letter, an item in the newspaper. Every day, I read the "Police and Fire Watch" column in the local paper. Every day, I am relieved that no body has been found. Of course this is ridiculous, and I know it. There's a name for it: *sympathetic magic*.

And there's that other matter too, for which Brian had a word: *synchronicities*.

What do they mean? I ask myself. What do they *mean*?

In the evenings, I read of doomed voyages.

The Relation of Christophe Regnaut concerning the martyrdom and blessed death of Father de Brébeuf ... captured on the 16th day of March, in the morning, with Father Lalemant, in the year 1649. Father de Brébeuf died the same day as his capture, about 4 o'clock in the afternoon ... I saw and touched the top of his scalped head ...

The Relation of 1702: Father Bineteau died there from exhaustion; but if he had had a few drops of Spanish wine, for which he asked us during his last illness ... or had we been able to procure some Fresh food for him, he would perhaps be still alive. Father Pinet and Father Marest are wearing out their strength; and they are two saints, who take pleasure in being deprived of everything ... But they do not fail to tell me and to write me that I must bring some little comforts for the sick

... For my part I am in good health, but I have no cassock, and I am in a sorry plight, and the others are hardly less so ...

I read also of survival against all odds.

The Relation of the First Voyage made by Father Marquette toward New Mexico in 1673: ... his Canoe having been upset below the sault, where he lost both his men and his papers, and whence he escaped only by a sort of Miracle ...

I check my e-mail every day, I send out messages, I wait. I spin theories and discard them, I shuffle sequences as I might shuffle a pack of cards.

The joker comes up every time. Any riddles for recycling? he grins. Any letters for uncertain destinations? Any unperformed experiments to go?

I'm not even going to answer that, I say.

OUR OWN LITTLE KAKADU

There must be, by Maggie's reckoning, upwards of fifty chooks running loose, but who would know? When she steps carefully between pineapple rows to test the fruit cones, she puts her foot on at least a dozen eggs. First comes the soft crunch, then the streaky corona-squirt of ochre and snot, then the ooze between her toes. The soles of her feet squelch against her sandals, she is practically skating on slick. Hah, she thinks. Walking on water, tiptoeing on eggshells, what's new?

"He took an axe to the chook house months ago," her mother said on the drive from the airport. At the stop light, her mother had lifted both hands from the wheel, palms up, and raised them toward the roof of the car, beseeching someone, something, to bear witness.

"Jug's violent again?" Maggie was startled. "I mean, *physically* violent?"

"Not toward me, no, no. Not at people. Not even at your brother. But there's something ... he *feels* violent, yes. He's against anything being penned in now. Against pruning. You should just see the passionfruit. I could rip miles of it off the laundry shed if I thought I'd get away with it. It's taking up all the clothesline space, I have to hang half our underwear on trees." She clasped her hands together, the interlaced fingers pressing the knuckles white. "Well, he's never done anything by halves, has he?"

"Juggernaut by name," Maggie said.

"You can say that again. I never know what it's going to be next. I'm terrified he'll decide *mowing's* forbidden. We've had two pythons on the verandah already, and god knows what's living out there in the bus with him."

"Mum, the light's green."

"What? Oh." The car leaped forward, stalled, rallied. "You don't know what it's been like, Maggie. Chooks roosting in the laundry, in the bananas, in the vegetables, in the —"

"Mum, mind the —! Would you like me to drive?"

"I had a smashed egg in my hair last week. They're laying on the rafters in all the sheds, you never know what's going to fall on you. Not to mention chicks hatching wherever you happen —"

"Mum, pull over. You're upset. Let me drive."

"I'm not upset, I'm scared. He won't talk to me, he won't talk to your brother, he's started drinking again, he does say things to his mates at the pub when he's pissed, and there's *talk*, there's plenty of talk, but nobody can make sense of it. Nobody knows what happened. That's why you had to come back, I'm counting on you."

"Oh yes," Maggie said drily. "We're famous for getting on famously, me and Jug."

"That's the point. You'll strike sparks. If he gets mad enough, he might blurt out some clue."

"Doesn't Ben strike enough sparks?"

"It's weird. They're totally silent with each other. Anyway I can't get your brother near the place now, I have to go to him and Liz. And this is a taboo subject with them. Look, I wouldn't have dragged you back from Melbourne for nothing."

"I think I was looking for an excuse to come back anyway."

"Yeah? The girl who couldn't wait to get out, couldn't wait to shake the dust —"

"Yeah, well."

"Melbourne people are so up themselves, I did warn you."

"Yeah," Maggie laughed. "Made a bet with myself you'd say 'I told you so' before we got home."

"And wasn't I right? Didn't they give you the pip?"

"Yeah. Well, you know, there's all kinds. I've got some good friends. It's just … I don't know … You can't even talk about Darwin down there. You might as well announce you've come from Mars."

"They give me the pip."

"Whew, I'd forgotten how sticky —" Maggie eased her damp shirt away from her skin and leaned out the window. She wouldn't forgive her body if it had switched allegiance, adjusted to Melbourne chill, lost the knack for wet heat.

And then they passed under the familiar tangle of mango, frangipani, bougainvillea, and she cried, "Hey! You can't see the house *at all*."

"I told you. Pruning's not allowed, no cutting back, nothing. What we've got here is five acres of new-growth jungle with room to walk sideways round the house. Our own little Kakadu."

Between the half acre of pineapple rows and the house, Maggie can see flashes of yellow, bits and pieces of the bus. It is almost entirely covered by passionfruit vine, though at the four points where its axles rest in the earth, pawpaw trees rise in thick spiky clumps. He must dump the seeds there, Maggie thinks; it's some new geometric ritual, the compass points of whatever this latest obsession is. He could live on pawpaw and passionfruit without leaving his rusty cocoon, she thinks. He could just reach out through the windows and pick. The light inside must be green now, like under water. He'd love that, Jug would, odd fish in his tank (shark in angelfish clothing? dolphin in sharkskin?), jugging it down, *jug jug*, tanking up in his tank, probably having a whale of a time, driving them all round the bend. As usual.

She sees now what was impossible about Melbourne. It was having to explain this, him, Darwin, all of it, any of it; trying to explain it without having to endure *how quaint, how awful, how bizarre, how exotic, how horrible, how* —. She couldn't bear to expose her perfectly ordinary strangeness, her loony family's ordinary Darwin madness, to people who knew so very little. *Everyone's a bit troppo up there, aren't they?* they would laugh, nudge, nudge. *The Top End's a bit over the top, wouldn't you say?* I could scratch you, she would think, and you wouldn't be one sweat layer thick. But she'd learned to do it herself, play the clown, betray a memory here, the self there, one drink, two, it was easy, pile the accent on thick, get the laughs. Besides, only two years earlier, let's admit it, she'd been frantic to flee, *frantic*, indecently keen to put as much distance as possible between herself and her own little haywired Top End bubble.

I can't *breathe* here, she'd said.

She breathes the damp air, sluggish with pineapple musk, frangipani, white gingerflower. I'll drown here, she thinks. I'll never get away. I'm just part of this blissed-out vegetable world, slumping into the Arafura Sea. We're all drugged. We're all troppo.

Hallelujah! as Jug would have said.

She steps on another egg.

The whole bloody garden must be protein-enriched, she thinks. It seems to be doing wonders for the pineapples. Almost every plant has a plumed cone at some stage of ripening, and when she looks down the throats of not-yet-fruited clumps, she sees the telltale blush of things underway. How sexually blatant plants are, she marvels. She twists four ripe fruits from their serrated nests and cradles them in her arms. Squashing eggs as she goes, scratching her legs on the pineapple swords, she makes for the bus.

"Jug?" she calls tentatively from the door.

It was a school bus once, long ago put out to pasture, deregistered, bought at auction, on whim, for a song. Maggie thinks the most telling census question in Darwin might be this: how many deregistered, de-wheeled vehicles are slowly listing into your five-acre lot? The Darwin average, she suspects, would be three. Beyond the pineapples, beyond the bananas, the mangos, the vast overgrown lawn, the avocados, somewhere down among the compost heaps, there are, she surmises, four earlier family cars now all but invisible, bleeding rust into jasmine that has run amok.

In Jug's bus, all the seats have been removed. There's a galley kitchen in the driver's niche, a bunk where the back seat used to be, a chemical lav in one corner, a hinged lift-up table along the side, a couple of armchairs spilling stuffing. Everywhere there are cobwebs with watchful spiders as large as poached eggs at their hubs. Chickens, eggs, ants: the floor seems busy. A harmless carpet snake, thick as a forearm, has coiled itself neatly into a chair.

"Jug?" There's no answer so she climbs in. She sees him lying on his back on the bunk at the rear of the bus, arms folded behind his head, staring at the ceiling. He is wearing khaki boxer shorts and a singlet, nothing else, and the bus is ripe with the smell of unwashed male. Light comes through the passionfruit leaves, amber green. "Four pineapples," she says brightly. "Real beauties." She puts them into the miniature stainless steel sink. "Mum says you've given up on roads and bridges and gone into vegies and fruit. The market man, the green-fingered genius, she says."

Speak, you stubborn old bastard, she wills him. She can feel the usual dual pull of rage and protectiveness. For a big blustering man, he looks unexpectedly frail, and she is alarmed by the sight of his skinny legs and bare feet. His face and shoulders and arms are like old leather, but the legs and feet — trousered and shod throughout his respectable years as a civil engineer — are as pale as the skin of young children. She feels embarrassed to see her father this way. It's like seeing some soft creature with its shell peeled off. Improper. She lifts the lid off his icebox and takes out two cans of beer, watching him. She peels the tab off one can. It makes a slight hiss, and brackish foam bubbles out and spills over her hand. She sees his eyes swivel in her direction and she walks down the bus: "Mum tell you I was coming home?"

"Nope. But I reckoned you would, sooner or later." He accepts a beer and swings himself upright. "Told you I was bonkers, did she?"

Maggie sits cross-legged on the floor in front of him. "Didn't need Mum to tell me that," she says, cuffing him on the leg. Tactful, she makes no comment about the beer, which he had so dramatically renounced ten years ago. Maggie had been fifteen at the time, her brother Ben, eighteen. "The Lord has delivered me," Jug told them. "I've been born again, pure as the driven snow."

"Not much call for snow round here," Ben said, asking for it. But there had been no oath, no swipe at Ben, no bash across the side of his son's head, so that they had all marvelled and had known something eerie had occurred. Only the rigging in his neck, corded tight, told them the old Jug was still down there somewhere, inside the new one.

"It's funny," Jug says meditatively now, looking around the bus. "Well, not bloody funny at all. Something plays bad jokes on us, eh? I lived in the back of a truck when I first ran away to Darwin, fourteen years old. Jeez, jeez, jeez. I hate the way stuff comes back. Like bloody spiders crawling into your head."

He never speaks of his childhood unless he's drunk, and it's a bad sign when he does. They know almost nothing about it. He began brand new on his wedding day, no baggage, no past, except for the bits that sometimes leaked out of beer-soaked cracks, or showed up, mangled, in rage. He was a famously hot-tempered boss on the road gangs, a short-fused husband and father, a weekend roisterer and larrikin of note.

And then the Lord spoke to him from a Gospel Hall pulpit. It was a steamy Sunday night, and Jug, guzzling from a large Darwin stubby of tarblack bitter, was weaving by the chapel's open door on the esplanade when the Lord shouted at the top of His Almighty lungs: "Jug Wilkins, it is required of you this night to be a juggernaut for God." Jug broke his teeth on the neck of the bottle in shock, and cut his lip, a potent sign. Blood streaming from his mouth, unnerved but belligerent, he staggered into the chapel and walked down its central aisle. "Who the fuck do you think you are?" he demanded, teetering on his feet. "I am the Lord your God, Jug Wilkins." God fixed him with His pulpit eye, and Jug just stood there, confused — like a kangaroo in truck lights, people said later, swaying at the lip of some steeply pitched gulley. "Decide!" God roared. And Jug did. He jumped. He crossed over. He became an enforcer for the Lord, a role that not infrequently brought him into collision with his rebel daughter and resisting son. Bible in hand — his surveyor's chart — he would chapter and verse them, laying down markers, calling the shots, mapping everyone's road to Eternity.

"Watch out," he tells Maggie now, fretfully. "I'm infectious. I got these old dreams, bad dreams, coming back." He bats vaguely at the air and she sees mosquito swarms of nightmares buzzing him, giving him no quarter. "Western Queensland somewhere," he says, ducking. "Must've been. Between Charleville and the Territory border, I reckon. I'd just nicked off, me old man didn't believe I'd ever do it. I hid in the back of a roadtrain, see." He is not so much talking to *her*, Maggie thinks, as talking in a waking sleep. His voice seems very far away, inside a bubble in his head. "It was cold as the bloody South Pole, that's the way it is out there, nights, June, July, cold as the bloody South Pole. You wouldn't believe the difference between night and day, she's an oven by day (you could fry an egg on the road), and deep freeze after dark. If you tripped over your foot in the dark, it'd snap right off, you'd get ice in your eye. Blimey, it's cold, it's cold." He huddles into himself and begins to shake. "I'm shivering under this tarp, which, let me tell you, stinks of bloody cowshit, *stinks*, and me old man steps out of nowhere with his whip in his hand. Steps out of the air, *abra*-bloody-*ca-dabra*, and into the back of the truck and rips off the tarp. He's got horns on his head." Jug drops the beer and puts his arms in front of his face, warding off blows. He is trembling violently.

"Jug!" Maggie says, alarmed. "Jug, you're drinking too much."

" '*Gotcha*,' he says. '*Gotcha, gotcha, gotcha.* You'll never get away from me, you little bugger, you little twerp.' "

"Jug, it's okay, it's all right." Maggie takes hold of his hands, which are clammy. He's sweating like a pig, but feels dangerously cold to the touch.

"He *laughs* when he does it," Jug says. "And I never did, I never did, he was right about that, I never got away from him." He's shivering, curled into himself, barricaded behind his arms. "He's back again," he says. "He's back. He's showing up after dark."

Maggie can't bear it. "Dad," she says, hugging him. "Oh Dad, you've got the DTs again."

But it's the wrong thing to say. Wrong word. A sort of spasm passes through his body, and lucidity, like a brilliant tropical bird, swoops down on him. He leans toward her and takes her chin in his hand. "I do not have the DTs," he says distinctly. He repeats himself intensely, enunciating each word as only challenged drunks can, exaggerating syllables to such a degree that Maggie, helplessly, thinks of stepping on eggshells, thinks of his chook-mad garden, thinks of the crusted goo on her feet.

"*Take my yolk upon you,*" she splutters, on the edge of something, anxiety, compassion, hilarity, fearful hysteria. But this does not help.

"That's cheap, Maggie, cheap. Is that what they taught you in Melbourne? Cheap blasphemy? Blasphemy is cheap. Making fun of the Bible is cheap, making fun of your father is cheap." His grip on her jaw is tighter, tighter. "Your father does not have the

DTs. Can you get that into your fucking head? I do not have the DTs. I know what's fucking real and what's not." Any second now, Maggie thinks, my jaw will crack. "This world," he says furiously, "is full of fucking people who don't know what's real and what's not. DTs, they say. Visions, they say. Bonkers, they say." For emphasis, he bears down on her face with rhythmic force as he makes each point. Because she cannot speak, quite literally *cannot* speak — she can feel her bones giving way — Maggie focuses her outrage in her eyes, and he glares right back. "Don't you look at me like that, young lady, with the devil between your eyes, and between your legs too, I reckon. Honour thy father, young lady, and fucking remember this: I fucking well know what I've seen and what I haven't, don't you fucking forget it."

"If I ever kill anyone," Maggie tells Ben and Liz. She's still crying. "If I ever kill anyone," she sobs.

"Yeah," Ben says. "I know. Hey, it's okay, kid. It's okay. We won't. I've thought it a thousand times, but we won't. We love the old bastard, and we won't."

"But I would've," she says. "If I'd had a gun or a knife in my hand, I would've aimed straight for his gut. I *wanted* to."

"Yeah, well you didn't, and you won't."

"Ben came close once, though," Liz says. "In high school, remember?" Ben frowns, a warning, but Liz barrels on. "The night he kicked Ben out. I nearly killed him myself that night."

"Yeah," Maggie says. "I remember."

She remembers the two of them standing there, Ben and Liz, and Jug screaming at Ben: "The beginning of the end, that's what it is. A man starts fucking *boongs*, that's it, he's into the sewer, mate, and it's all downhill, all fucking downhill from there." This was before God had grabbed Jug by the scruff of the neck. Weeks before. "No son of mine," Jug had roared, "is going to screw around with some black fucking gin. You wanna fuck *boongs*, go and live in their stinking camps."

There had been fists and blood and mayhem.

"Get out," Jug had yelled. "Get out, and take your black slut with you, and don't ever come back."

"Too bloody right," Ben yelled. "You can count on it, mate."

Weeks of storm weather had prevailed, weeks of walking on eggshells.

And then God had spoken.

And then Jug had pulled in his horns.

"She's all right," he'd say gruffly of Liz. *For a boong:* you could hear him refuse to think the thought. "Red and yellow, black and white, All are precious in His sight," he'd say. In fact, Liz got on better with the born-again Jug than his son or his daughter did. It's my Mission School background, she'd say. I know that country.

"How long's he been like this again?" Maggie asks.

"Didn't Mum tell you?"

"No. She never said a word in letters till the chooks got her down. So how long has it been?"

"Since the new road from Jabiru," Ben says.

"Mum says nobody knows what happened."

Ben says nothing.

"Well?" she says, watching him closely. "Is that true?"

"Yes and no," he says. "I don't want to comment. I can't comment."

"I can," Liz says. "He's been sung."

"What?" Maggie blinks at her. "By who?"

"By my mob," Liz says. "By the elders of the tribe."

"Why?"

"The road," Ben says. "The mining company. The new road through Kakadu. It runs through sacred sites."

"He knew that," Liz says. "We made depositions. The press refused to cover it, per usual, but everyone knew. I faced him one day, with the demonstrators. Nose to nose."

"So that's it," Ben says. "You never told me."

"No."

"What'd he do?"

"We just stood there staring at each other. And he said: 'What can I do, Liz? I'm a working man, I build roads, what else can I do?' And I said: 'You can cross the line, Jug.' And he said: 'Easy to say, Liz. Easy for you.' And I said: 'Don't do this, Jug, please. It's our land, it's our Dreaming, it's our old people, you're tearing us up, it's our country.' And we just kept standing there, looking at each other, eye to eye, people pushing and shoving, but it was just us two, him and me."

She is staring at the backs of her hands.

"Yes?" Ben prompts.

"I don't know," she says. "I felt he was standing right on the line, I felt he was thinking about it, I thought maybe he just might step over and join me, he just wanted a nudge, so I said …"

Maggie pictures the scene: the graders, the steamrollers, the tiptrucks of crushed stone, the sharp smell of tar, the demonstrators, the workmen in their heavy boots and singlets, the heat. She watches Liz remember it. She watches Ben watching Liz. *This is a taboo subject with them*, she hears her mother say.

"What happened?" Ben nudges.

"I said something ..."

They wait. Liz studies her hands. "*What?*" Ben says. "What did you say?"

Liz sighs heavily. "I said the wrong thing, I reckon."

"What was it?"

But she's back at that line, nose to nose with Jug, her mob and his mob, stalemate.

"What, dammit! What did you say?"

"I said: 'You've got a grandchild coming, Jug. It's his Dreaming you're messing up. It's his place, it's his country, your own *grandchild's*. You're desecrating his birthright, Jug.' "

Maggie watches Liz breathing, she knows the way of it, how the ragged tempo takes you over, it's like a weather pattern that you enter when you get too close to Jug. "What did he say?" she asks.

"He said: 'You fucking manipulative *boong.*' "

Ben puts a hand over his face.

"And I told him, I hissed it at him. I said, 'You're being sung, Jug Wilkins. You'd better make arrangements, because you're gonna be sung.' " She starts collecting dishes with extraordinary vehemence and banging them into the sink. "Fucking boong-hater," she keeps saying. "Fucking boong-haters, all of you, deep down."

When she passes by him, Ben lifts a hand to touch her, but drops it again. Maggie has a sudden lurch of panic: they'll fight, she thinks; they'll say things they can't take back; he'll turn into Dad. Maggie wants a lightning bolt, she wants to point the bone somewhere, she wants someone to unsing the country, she wants to stop all of this. She gets up and puts her arms around Liz, but Liz pushes her away, furious. "Don't you bloody *touch* me!"

Liz yells, but the words puncture her rage which leaves her in a sudden rush, half sob. She looks deflated and unutterably weary. "Oh shit," she says helplessly to Ben: "I'm sorry, mate. I really thought, you know, he was going to cross the line. I was so fucking *disappointed*."

She says to Maggie: "Anyway, they did. Sing him, I mean. They did it. He's been sung, and he knows it."

Maggie is standing at the very back edge of their lot. It's night, still stiflingly hot and humid, but there's a full moon and just the suggestion of a breeze beginning to snuffle in off the sea. Around her rise the burial mounds of old cars. What would an archaeologist make of this? she wonders, this humpy terrain of rusted frames and compost heaps, all smothered and choked with jasmine, al-lamander, bougainvillea, and the ever rapacious morning glory, all of it sliding back into bush. Who knows where the boundary lies? What mad surveyor ever tried to mark such a thing?

"So wha'd'ya reckon, Maggie?" His voice is slurred, rising from somewhere in the smothered heaps of junk.

"Oh god, Jug, don't *do* that, you nearly gave me a heart attack. Where are you?"

"Where you gonna place your bet, Maggie?" He knocks on a creeper-clothed mound, and it gives back a hollow note, faintly metallic. "The Earth our Mum? Or the cars? Wha'd'ya reckon?"

She's still too angry with him for patience, she wants to hurt. "I've been to Ben and Liz's," she says. "You shouldn't've worked on the road. I know why you've gone loco, you've been sung."

"On the road to Ka-ka-du-uu," he sings drunkenly, "where the crocs and the jabiru play —"

She will make him bleed. She will. "They've turned you into the fruit and vegie man," she says.

But he's not listening to her. He's not paying attention. He comes crawling out of the undergrowth on all fours, his head cocked to one side. He's listening for something else. She thinks of the cats watching invisible birds in the bush, that fixed intensity, his concentration focused at the point where the car humps merge into impenetrable wetland scrub. She peers into the moon-washed darkness, curious. "What are you looking for?"

He gives no reaction, no sign, she might as well have ceased to exist.

"*Jug*," she says, irritable. She wades through ground cover, creepers, rotting matter, she crunches sticks and eggs as she goes. "What are you looking at?" And when he ignores her, she pummels his shoulders with her fists. He yelps, and throws her a brief startled glance, but whirls back again as though he dare not waver in his attentiveness. She has the creepy sensation that they are both being watched.

"What are you looking at, for god's sake?"

"Them," he says.

"Who?" She batters him with her fists, years of rage, anxiety, helpless compassion all shouting through her white tight knuckles. "Wha'd'ya mean, *them*, you bloody loony?"

He catches hold of her wrists. She can see he's snapped out of it now. He's with her again. He's just Jug. "You see, Maggie," he says quietly, "that's why I can't tell you. I can't tell anyone. You'll say drunk, loony, the DTs. It's too big for that. It's too —"
He can't even find a word.

But she knows suddenly, intuitively, what he's talking about. She has a sharp vision of a Melbourne dinner party, the usual little terrace house, cast-iron lace balconies, North Carlton, candlelit table, a whole roomful of elegance, brittle wit, and glibness. Maggie's in mid-flight, and all eyes are upon her, waiting. They are waiting for the laugh. *And as for Jug ...?* someone prompts, but Maggie has fallen silent. There's a line she won't cross. She has bumped into sacrilege and recognised it in time. I forget, she says politely. I forget what I was going to say.

"Except maybe Liz," Jug says. "I could tell Liz, but I won't give her the satisfaction, me pride won't let me. And I can't tell anyone else."

"It's okay, Dad," Maggie says. "I know what you're talking about."

He puts out a hand to steady himself. "I got vertigo," he says. "Comes and goes. Ever stood over a crack into nothing?"

"Yeah," she sighs.

He holds his two hands up against the moon and brings them slowly together. He matches them carefully, palm to palm, finger to finger, thumb to thumb. "There's two worlds," he says, trying to explain something to himself. "They're both as real as can be. They match exactly, so you can only see one at a time." They both study his hands against the moon, a single dark silhouette. He could be someone praying, Maggie thinks. He sighs heavily. "They match exactly," he says, "but they don't fit."

"Yeah," she says. "I know."

He looks at her warily and she gestures with her hands, palms up. Who has answers? her shrug implies.

He is assessing something. He reads her gestures and her eyes. He makes a decision. "I saw something," he says.

She nods.

"But I can't tell you. It's too —"

"I know," she says. "It's okay."

They watch each other for a long time in silence. Then she raises her hands, palms facing him, and he brings his up to meet hers. They sit there like two children, fingertip to fingertip, palm pushing lightly against palm, an imperfect fit.

"If I told you ..." he says gruffly.

"You don't have to tell me. It's okay."

"If I tell you, you gotta promise —"

"Cross my heart." She licks an index finger and gestures over her breast.

"It was before they sung me anyway," he says. "It was just after me and Liz — well, I blew me top."

"Yeah, she told us."

"Didn't mean to. And then afterwards, I just wanted to smash something. I climbed up on the steamroller. We had the first bed of gravel down, I wanted to crush it meself, I wanted to mash it in, flatten it. I saw Liz leave with her mob. Good riddance, I thought, and I moved 'er up to full throttle. You could hear the road crunching into dirt, it's a good sound that. I was up there behind the wheel, and I suddenly had this giddy feeling I was on the spine of a razorback. Each side of me there was nothing. *Nothing*. I mean, if I moved, I could've fallen right off the world. And then I got this funny feeling on the back of me neck, this prickle, like when you know someone's watching you."

He opens his eyes very wide, the pupils dilated. The moon, bright orange, sits behind his head like a plate. Maggie sees herself, twice over, in his eyes.

"I turned around," he says, whispering now, "and there were hundreds and hundreds of them, thousands maybe, just standing there with their spears in their hands, watching me. They didn't make a sound. They were naked except for those little things they wear, and white bodypaint."

He clutches at his heart, a sharp pain grabbing him again. "It spooked me," he whispers. "The way they just stood there watching. They never made a sound, but I knew what they were waiting for."

He looks at Maggie intently. "They are *with* us," he said. "I never realised before, but they're with us."

Maggie swallows.

"I climbed down off the steamroller," he says. "And I walked away. I never went back."

"Dad," Maggie says gently. "Let's go back to the house."

But he doesn't want to. He stands there staring into the wetlands. "Alpha and Omega," he murmurs. He seems to be sifting through clutter in his mind. "The first and the last," he says. "The First Ones. *The last shall be first.*"

Maggie tugs at his hand. "Dad," she says.

"*Seeing we also are compassed about with so great a cloud of witnesses,*" he says, pulling at a creeper from the scrub of his Gospel Hall decade. He thinks he's got hold of something. "And in those days, the last shall be the First Ones, and they shall be with us in the land."

"Dad, you're mixing things up."

"Nothing fits," he says, turning to offer his puzzled benediction. "That's the problem, Maggie. Nothing fits. But I know what's real and what's not, and they are with us."

CAPE TRIBULATION

This is how it is, Brian sees, nip and tuck, he has to be quick, and the sheets are no protection whatsoever. When the bats swoop they give off a high-pitched sound like email, or perhaps he imagines that, but he does not imagine the velvet pelting, there must be dozens of them, *dozens*, he has to crouch into himself and roll on the bed, this way, that way, arms over his head. "It's your hair that you have to watch out for," Philippa told him once, over a restaurant table somewhere. She was gesturing violently with her hands. She always did that, oblivious, knocking wine glasses over, knives off the table.

"For God's sake, Philippa," he'd said.

"Did I do that?" She'd stared at her hands, puzzled.

"Don't," he said, agitated.

"Don't what?"

"Drift off like that. For God's sake, keep hold of the reins."

He had seen a painting somewhere, he could not remember where, an Arthur Boyd, he thought. There was a woman in a horse-and-carriage rising out of nowhere, out of ocean, out of water and fog and cloud. It was Philippa to a T, dreamy, parasol-twirling, somewhere else. "It's a kind of Australian *Birth of Venus*," he said. "It's you, arriving with your usual splash —". She, after all, was the one who rattled blithely on, inattentive but unsinkable, tooling through fog and floodway, through interruptions, smashed glasses, absences, shipwreck, nightmare, whatever, pulled by a galloping horse who knew the way home; which was why he, Brian, could hive off on mysterious routes, sniffing and testing, getting lost, knowing she'd keep an eye out for him, that she'd reach for him and haul him in, or turn back and come looking if need be. "Hurtling along the fingertip of Queensland and planting your lace umbrella like a flag."

"What are you talking about?"

"A painting. I'm going under, you go barrelling over the skin of the water in a horse-and-buggy and rescue me."

"I have no idea what you're talking about." She'd folded her hands and rested them on the edge of the table, studying him, blinking. "You're nuts."

"Probably," he'd said.

"Where was I?" she'd asked vaguely.

"Bats. You were rattling on about bats."

"Ah yes, bats," and her hands had flown up and hovered and dipped. "It's your hair," she'd insisted. "The little hooks on their wings, they catch in your hair, and then they panic, see, they whip it into snarled coir. In three ticks, your hair's a mesh of old mattress fibre, it's excruciating."

"Rubbish," he'd said, relieved. "What bullshit. That's a children's myth, Philippa, like frogs causing warts. It's amazing, the stuff you'll believe. Bats don't touch *anything*, they're masters of the art of evasion, believe me, they have the most highly developed radar —"

"It is not a myth," she'd said. "How would you know, Brian? You're a dot-matrix person. Japan or here in Melbourne, what's the difference? You have a *virtual* life, and what would you know" — as her fork curved into the question mark; her fork, like her hands and her argument, in shimmering flight — "what does anyone know about errors that might have been breeding themselves for decades?" She rummaged under the tablecloth. "I'll bet there's misinformation that travels like a virus from one data bank to the next. I can't find my … oh there it is. Whereas me," she said, "I live by touch and sight and … Anyway, I was with this group once — maybe I've told you this? — in South India."

"Yes," he said. "The temple tower, the dark spiral stairs. You've told me."

"— and this cloud of bats came for us," she said. "We dislodged them or something, this little black cloud, it was horrible. There was a woman in a sari with hair down to her bum and the bats settled on it like rabid moths. She screamed and screamed and they had to hold her down and practically shave her head. I still have nightmares."

"I'll bet," Brian said. "I believe you. But you make them up afterwards."

"Right. I dream them up. Exactly."

"Yes, you do, you dream them up, you invent —"

"Dreams are dreamed up," she said. "That's the way they happen, Brian."

"And your stories get more detailed with each retelling, are you aware of that? They thicken out."

"One of the German tourists had a Swiss army knife," she said, "and someone else, someone from Bangalore I think, had a dagger, but it must have been blunt, because they had to hack, the two men I mean, they hacked her hair —"

"You come up with more amazing details each time," he said. "You embroider everything, Philippa."

"The dagger had a beautiful handle. Quite extraordinary, I remember." She stroked the curves of the fork she had retrieved and held it against her cheek. "Silver and gold filigree, it was, like fig roots scabbling a tree —"

"Scabbling?"

"Yes. Rainforest style. I asked if I could hold it, but the man from Bangalore wouldn't let me. And I remember there was another man who wept, the woman's husband, I think. It's a disgrace, you know, in India, to have your hair cut off."

"You're hopeless," Brian said. "You've got Galloping Invention, it's a kind of disease, and you can't even hold your own reins."

"And you," she countered, witheringly. "Packing the jack-in-a-box world into numbers. Better keep the lid on tight, Brian."

And now this come-uppance: he is having her nightmares. Her bats are arriving by email; also memos from his funding committees, the university administration, the Physics Department, his research partners, his labs in Melbourne and Japan, his computer technicians, his alarmed colleagues, his frustrated students, his frightened and angry ex-wife. He answers none of them, he ducks and brushes them away with his arms. He pulls the sheet over his head, then drags it with him and tents it over his desk.

Philippa, he emails, *there's no such word as scabbling. Bats never hit anything. Your memory is cockeyed, your knowledge of science is at the level of old wives' tales. Love, Brian.*

He wants to establish one fixed compass point. He would wait for her to come galloping in for the gauntlet if he could wait.

Philippa, he emails one hour later. *Help! I can't keep the lid on any more. Brian.*

He watches for the flicker of her arrival on his screen, and yes he thinks he's receiving, yes, she is splashing out of digital fog, rising from the cyberflecked sea. She sits high in the trap, waving. He can see foam on the horse's flank, then a whitish blur, *It's a trap*, she winks, *system error*, damn damn damn, they are blinked out, gone, trailing streamers of ghostwords. He has to fish for them.

Brian, where are you? I've been trying to reach you for two years. I heard you were terribly ill, and then you just disappeared. For God's sake, where have you been? Love, Philippa.

I don't know, he tries to answer. *I'm lost.* But now the bats intervene and he cannot even find his keyboard in the dark.

He could be in Japan. By the roar, he thinks it must be Japan. Outside his fifth-storey window, the concrete pretzel of freeway looms like a reef, so yes, it's definitely Osaka, and the noise would drive him crazy within hours had he not invented a device to outwit it. Beneath his bunk (which must be raised and hooked against the wall when he wishes to use his desk), he nestles a hair-dryer in the crook of a ceramic bowl. All day while he works, and all night while he tries to sleep, to make white noise he leaves the hair-dryer on, full blast. The ceramic bowl safely disperses the heat, he is proud of that touch. He burns out one appliance per month but considers the solace cheap. His room, in the building for visiting professors, is so small that he fears the walls will implode if he sucks in too deep a breath.

He twists and holds the pillow over his head. Who would have thought that bats could come right off the freeway stack, straight out of the hot urban night? The hooks on their wings are tiny, as delicate and vicious as the fishhooks he and Richard used in coral-reef pools when the tide was out. They would never let Philippa hold the lines. "See if I care," she'd say bitterly. They were all kids then, all from the same neighbourhood, the same school. They all still lived on the sunshine coast of never-never land, in Queensland, and he wonders why it was they all left. Perhaps that was the original mistake, he thinks, though there was a time when they couldn't wait to get away. Before that time, back in the childhood zone, there were no clouds in the sky, no shadows, and no one was lost. Zebra-striped minnows, they sometimes caught; golden hammerfish; cobalt-coloured zitherfish; fish smaller than a finger but shockingly bright as they zipped between the antlers of the coral. There were no obstacles, no collisions. They knew their way then, they all swam as safely as reef trout.

"Anyway," Philippa said, "they're horrid, those hooks. The fish are too pretty, and it's cruel."

"We're going to swim to the Outer Reef now," he said, "me and Richard. You can't come, because you swim like a girl and you'd drown."

"I don't want to," she claimed, furious, dabbing at trickles of blood on her legs. "It's dangerous. There's coral underneath you, that you can't see, and if you don't watch out, you'll get scraped."

"Only girls get scraped," he said.

"Don't be stupid," she said. "Everyone gets scraped. What about Captain Cook? He got scraped."

"Because he didn't have charts," Brian said. "That's why. But we know where we're going, so we won't."

"Bet you don't know the date Cook got scraped."

"Bet you don't either."

"Bet I do," she said. "Eleventh of June, 1770."

"Smarty pants," Richard accused.

"Show-off," Brian said. "Anyway," he added loftily, "it was the other end of the reef, up near the equator, where he got wrecked."

"Not wrecked," she claimed. "Keelhauled."

Brian laughed. "*Sailors* got keelhauled, dummy, not ships."

"Keelhauled by the reef," she insisted. "Then they got into the Endeavour River and fixed the ship with oakum and … and —"

"Show-off!"

"— and sheep's dung," she spluttered defiantly, fighting the dunking. "I hate you, Brian."

Naturally Brian has read Cook's journals since then. He has read them a number of times, waiting for the right moment, the right year, the right trivia quiz, to trump Philippa. They're still at it, forty years later. But also: the matter of sailing into unmapped waters, which has turned out to be the business of Brian's own life, has him hooked. He licks his lips. He has tasted that particular excitement, the edging into blank space, and his tongue is equally familiar with the salt tang of risk. He has known deceptive nights like that of June 11, 1770. They line themselves up like rude marker buoys, such nights, *in clear moonlight and with a fine breeze*, as Cook plaintively wrote, Cape Tribulation on the port side licked with gold, the coral cays gleaming low to the east. The *Endeavour* floats as carefree as a painted ship upon a painted sea and naturally Brian will stay on the bridge, excited, peering into the dark where no one has ever sailed before, and there is no need for him to sleep or eat or pay any attention whatsoever to obsession or exhaustion or the expostulations of the crew or of neglected students, for the goal of all his exploration is in sight and he can taste it, he can sense the rigging of his calculations falling into perfect — and then the sails hesitate. He feels the change in the slap of ocean, wave patterns gone manic. He hears the sickening crunch of hull against reef.

I have called the point Cape Tribulation, Cook wrote in his journal, *for here began all our troubles.*

Philippa, Brian emails. *I've been keelhauled. I'm all at sea. I'm stranded somewhere off Cape Tribulation, and I'm not sure if I can patch the vessel up. Please write. Any old clap-trap and galloping horse-thoughts will do. Brian.*

He puts his message in a bottle and floats it in the flickergreen cyberslick sea. The fingers of coral reach for it. They make a bony internet that is dangerously below the line of sight.

I did not think it safe to run in among the shoals, Brian reads in Cook's Coral Sea log, *until I had well viewed them at low water from the masthead, that I might be better able to judge which way to steer, for ... all passages appeared to be equally difficult and dangerous.*

Brian gropes among the antlered reefs for his keyboard. Glaucous light, like the sun seen from under water, or like the glow from a monitor or from fluorescent tubes in some institutional building, falls on his gashed hands. The blood on his sheets frightens him.

Philippa, he emails, panicked. *I can't see any way out.*

"Row, row, row," a man says. He has the build of a football player but is strangely dressed in white canvas. "It's gonna go easier for you, mate, if you give it some slack."

"Are you sailors?" Brian splutters, going under.

"That's a good one," the man laughs. "Not sailors, mate. Orderlies. One, two, and we'll have you unwrapped."

"Cardinal," Brian corrects. "Those are *cardinal* numbers, not ordinal."

"Pin 'is arms, Joe, till we're sure. Bugger's scraped me skin off more than once. Not to mention what he's done to himself."

"Yeah. Weird, innit? Like birds or bats have been at 'im. Wonder why the high and mighty go nuts when they go nuts. Hey, that's funny. Get it? They go nuts when they go nuts. But more nutso than your ordinary nut case, I mean. You noticed that, Mac?"

"Hold his arm, Joe, while I jab 'im."

Brian is wedged into the reef, he cannot move. He can feel the spiked coral, the way the panic fish dart, the clamshell pincer at his heart. Brian's under, he is fighting for his life.

I cannot have come to this, Brian emails Philippa. *I cannot have come to this. This is intolerable. I do not believe I have come to this. I am having a nightmare. This is your nightmare, not mine. I've been keelhauled. I'll drown. I'll go mad.*

He wears gray pyjamas, much too large, and the room smells horribly of disinfectant. A line stretches ahead and behind. Every thirty seconds it shuffles forward in its slippered feet. Brian can feel a small flock of screams, trapped, batting against the inner scaffolding of his ribs.

"Next," Dr Someone says.

The screams' batwings are frantic. They whir and rise and beat so hard against the rigging that Brian has to press a hand to his mouth. The little hooks tear at him.

"Ah, Professor. How are we doing?"

Brian reaches behind him and arcs the pyjama coat over his head like pinions. A small cry vents itself, unbidden, but he manages to imbue it with contempt.

Dr Someone sighs. "If you could forgive yourself, Professor, you'd recuperate faster. The mind's a hard taskmaster."

"Hands," says the nurse, sharply.

Brian extends them, cupped, and the nurse fills one palm with a little cascade of pills, the other with a small paper cup.

"Down the hatch," she says.

"Amen," Brian says. And also with you, and up yours. He lifts his hand to his mouth and works the tablets under his tongue. He lifts the cup. Drink ye all of it, says the watchful eye of the nurse. Brian swallows.

"We'll see what this lot does," the doctor says. "I'm experimenting with your dosage."

Brian shunts the pills into the pink back pocket of his lower gum. "Me guinea pig, you Dr Mengele," he says, incautiously.

"I'd advise against making trouble, Professor. We are not on your research team, and your obsessions have no currency here." Then the doctor smiles. "You would do well to remember," he says gently, "that resumption of your career rests entirely on my recommendations."

"Blackmail now, is it?" Brian shouts.

"We know you're not taking your medication," says the nurse. "If this continues, we'll put you back on injections."

"Blackbirds and blackmail," Brian sings, letting his eyes go blank. "All baked in a four-and-twenty pie."

The doctor pats Brian on the shoulder. "Give it time."

"Next," the nurse says.

Every day I climb the masthead, Brian writes in the log which he emails to Philippa each night, *to inspect the atolls and shoals. At*

*present, I can see no way out, though I make a close study of the rise
and fall of the tides.*

The tides rise and foam with white horses that pull cursors
behind them, too fast. The reins are loose in Philippa's hands.
She leans back in the trap. "Cook was a dreamer, you know,"
she calls over her shoulder. "They say he had visions. His siren
rode the whitecaps and sang up a storm and St Elmo's fire lit
up the channels. That's how he got out."

What bullshit, Philippa, he emails, laughing. Blue fire shivers
down the length of his spine. In fact, he believes, it is the natives
who hold the key, because they know the waters so well. He
studies them. There is one, a young woman, who hides her
medication beneath her tongue for hours at a time before she
spits it into the bushes during outdoor time. *We resisters are easy
to spot, Philippa, in spite of our cunning Deadman's Shuffle. It's the
sudden dart of the eyes that gives us away, at least to each other. We
are too focused, too quick. She was crying this morning, silently. I could
feel her sobs in my bones. So I whispered: "We can get out. But only
if we play by their rules."*

"*I'm afraid I'll go mad before then,*" *she said.*

"*Me too.*"

"*How'd you get in here?*" *she asked.*

"*Hard to trace exactly.*"

*I tried to recall that glorious rush of wind, Philippa, when I couldn't
eat, couldn't sleep, couldn't stand interruptions, when I locked the door
and unplugged the phone. I was almost there. I skipped a few weeks'
classes, I think, but it could have been longer. Frantic students and all
that, appointments to discuss dissertations and I didn't show up. No one
could reach me.*

"*My colleagues thought a heart attack,*" *I told the girl. "And my ex-wife thought suicide. Next thing I knew, police were kicking in my door."*

"Oh, the police," the girl said, rolling her eyes. "Yeah."

"They arrested me," I told her. It still astonishes me, Philippa. Charged me with 'threat to my own safety'. I could have killed them for interrupting at such a crucial ... "Don't get cute," they said. "You're coming with us." "What about my rights?" I shouted, dumbfounded. "You've forfeited your rights, mate," they said. "There's been two people signed a form. You're being committed."

"Yeah," the girl sighed. "I know. Runaway, I was charged with. I said I'd kill myself rather than go back home, so then, you know ... because that's a crime ..." She chewed her hands. "Your mum's boyfriend, the police, anyone can hurt you," she said. "Except yourself. And if you try to, no matter what reason ... Those are the rules."

"We'll get out," I promised her. "They can't keep us long. They can't. Because we're so obviously sane."

"I dunno," she sighed. "I dunno anymore if I am. The policeman who brought me here ... he felt me up in the car and I bit him."

"There you go," I said. "That proves you're sane."

She stared at me and then she began to laugh. It was the most astonishing sound, like the sound of oakum and sheep's dung being slapped against a hull. I laughed and she laughed, we couldn't stop, and even the sleepwalkers stirred. Our laughter whirled us up through the rigging, and just before the orderlies came, I thought I glimpsed a passage between the reefs.

"God, it's good to see you," Philippa says. "I was afraid we'd lost you. You were so manic the last time ... you know, fidgeting, and knocking things over —"

"*Me* knocking things?"

"I thought you were dangerously wound up about your research. I was afraid you'd ... you know ..."

"Crack up?"

"I was afraid it was worse than that."

"Nothing's worse than that."

"I was afraid you'd have a heart attack in Japan or somewhere. It's been such a long silence. Two years!"

"I'm a bit hazy about timespans myself."

"And not even your department or your ex knew where you were."

"They did. Oh believe me, they did. They had me committed."

"Brian!" Her hand flies to her mouth.

He shrugs. "They believed they had to. They thought it was for the best. Anyway, I'm seaworthy again. Less wind in my sails, but I manage. I'm patched up with oakum and sheep's dung, it works well enough."

"Patched up with *what?*"

"Don't tell me you've forgotten Cook's journals?"

"Never read them," Philippa says.

"You did so. We did extracts in school. You used to reel off dates and data like the obnoxious know-it-all you always were."

"I did not, Brian. That was you."

"I can remember the exact day," he says. "We were fishing in pools on the reef."

"I never went fishing with you. You never let me."

"And you got up on your high horse and trotted off in a cloud of history-book trivia and dates. When did Cook get wrecked?"

She stares past him, and he can feel the fog of childhood settling in.

"Don't," he says urgently.

"What?"

"Drift."

"Sorry. I was thinking about those divers finding the *Endeavour*'s cannon on the reef. You know, from when they threw everything over, to lighten the ship. Did you see that on TV?"

Brian feels seasick. "All the stuff that's been lost," he says, queasy.

"After two hundred years," Philippa marvels. "It's eerie, isn't it?"

"Stuff that will never be recovered." He buries his head in his hands. "How much went overboard? That's the question. I have no way of even knowing what's been lost."

"It will surface," Philippa murmurs. She puts her hand on his arm. "It might all be found again. One day. You never know."

You never know, Brian thinks, stricken. You will never know.

FLIGHT

"Yes, I'm coming," Cecily promises, breathless, hearing Robert's urgent voice above the wind. She runs barefoot, tripping on something in the early morning dusk. The wind beats against the bedroom window and beyond she can see thousands of dead leaves whipped into squalls, no, not leaves, she sees with astonishment, not leaves but birds, wheeling galaxies of small brown birds. The air is thick with them. The air sways and tilts with the soft spirals of their flight, a Milky Way of migration so dense she can see nothing but wings. She can hear Robert, she can hear the edge of panic in his voice, but she cannot see him. She can hear the other man, the passenger, the one they have brought with them. "I'm coming!" she promises, fumbling with the lock on the window.

The birds spin like a nebula. It must be winter that drives them like this: the sudden onset of frosts and the sharp unseasonable plummeting of the mercury; it must be panic.

The velvet folds of the birdswarm brush the glass. The sash window is old and heavy, she cannot lift it. Robert calls her name again, his alarm transposed up to a higher key. "I'm *trying*," she cries, almost sobbing. She hears the passenger, the man they do not know. The window is impossibly heavy. "I'm coming!"

she promises, but very likely years have passed since the sash was last opened, and it will not budge. She hammers on the glass with her fists, a stammer of rage, because it is pointless, she will not be in time, she is never going to be in time, she will always be a second too late, there will always be the sickening thump, the shower of glass ...

The sound, when it comes, is like gunshot.

She will not look.

There is blood on her arms from the glass but she ignores that, she crawls back into bed, she tosses, she wakes — she *wakes! oh, thank God* — but the waking brings no more than a second's relief. Her days come and go like birds, her dreams like days.

She shivers and reaches for her robe.

What time is it? What day? What week?

In the refrigerator she finds a loaf of bread flecked with blue and green and whitish circles, quite interesting. The bread gives off the yeasty smell of a forest floor. There is also a tomato delicately slumping into one corner of the vegetable drawer and leaking pale red fluid. I have to buy food, she thinks. I have to walk into the village to buy food. She frowns, concentrating. First I have to get dressed, she remembers. She concentrates again. Which language, which country? English, she remembers. England. I am in an old farm house near the Channel coast.

"This one's been round a bit," the man in the General Store and Post Office says, proffering a postcard. "Crossed a few oceans. Been re-addressed three times. They ought to call you the Artful Dodger."

Cecily smiles and slips into her flippant voice. Nothing in her wardrobe fits well anymore, but she can always make do with flippancy, a hitch here, a tuck there, the lightness is all. "Fleeing the scene of a crime," she says. "Got to cover my tracks."

"You Australians." But he has no complaints with her shopping list, cans of this and that, Sussex cheese that smells like old socks, a jug of cider. "Don't you want to know what it says?" he prods. "The postcard, I mean." She smiles at him. She is tempted to ask who it's from. Of course he has read it. Of course the whole village is involved in exegetical debate at this very hour in the Brewers' Arms. "Came five days ago," he says with a hint of reproach. "Is it dust you're looking for?"

"Pardon?"

"Why d'you always run your fingers along the sides of my shelves like that?"

"Oh," Cecily says, embarrassed. "Do I?" She studies the pink cushions of her fingertips vaguely.

"They've been asking about you down at the pub. We thought you must have moved on."

"No. Not yet." She tucks the vegetables into her knapsack, between the cans, and starts putting the apples on top. "But maybe now that my mail has found me."

The old man throws his hands up in mock despair and laughs.

"*Dear Cec,*" says the back of the postcard, in a neat minute hand. "*This photograph seemed appropriate. If I didn't know better, I'd say it was you. Bought it in Sydney on a back street in Glebe. Actually it leaped out from a rack in a bookstore and assaulted me, clobbered me, made me go weak at the knees, but since the setting's France and you're in south-east Asia (aren't you?), it seems unlikely. If you steam off the airmail sticker (didn't want to waste valuable space), the fine print will tell you the staircase is in Chateau Chambord. You have a doppelgänger in the Loire Valley, and what is she doing on the racks of a bookstore in Sydney? you may well ask — the jackpot answer being that some graphics company in Paris, bunch of art students, has cornered a niche market worldwide. Seriously. I read it somewhere. Artsy photo-cards selling like hot cakes from New York to New South Wales. Anyway, the symbolism seems just right.* FLIGHT OF FOLLY. WOMAN TRAPPED IN CAGE OF OPEN DOORS. *Hope this finds you. Hope you have a magnifying glass to read my wingèd words. Hope no one else is not missing you as much as I don't miss you. Hope your life is as shitty as the bottom of a birdcage, like mine. Hope somebody clips your wings. Hope the brakes fail in all your nightmares. As for myself, I'm down to one car-crash dream per month. Sorry, sorry, sorry, that is really below the belt, but that's what you get for running away. Hope you rot in the jungle, and afterwards I hope you come back. Love, Robert."*

Cecily does not believe in the postcard, in spite of the apparent external evidence of the old man in the general store. She knows the mind is a very queer bird and an artful dodger of exceptional skill. There are, for example, highly intelligent people who believe they can fly; there are others, well read and well travelled, who see revenants in doorways and under stairwells and tell no one; there are those who believe they receive messages from the dead; there are crazy people who read coded information in raindrops on a window or in the migratory patterns of birds.

She pins the trick photograph to her bulletin board, and stares at it. What is shown is a luminous corkscrew of nothingness, an arrangement of delicate openings in a curved limestone wall: the famous double spiral of Leonardo, the central staircase in Chateau Chambord. Through the openings, she sees stairs fanning upwards into light. In the upper left corner of the photograph, a bird is poised on a blur of wings. In the lower right foreground, framed by one of the openings, is the face of a woman, startled, her lips parted. She is caught in the act of turning towards — or perhaps away from— the camera.

At first the bird had seemed to Cecily to be there by design, well aware of the complicated updrafts of air and the whorls of light. There are complicated people, though Cecily is not one of them, who can step back inside the frames they once inhabited and decode the whirling updrafts of design. There are others who can step out of photographs to haunt us, and still others who are not so free to leave. (The wind changed, perhaps, as the shutter clicked, and the subject was stuck forever in the blink of a particular moment in time.) At first, it had seemed to Cecily, the bird was not at all trapped but was there by choice, by design, she remembers that, she remembers thinking that. She remembers thinking that the bird knew the stairwell intimately.

She remembers wondering how the passenger (a stranger casually met) could be following her so relentlessly, watching so closely, sending (out of malice or desire?) such heavy messages. She remembers fearing that her paranoia was out of hand.

She remembers thinking of the Venerable Bede, his monkish Latin winging by, *Talis mihi videtur, rex*, feathered words from the seventh century, a quick flash of history, King Edwin in the mead hall with his thanes, *This life of man, O King, is like the flight of a sparrow through a lighted hall*, and there is nothing like a well-shaped line to move through time, so Cecily thinks, so the Venerable Bede confirms, *and outside it hails and snows and storms ... and the bird flyeth in one door, and while it hovers inside the hearth-bright wine-heated hall it knows nothing of winter, and it is warmed by the fire, and its wings are bright in the torchlight, but then it flyeth out through another door and the winter night swalloweth it again and we know not whither it goeth* ... and where does it come from, all this arcane knowledge, where does Cecily keep this gilded bric-a-brac?

This is her problem precisely, she remembers too much, she cannot jettison knowledge, she has a brainful of junk, and what use is King Edwin? of what possible use are his thanes in his lighted hall? With respect to her present situation, Cecily is unable to list a single advantage springing from her intimacy with assorted medieval manuscripts, and therefore King Edwin's sparrow should put itself back in its venerable bede-box where it belongs as far as she is concerned, yes, it should fold itself quietly away because there is much that Cecily would like to forget. This freefall into photographs is for the birds, and she does not want to be there again, with the bird again, in the stairwell, there, *here*, at Chateau Chambord, because in fact, o tourists, this life of birds is like the short ridiculous flicker of desire and we know not whither it goeth.

The limestone, cunningly lit, is the colour of butter. Against it, the bird is like a quick black thought of death, and Cecily notes that it is bloody marvellous the way forbidden words will come winging in without any provocation whatsoever. Give them an opening in a stairwell and they stage a stunt-flying display at the moult of a feather.

Excusez-moi, excusez-moi, a man says, and that must be a Portuguese accent, or Basque maybe, or at any rate from somewhere south of the Pyrenees, and Cecily must be making progress after all if she is detecting these finer linguistic shadings, or thinks she is, and please, she says, think nothing of it, *ça ne me gêne pas,* something I've always dreamed of, catapulting down a few hundred corkscrew stairs in the Latin arms of a stranger. No, really, it's nothing, monsieur, it's nothing, Pedro then, *enchantée*, really Pedro, don't give it a thought, *Cécélie, je m'apelle Cécélie*, Cecilia, Cecily, Cec, Cess (and Cesspool during certain early years in school), though Cecily embarrasses herself beyond endurance when she babbles on like this, and she does not think her ankle is twisted, at least not badly, and in any case accidents arrive, and the crowds are *affreux, schrecklich*, whatever, isn't it? she is sorry, she is afraid she doesn't know a single word of Portuguese, she's just recently arrived in France herself, from Malaya as a matter of fact, but this business of daily living, o pushers and shovers, is like wading through a cesspool, is it not? and this life, this life, o Pedro, is for the birds.

The bird brushes her cheek. From outer darkness to outer darkness, a feathered meteor through a moment of light, what a daredevil, Cecily thinks. What tenacity. *What comes before and after, we know not.*

François I, says a guide in too careful English, and Cecily has to flatten herself against the luminous outer wall to let the group pass, *was bringing Leonardo to France for this express purpose ... the design of the staircase, it is his, Leonardo's, of the double spiral around the nothingness.*

The bird is flirting with the nothingness now. It drops in odd little freefalls, hovers, flutters, plummets another meter or so, a plumbline down the pale gold windpipe of the double stair. It is level, now, with Cecily's eyes and she sees, with sudden anguish, that this has nothing to do with the sport of tormenting *her.* You poor little thing, she whispers, and leans out into the core, a precipitous and dangerous and altogether pointless move. "Here," she murmurs urgently, "here, little bird," straining across the limestone sill, offering her hand, her wrist — and then she sees the man at the opposite opening, on the opposite arm of the stair. Watchful. Watching. More than watching. Is it surveillance? No. She has no word for the meaning of his gaze or for its intensity.

His eyes, her eyes ... she feels as helpless as the bird, and what is strange, what is frightening, what is as exhilarating and terrifying as a brush with death, is this weird sense of fusion, this sense that they have entered the same tailspin, she and the man, that it is not his freefall, not hers, not the bird's, but *theirs*, the same one, same delirium, same shock, same euphoria, same express trip to unknown end.

What comes before and after, we know not ...

Days and months later she spins theories. It is possible, for example, that random arrangements of certain objects constitute some kind of magnetic field. It is possible that currents pass through the poles of such a field. It is possible that shifts occur, earthquakes, upheavals of the magnetic poles, irreversible changes ... Or it is possible, yes, it certainly could be possible, why not? as good an explanation as any, didn't Leonardo himself, after all, believe in potent alignments and perfect symmetries and numerologies and arcane geometrical powers, so yes it is possible that spells are generated spontaneously from certain precise mathematical configurations, for example from the axis that begins with Cecily's eyes and passes through the hovering bird to the eyes of the man.

The man seems to be there by design. He seems to know her, and for a moment it seems to her that she knows him, that it is all happening again, that he is the passenger, that he was the man that she and Robert had brought with them, but no, no, actually he does not resemble the passenger in the least, she does not know why she thought that stupid thought.

The man in Leonardo's staircase continues to stare at her with a slightly stunned look, the look perhaps of a man who has loved a woman passionately, lost her, and is stupefied to see her again after many years. Cecily has the lunatic sensation that he must indeed know her. She has the impression that he comes here often, that he returns, just as she herself seems to return, for reasons private and dangerous, to places it would be wiser to forget.

But she is sure she has never seen the man before. She has never been to Chambord, nor indeed to the valley of the Loire, before. Her mouth is dry. She swallows.

Excusez-moi, excusez-moi, someone says, and she feels faint, gripping the limestone sill because there is shuffling, pushing, there are people behind him, behind her, there is a swarm of languages, cameras, flashbulbs, yes, and collisions occur between particles of light and bewilderment. He too has a camera in his hands. She blinks and sees white circles, lightning, the quick black spark of the bird.

Oh, the bird! someone says, and talk ricochets off the walls. *Got it, I think. Good shot ... What shutter speed ...? Do you think the light ...?*

Distressed, Cecily brushes the voices off like flies.

"Don't move," the man says softly, urgently, in French, no, in English, no, she feels the words as feathers against her skin. But she is pinned by a torrent of people and the rising tide of the tour groups on the opposite stair is lapping and pulling at the man.

Don't go, she pleads silently.

He smiles very slightly, a half smile, the shadow of a smile, and points upwards. She nods. She begins to climb. He is on the other coil of the double stair. The two flights twist around and around each other, but never meet. At each turn of the twinned whorls, at each matched pair of openings, the man and the woman pause for ten seconds, twenty, sometimes thirty. At each turn of the stair, the air is heavier. Cecily can feel the drugged weight of it in her lungs, on her eyelids, between her legs. When we get to the top, she thinks, we will meet on the great balcony. It seems certain to her that afterwards nothing will be the same.

Nothing, however, is certain except uncertainty and there is always interference in the lines of flight. A man and a woman may meet in Sydney or in Paris or wherever, signals may be exchanged, heat of various kinds given off, future possibilities intimated ... but then ... But then a bird and a car may meet without warning and throw all flight paths into drastic disarray. There are no guarantees that desired effect will follow the cause or the course of desire.

Near the top of the double staircase, the congestion of the tour groups is extreme. *Americans*, Cecily thinks with exasperation, already breathing French attitudes and air. There should be certain hours for noisy American groups, and other hours for contemplatives, she thinks, then she sees the Australian flags on several backpacks. Once, before she became so flighty, she would have felt a leap of happiness. She would have tapped the traveller on the shoulder, *G'day, mate*, just to hear the dear diphthongs again, the muddy vowels. Now she makes herself invisible. Swimming against the current, slipping sleekly through hollows in the tide, she slithers through to the labyrinth of outdoor galleries and the pinnacle-forested roof.

There is no further sign of the bird.

The man has flown.

Cecily leans against the outer wall of Leonardo's lantern, breathing raggedly, and stares across parklands and parterres into the dark wood of François I. She feels weak with relief. I must run, she thinks. I must leave before I see that man again.

"Excuse me," he says, touching her shoulder, and Cecily startles violently and turns and their eyes meet.

She cannot breathe for sheer panic.

She runs toward the stairs and keeps running.

In a farmhouse in the rural south of England, Cecily stares at the postcard on her wall. For some reason, she is shivering. She takes the quilt from the bed and wraps herself in it and huddles in a chair, but she still feels cold. Then she pulls open the drawer in the small oak desk. For a whole minute, maybe two, she sits there, indecisive, her hand in the drawer. Her fingers read the large brown envelope like braille — the grainy outside, the gummed flap, the smooth lining. *It's shock, that's all*, she hears Robert say. *It wears off.* She extracts the envelope, and for a long time sits with it unopened in her lap. Then she takes out the 8 x 10 inch black-and-white photograph, the one from the inquest, the one the lawyer had given her. She pins it to the wall beside Robert's card.

A tree is growing through the middle of a car, and the car has split open like a well-charred seed. The tree grows through the place where a front passenger might have sat. No photograph exists of the passenger, the man to whom they had offered a ride.

It is dark, but Cecily lights a candle and stares at the two photographs all night.

In the morning, she takes pen and paper.

Dear Robert, she writes. *You think I am running from misplaced guilt about the accident. You think that I think I caused it because of the birds, because I distracted you. I did cause it. But not in any way you could know ...*

The sheer randomness of desire, its casual ruthlessness, is what frightens Cecily. She did not know the man. She heard that he came with the friend of a friend of someone, not that she would ask. He is in Political Science, she has overheard, or maybe it is the History Department, a new appointment freshly arrived in Sydney from somewhere else, Melbourne, Brisbane, nobody seems quite sure. There is such a crush at the party, such a thick fog of bodies and smoke, people flattened against walls, people falling over coats in the hall, people pressing up against one another (sometimes by design, sometimes not), people spilling champagne or good Australian beer.

But no one has introduced Cecily and the man from Brisbane or wherever, and they have not yet brushed up against each other. In fact, she has been going to absurd lengths to avoid him, she has no idea why. There is something about the soft skin at the back of his neck, just above his jacket collar, and something about the way a curl falls across his forehead, which affects her breathing. With whom has he come to the party? With which woman? She cannot believe she is asking these ridiculous questions of herself.

If she stands by the tub of ice from which bottles jut like porcupine quills, she can swap small talk with the bartender.

Behind him is a wall of mirrored tiles. She waves to Robert's reflection. Robert blows her a kiss. In the mirror, she sees a woman, laughing, lean in close to the man from somewhere else and brush invisible lint from his sleeve. Cecily turns away.

People come and go. Into the brief spaces of monologues, Cecily makes sounds of approval. "It's so refreshing," a man tells her, slurring his words a little, "to talk to someone so interested in the kind of research I do." *Yes?* she murmurs. Through the crook of the researcher's drinking arm, she watches the man from Brisbane — she has decided it must be Brisbane because of the tan — she sees him move away from the woman who touched his jacket. He is watching someone in the mirror, watching with an intense, demanding, look-at-me look. Out of simple curiosity, she turns.

And who knows how long they stood like that, reflecting? His eyes, her eyes: how could movements so tiny throw so many lives off course? She concentrates on setting her champagne flute delicately down on the bookshelf beside her. Everything is in slow motion now, the way the man walks through the mirror and takes her glass from the bookshelf and tips his head back and drinks, watching her.

"That is a dangerous thing to do," she says in a small voice, and now Robert is waving from the mirror, signalling, and the man says: "Ah, you belong to someone then," and she says, "Well, uh, we've been together a while ..." and everything speeds up, everything goes to Fast Forward, Robert is explaining that it's two in the morning and they really must, "... but I don't *belong* to anyone," she says, and then suddenly it's flight she wants, yes, she agrees with Robert, we have to leave, but Robert is saying "You're Joe's friend. From Brisbane, right? Good to have you

here, can we give you a lift, are we heading in the same direction?"
and as a matter of fact, what do you know? they are indeed, but
there's absolutely no need, except that Robert of course is his
always generous self and insists, he *insists*, no problem. And then
Cecily says, well in that case the passenger should take the front
seat, yes, this time it is she who puts her foot down. Absolutely.
Because, because. So the two men can talk.

"Oh look!" she says, as they leave the city behind and skim
along the shore road north of Manly. To their right are the dunes,
and beyond them the curl of Pacific surf. Cecily leans forward,
pushing slightly between the bucket seats. She is pressed up against
the passenger from the sway of the car. "Look at the nightbirds!"

"Where?" Robert asks, and swerves, and the birds come at
them like leaves. Instinctively Robert puts his hands in front of
his face. "Cec!" he shouts, and she lunges forward between the
seats and she tries, she tries, to reach the wheel.

Dear Robert, she writes. *Accidents are accidents, as the inquest ruled,
and as you have said a thousand times. They are nobody's fault. Nevertheless
there is something I've never told you ...*

She crushes the sheet of paper into a ball and takes another.

Dear Robert, she writes. *I have a confession to make. It is desire,
that careless predator, that outlaw, I am running from ...*

She tears the page neatly and precisely into shreds and begins
again.

Dear Robert, she writes. She leaves the sheet blank and signs
her name at the bottom. *PS*, she writes. *Thank you for the card.
You are dear to me, and always will be. As you'll see from the stamp,
I'm in England at present, but please don't try to write as I'm moving
on. Love, Cecily.*

Yes, she has the right street. She takes the postcard from her pocket: the luminous staircase, the bird, the woman's face. She checks the back of the card again: yes, right street, right number. And there is the place, *Graphique de Paris*. But perhaps she will come again another day. She turns back to the Métro entrance. Then again, maybe she should lay the matter to rest and have done with it. People are looking at her strangely. She leans against the stairwell and watches them pass up and down, whole flocks of them, like birds.

What have I got to lose? she asks herself.

And in fact it is all very brisk and businesslike in *Graphique de Paris*. An elegant young woman studies the postcard, turns it over to find the title of the photograph, and then types *L'envolée* on a keyboard. Her computer hums thoughtfully for several seconds. She looks from the screen to Cecily and back again. She swivels the monitor around so that Cecily can see the image, enlarged, in digital clarity. "Is it you?" the young woman asks curiously.

"I think so," Cecily says.

The young woman swings the monitor back to herself and presses another key. "Hmm. The photographer's one of our freelancers. Lives in the Marais. Here." She swivels the monitor again. "You can copy down his address and phone number if you like."

Cecily sits in a coffee shop near the Place des Vosges in the Marais, watching the building across the street. If she were to push open its large wooden door, and cross its courtyard, and climb Staircase B, and ring the bell on the second floor, what would she say?

She pays for her coffee. She crosses the street and pushes open the great wooden door. She walks through the courtyard, she climbs Staircase B, she rings the bell. But when he opens the door, she is unable to say a word.

"Ah," he says, nodding. Seconds pass. He is smiling slightly. He scarcely even seems surprised. "So you got my message," he says. He says it in French and she has to play back the words inside her head and then translate.

"Why did you look at me like that, at Chambord?" Her French is inordinately careful and slow.

He shrugs. "I don't know. You reminded me of someone." He rakes a hand through his hair. "I don't know why I say that. You don't really look like her at all. It was just something ... It was something fugitive about you."

They stand there staring at each other.

"I'll confess something," he says. "I willed you to come back. I planned it. I've been waiting."

"That's crazy," she says shakily.

"I know."

"The odds were overwhelmingly against you."

"Yes, they were, weren't they? Just the same, I believed you would come."

"I have to warn you," she says, and there is something the matter with her voice, she has to struggle to make herself heard. "I have a dangerous record. I'm a very bad risk."

"*Le seul risque est de ne pas en prendre*," he says gravely.

And she feels like a bird that has accidentally, miraculously, been blown into a radiant hall on a rush of air. *What comes before and after we know not* ... Oh, almost certainly there will be another door, she knows that, and some future current of air will push her, or suck her, into darkness again. But she doesn't care.

FRAMES AND WONDERS

1. Frame of Reference

"No," the man says, "we're not interested."

"We might be," the woman demurs. "Let me see."

"Don't indulge him. He'll expect to be paid." The man catches his reflection in plate glass and looks away. Though he thinks he is aging well, he does not like growing old. He does not like to have a record kept. "They are parasites," he says irritably. "Public nuisances. As bad as the beggars, and such amateur work."

"Look," she says. "Double exposure." She leans across the bistro table, the Polaroid snapshot in her hand. In the photograph, a man and a woman are drinking wine at a sidewalk café. They could be lovers.

Reluctantly, the man looks and then smiles. "*Les yeux dans les yeux,*" he says.

"Mm. And look." She points. Behind the figures in the photograph, ghostly beneath the window-painted lettering of Brasserie Bastille, their reflections mimic and float. "It's us, exactly. Don't you think that's perfect? Multiple selves, anchored nowhere. After all these years, same café, same regrets, same high-voltage gaze, same old impossible shadow dance. Except that we've never both been in the same frame before. And except that we're old."

"*Non,*" he says. "*Mûr. Nous sommes mûrs,* Odette."

"Sounds much better," she agrees. "Ripeness is all."

"*Tu es encore belle.*"

She smiles and touches the smudge of birthmark beneath his eye. "I am a sucker for perfect imperfections."

"*Excusez-moi, madame.*" The street photographer coughs deferentially and eases a second snapshot between one glass and the bottle of wine. This photograph shows a man and a woman leaning close to look at a photograph which shows a man and a woman leaning close.

"Here we go round the mulberry bush," she says.

He closes his eyes. "Do you remember the summer we found the lost village?"

"I remember we went in search of a place for one whole summer. We never found it."

"What?" He stares at her. "How can you say that?"

"Because it's true. You know the place doesn't exist."

"We spent a whole day there, and a night. Why don't you want to remember? We had wine and apples."

"And we picnicked beside the pond?"

"Yes, yes, exactly."

"But we never did sleep in the king's hunting lodge."

"*Si, si.* We made love in the royal bed. You cannot have forgotten. You must remember that."

"I remember your fantasy. You embellished it every night."

He is agitated. He tears a *Pastis* coaster in half. "*C'est incroyable.* It is because my English was so poor then, and your French was not yet good." He puts his head in his hands. "So much I explained to you, so much you never understood."

"Swann," she says. "Dear Swann." She takes his hands and kisses his fingertips. "Half the time, we were lost in mistranslation, that's true, but I did understand your obsession with that place. We found no trace of it. It did not exist."

"I took photographs," he insists. "When you left, so brutally, I sent you copies."

"You took photographs of wishes and birds in flight. You sent a postcard of an empty cage."

"It is very revealing," he says bitterly, "this repression. This need to deny. It is very Puritan, very Australian. Very damned Anglo-Saxon. You are all terrified of desire."

"Are we going to fight again? It's the way you confuse passion with possession that scares me. It's that insane French jealousy, that need to control. I felt caged. "

"Love is a cage, yes, and the Anglo-Saxons lock themselves outside it." He is angry. He sweeps the importunate street photographer aside. "And so you wipe passion from your memory. The past, you erase."

"Swann," she says wearily. "You invent the past."

"In the king's hunting lodge," he says, "in the photograph, you look as you should always look. The face of a woman well-loved is like the face of a *biche*, how do you say?"

"A fallow doe."

"Yes. Soft and most beautiful. I keep that photograph always in my wallet since that day."

"This is impossible, as usual," she says. "You don't know what you make up and what is real."

2. This Is Not a Sign

First photograph: the woman is framed by the sign. There is a stone wall, a saint's niche, a Saint Someone—benefactor of pigeons— chalked with shit. Wild rose has choked the gate open. The woman sits on the ground between two posts, the gate behind her. Above her head, on the cross-piece, the name of the village is scored. The woman is pointing up at the black letters. She speaks to someone outside the frame, the tilt of her chin suggesting challenge. Can you read me? she seems to be asking. Or possibly: Can you translate this sign?

The sign says: LA FORÊT LE ROI.

Second photograph: a man leans on the same sign from the other side. He looks directly and intensely at the viewer. Below one of his eyes, a small birthstain, attractive, resembles the map of France. The man smiles, but sadness clings to his smile. Because his arms are hooked over the cross-board, and because his chin rests just above the T, he has the air of a man in the village stocks.

The words on the other side of the sign remain the same, but a red diagonal line runs from the lower left corner of the cross-piece to the upper right. Decoded, the slashed letters mean: *You are leaving the village of La Forêt le Roi.*

Other translations, however, are possible. For example: *This sign is inaccurate. It is forbidden to use these words. This village has been discontinued. Translation unavailable. Not to be read.*

The woman cannot find the photographs but she knows they exist. She can remember, yes, in some detail, the last time she held them in her hands. The day was cloudy. She was indoors, reading a book, and the photographs slithered out from between the pages and fell to the floor. She thought the book faintly ridiculous, though absorbing. It was in French, a nineteenth-century traveller's meditations on the world. *In Asia and the exotic lands of the South Pacific,* the observer wrote, *the appreciation of fine wine does not exist. This is due to a diet of fiery spices and boiled food, two barbarisms which have destroyed the palate in the contrary hemisphere. Such lands, one might say, constitute the realm of bad taste, for below the equator and east of Constantinople, one of the five senses is extinct. In Australia, there is a bird that laughs when people eat.*

She had gathered the photographs up from the floor and studied them. Time passed; an hour, two hours, she does not know. Darkness surprised her. She turned on the lamp and closed the book. She has a clear image of pages 56 and 57 shutting themselves over the prints, and of her hand reshelving the book. The rest is hazy. She cannot remember the book's title or the author, though the minute she sees them she will know. She remembers the shape of the volume and the colour. Cloth-bound. Red, with bleached patches where silverfish had dined. She has searched high and low, in all the likely and unlikely places. For the Nth time, she is working her way through her library, A to Z and Z to A.

3. Afternoon of a Faun

"It's getting dark. We must have taken the wrong path again."

"Shh." He presses his fingers against her mouth. "Don't move!" Behind his shoulder, the wheel of sun skims the vast beech-tree crowns. Her eyes water. "*Bouge pas, chérie*," he whispers, and steps backwards through long grass, two paces, three. He is quiet and careful as a cat. Behind her: the abrupt wall of forest. Behind him: wheat fields, red scatter of poppies, black crows against blinding gold.

He whispers, "Look this way. Look at me."

"I can't. The sun."

"Shh." At the soft click of the shutter, she hears leaf swish, the shuffle of a branch, deer again. They are always watching but never stay. Before she turns they have gone, white behinds scudding away through the shadows like cirrus fluff.

"Two *biches*, very young." He indicates a square with his index finger and thumb. "It will be perfect. Everyone in my same ..." He emphasises the shape made by his hand.

"Frame," she says.

"Frame, yes." He strokes the camera. He draws spatial arrangements in air. "Three pairs of eyes, the white tails, your white shirt. It will be excellent. One can wait years for such a moment."

"I think I spoiled it. I think I moved."

"No, *ma petite biche*. High shutter speed, it doesn't matter. I will call it *Secrets du bois*."

She begins to sing, "*Down there came a fallow doe, As great with young as she maun go*," but trails off.

"Is it an Australian *chanson*?"

She laughs. "No. It's a ballad. Old English. Train of association with the deer."

He frowns, deciphering this.

"Fallow doe," she explains. "*Une biche*. It's a song about secrets and death in the forest."

"Always in forests there are secrets and death." He reverts to French; she speaks English; it is simpler that way, though often they move erratically back and forth, new language to old, old to new.

"Maybe if we follow the deer scat," she says. "Maybe that's the right path. Maybe the deer will lead us to the village." She walks out of sunlight, into the cavern of beech and oak. Instantly the light changes, fails, turns aqueous. The temperature drops. All around her are low unnerving sounds. She shivers. "It's spooky in here."

He is changing film, kneeling on the narrow grass levee between forest and wheat. He nods into the woods. "The deer trail might lead to a body. There was a murder last year."

"What? Here?"

"A woman from our village and the *curé* from La Thierry."

"From *our* village? From St Sulpice-des-Bois?"

"Yes," he says in English. "It was a scandal. She was *enceinte.*"

"Pregnant."

"Yes. She was ..." He searches for the English word but gives up. "*Absente,*" he says, frustrated, and turns back to French. "She was missing for weeks, and then a hunter found the bodies in there."

"Now you tell me." She steps back into the light.

"*En fait*, the deer found the bodies and the hunter found the deer."

She looks warily into the trees. "A priest and a pregnant woman. Were they lovers?"

"What do you think? They were found naked."

"Ah." She begins humming the ballad to herself and breaks off. "There's a murder in the ballad too, and lovers, a knight and a maiden. I wonder why something like that gives us such a — *frisson*? There's not an English word, isn't that interesting? *Un tel frisson.* But it seems indecent to feel it, it seems obscene."

He is checking his light meter, holding it close to the trees. "The forest is erotic," he says. "And so is death. And so is mystery."

"*Down in yonder green field,*" she sings, "*there lies a knight slain under his shield, with a down* — Did they find out who did it?"

"No."

"Nothing? No clues?"

"Yes, a clue. Another body in the forest near La Thierry. The *chef de police* in Etampes thinks the same killer, *quelqu'un du coin.*"

"Someone local."

"Yes. Now you see why I do not let you walk alone."

She bridles at this. "No one *lets* me or *doesn't let* me. I do what I choose."

"No, I forbid it. The killer could be anyone you meet."

"He could be you."

"He could be me."

"*Down in yonder green field,*" she sings, the notes low and annoyed. "*With a down, hey down. There lies a knight slain under his shield, With a down, derry derry derry down down ...*" She leaves the boundary line between forest and field and moves out between the wheat rows where the light is still golden as butter. "Haven't you finished reloading yet? I'm starting back. I think we're lost."

"You cannot cross the field, that is trespassing. We are not lost."

"Well then, the village is lost. Forgive us our trespasses or we won't be home before dark. And we're not going to find La Forêt le Roi, that's certain. Not today."

"We are not lost," he repeats. "Simply, we have not yet found the right path."

"Precisely my point. And we're not going to find it in the dark. Let's go."

"No, we wait for the partridges. They will arrive now, momently."

"At any moment," she corrects. "We must be at least ten kilometres from St Sulpice. Once the sun goes —"

"*Et voilà. Des perdreaux.*" They always appear close to dusk, the fledgling partridges, and always in pairs, nervy, intense, small high-speed feathered propellers, flying low over the wheat fields and into the black trees where death waits: hawks, hunters' guns, owls. She watches the pearled blur of wings and the birds seem to her unbearably vulnerable. "*Venez, venez, mes petits,*" he murmurs, excited. He points the camera like a gun. A high thrumming rises from him, and she turns away, disturbed. The fledglings vanish between the trees. Panic, unaccountable, swoops down on her. She begins to run through the wheat toward St Sulpice.

"*Chérie,* what are you doing?"

In minutes, he catches her and reaches for the back of her shirt. She tears loose, hears the ripping, then he has her again. He covers the back of her neck with savage kisses.

"Stop it. You're hurting me."

"*Un chasseur aime chasser,*" he murmurs. A hunter loves to hunt. She can feel the camera against the curve of her spine. "You should not provoke," he says. "But you like to provoke."

"I don't like to be hunted as though I'm wild game, nor do I like to be lost. Look what you've done to my shirt."

He runs his fingertips over her breasts. "You look better this way."

"This is insane. It's nearly dark. You got partridges yesterday, and the day before."

"Sometimes from six rolls of film, I do not find one single shot which pleases me."

"You're obsessive. You're more interested in your wretched Nikon than in me."

"To be jealous of a camera, *c'est ridicule, chérie.*"

It's not jealousy, she does not say, her heart thudding. It has nothing to do with jealousy. She does not know what it is. It is something shapeless and dark, like the black spaces deep inside the woods.

"*Bouge pas.*" He focuses, clicks.

"Don't," she says, angry, covering herself.

He pulls the shirt from her, rams it into his camera case. "I am an eye, *chérie*, this is what I am. Please. Like this. Or running, yes, if you want, that's good, *c'est magnifique!*"

They are both gasping now, the wheat in tumult as they pass. She cannot tell if the tolling bell is a church or her heart or the blink of shutter or thudding feet. She trips and falls and rolls into darkness. His weight crushes her, the wheat stubble scratches her back. "Perfect," he is laughing. "The light is perfect. I will call it *Nymph fleeing, with bare breasts.* Or *Diana the Huntress.*"

She beats at him with her fists, she tears at his clothes, they bite, their embrace is violent and smells of soil and want and hay. Afterwards, spent, they look up through the smashed wheat at the darkening sky.

"*Nymph and Satyr,*" he murmurs. "But no one to put us in the same frame."

She rolls onto her side and stares at him. "You arrange us in your head the whole damn time," she says, furious. She bites his shoulder. "You weren't even here. You're an *onlooker*, you know that? a bloody voyeur. You're always some place else, inventing us."

"I am not guilty as charged. I have been framed."

"Oh, that's good. A pun in English, that's very good. Everything's just a game inside your head."

"*Just* a game? I am very serious about games, *mon petit joujou.*"

"I'm not your toy. We've been walking all afternoon and we never even found the right path, let alone your precious village."

He laughs. "Is it Australian? You cannot enjoy the game without kicking the goal?"

"Is it French, forgetting which fucking game you're playing?"

"*Mais c'est toi.* You are my fucking game. I never forget."

"Lose the time clock, lose count of the score, change the rules as you go, declare yourself winner anyway."

"*Bien sûr.* I always win."

"If that's a dare, you're playing a dangerous game."

"You like dangerous games. We both like dangerous games."

She shivers.

"What are you frightened of?" He strokes her neck with his fingertips. He bites her lip. "Are you frightened of me?"

4. *Swann and Odette*

She calls him Swann because he calls her Odette.

"Odette?" she says. "Why? Because you stalked me?"

"Because Odette played with men the way cats play with birds, and because Swann won her back against all odds."

"A trophy. And then he walled her in *chez Swann* and she had to drop right out of the world. I don't like the sound of it."

"It was you who came looking for me. It was you who came back."

"Because you sent signals. You set out lures."

"Yes," he acknowledges. "And you were looking for them. You knew where they led. You flew right into my cage."

"I can fly right out again."

"Or you might not want to. Or I could stop you. That is the game."

5. *Swann's Way*

"We will stay longer on the road," he decides, his finger on the old map. "This time, we will follow the road to here, *direction* Etampes, but since Boissy-le-sec we will cross the fields."

"I thought that was trespassing."

"We will cross *between* the fields. On the right-of-way."

The shutter clicks. She has him, profile against afternoon light, both maps unfolding their wings. She can see the bright plume of obsession. He believes it means something, that they found the map in the wine cave beneath their house. He believes it means something extraordinary. The map is cobwebbed and water-stained. When they unfold it, pieces fall away like ash. In the lower right corner is a royal seal and a stamp:

Propriété de Monsieur Bousquet, forestier du roi, 1681.
Pavillon de chasse du Roi.
La Forêt le Roi.

She moves closer and presses the shutter again.

"Since Boissy-le-sec," he says, "we will search closely for the path. It should show itself here."

"*After* Boissy-le-sec." She moves, focuses, clicks.

He raises his eyes, reproachful. "You are wasting my film."

"You said 'since'. You can only use 'since' for time, not place."

" 'After' is place?"

"Okay, so English isn't logical. 'After' *can* be place. For example: before the wine cave, after the wine cave. As in: After the wine cave, Swann became obsessed with the king's hunting lodge."

"Because the steps to the wine cave go down to the seventeenth century," he says. He runs his index finger along the margin of the map. "*Forestier du roi*, 1681. The question is, how has it arrived in our *cave du vin*, the map of the king's forester? Why has it travelled fifteen kilometres, maybe twenty, from La Forêt le Roi?"

"Maybe the forester was Protestant? Maybe he was appointed by Henri IV and Louis XIV inherited him? And then bang,1685, Revocation of the Edict of Nantes by Louis, and the Huguenots had to flee for their lives."

"How do you know these things of French history?" he asks, amazed.

She thinks about it and shrugs. "Must be one of the oddities of an Australian education, a passion for dates. Mention a king or a war, and a year pops out like a cuckoo from a clock: 1066, 1215, 1337-1453, that's the Hundred Years War in case you don't know your own past."

He says, offended: "Those scars on the bell tower of St Sulpice? English catapults, 1405. Our grandmothers tell us the stories."

"You're joking. Of the Hundred Years' War?"

"The stories are passed down and down, and in the *mairie* records are kept from the twelfth century. Children find pieces of armour."

"They do? Still?"

"Si, si. Chain mail, coins, it is very bad luck to put an English coin in your pocket. They find Roman coins too, but that is lucky."

In St Sulpice-des-Bois, she is subject to a kind of vertigo. History floats. Time flutters like partridge wings. Monsieur Bousquet hovers over the king's hunting map while William Dampier, buccaneer, maps the north-west coast of Terra Incognita, inventing the shape of Australia as he goes.

The house itself, the house of Swann and Odette, once a

stable, is three centuries older than the royal forester's map. Some-times Odette presses her ear to the thick stone wall (it is cold; it is never warm, not on the hottest day; it is never light inside the house; they live in dusk), sometimes she holds the former stable like a shell to her ear and hears Crusaders thundering by, hears kings on hunting trips, hears the guillotine in the village square.

"On the old map," Swann says. "There is still the *s*. Do you see?" He points to the curled baroque script: *La Forest le Roi*.

"When did that change? The circumflex accent instead of the *s*?"

"I don't know. A long time ago. And on the map of the *département*, latest edition, here it is, the same village. La Forêt le Roi."

"Either way, it doesn't really make sense. The Forest the King. Why no partitive?"

"For the Sun King? Redundant, I suppose."

"Anyway, we've driven along every back road and every country track in that area. There's nothing there."

"It is on the map. The *mairie* is very exact."

"That doesn't prove the village still exists. Probably ten gen-erations of *fonctionnaires* transferred the old to the new, year by year, without checking."

"In the *mairie*, they always check. The road is not transferred," he points out. "In the old map, you see? the village is on the main highway from Etampes to Versailles. Now, on the map of the *département*, you see how the autoroute is very far from the villages. La Forêt le Roi is here, but there is no road that leads to it."

"Proof enough that the village has gone the way of the king's forester."

"No. Not proof enough," he says. "Not in France. There are footpaths and bicycles and canal boats and horses and carts."

On the seventeenth-century map, the footpaths are marked. On the map of the *département*, they are also marked. Some of the paths correspond. Some do not. In any case, the translation of lines from map to terrain is a highly intuitive skill, like water divining.

"We will find it," he says confidently. He measures something with thumb and forefinger on the royal forester's map and checks it against the modern map for scale. "The path should arrive somewhere here, when we can see the steeple of La Thierry."

"Why does it matter? What do you think you'll find?"

"It was where the king took his mistresses, the hunting lodge. *Un grand chasseur, le roi soleil.* Of women and of deer."

"So that's it. Hunting where the king hunted, and fucking where he fucked. That turns you on?"

"*Certainement.*" He is gathering up the maps and setting them aside, his hands trembling. She is awed, she is bemused, she is sometimes frightened by his flash floods of desire, the way appetite seizes him as a hawk might seize a quail. She cannot tell who is hunter and who is prey. She cannot tell which one of them has power and which has none.

"All you really want," she murmurs, "is a photograph of me in the lodge where Louise de la Vallière got laid."

"*Tais-toi, chérie. Tais-toi.*"

The table creaks and groans with their weight. Time slithers, maps realign themselves, kings watch, the forest lures.

6. *After the Hunt*

"After the hunt," he says, drowsy, "they say the king was inflamed. He liked to make love with the stag hung outside his window, dripping blood."

"Charming. Eros and death again, that really turns the French on."

"It turns everyone on. The French are honest about this, the puritan English are not."

"I am not English."

"Australian, English." He shrugs to indicate the splitting of hairs. "Anglo-Saxon, protestant, puritan, *inhibé, tendu* … How do you say it?"

"Uptight."

"Uptight, yes. But now …" He kisses her. "Now you are more *décontractée.*"

"In French, I am someone else."

"Now you have the face of a *biche*. You should look always like this. *Et voilà*, I have you on film. I will keep you this way."

7. *Secrets du Bois*

"Here is where we will search," he says, trailing an index finger across the map of the *département*, "after we leave the rue d'Etampes."

"Through the forest? But the old highway would not have gone through the forest."

"Three hundred years," he says. "Trees grow again."

"The forest where the bodies …? and the hunters? Where you told me they still hunt wild boar?"

"We won't be in danger. The hunting season hasn't begun."

8. Rue d'Etampes

Along the route to Etampes, each village is quiet as death. Stone house-fronts and high walls hug the road. Rambler roses suck at the mortar and the walls are thorn-barbed and honeysuckle-choked, but beyond all that noisy colour, hush crouches.

"No one lives in France," Odette says. "Not outside Paris. That's my theory. The villages are decoys left over from the Hundred Years War."

"Listen." Swann pulls her close and turns her to the wall that rises sudden as a rampart from the street. He presses his body against hers, and presses hers hard against the wall. "Listen," he says against her ear and his hot breath is like waves breaking in her head. "What do you hear?"

"Surf. Ocean. The sea of you."

"It's the law of village and not-village. You can hear it behind every wall. Someone is whispering to someone else: *C'est l'anglaise et le parisien.* Again."

"Then tell them I'm not *l'anglaise*. I wouldn't be English if you paid me. *Je suis l'australienne.*"

"It's all the same to them. It is slicing the hair. You speak English."

"Anyway, there's no one here. It's a ghost village," she insists. "If we ever find La Forêt le Roi, there'll be no way to tell if it's abandoned or alive."

"You are wrong. Already everyone in St Sulpice knows. Listen." He puts his ear to the wall and pretends to repeat what he hears. *"They are taking the direction Etampes, they have passed through Venant,*

they are in Boissy-le-Sec, they are leaving the road. Even in La Forêt
le Roi they know. They are waiting for us."

"Then the baker tells them."

9. The Butcher, the Baker

Each day, when the baker leans on his horn, she opens the gate
in their wall. It is ten exactly by the church-tower clock. The
baker parks in the cobbled square where the guillotine stood,
opens the back doors of his van, and leans against the shrine to
Our Lady who wears white, a powdering of pigeon-shit centuries
thick. The hot fresh smell of yeast pulls people like ribbons
through the gates on all sides of the square.

"*Ah, l'anglaise!*" the baker says every day. "*Bonjour, madame.
Combien de baguettes aujourd'hui?*"

"*Deux, s'il vous plaît, monsieur. Je ne suis pas anglaise. Je suis
australienne.*"

Day after day, not a word, not an intonation changes.

"No one lives in France," she says, "and nothing changes.
Ever."

"That is how we know we will find the village," he explains.
"And how we know they will be waiting for us."

She says: "I dreamed there was blood on the baker's hands."

10. Souls of the Damned

"It's so dark in here," she says. "I used to love forests. Rainforests.
But this one scares me."

"Look! Look there. A hunter's *abri.*"

"It's the hunters more than the murders. I'm scared of guns."

"Look." He points to a small dam, a drinking trough. It is a lure. As they watch, a fawn pricks its way across moss on dainty unsteady legs. At the trough it pauses, sensing something, and stares at them with its huge and lustrous eyes, and then it is gone, a streak of taupe and white.

"The hunters stay downwind," he explains. "They wait till the deer start to drink."

"That's so cruel. That's so unfair." She examines the water hole. "It's quite steep. It's very — *merde!*" She slips and falls into the mud.

Swann laughs, changing light reading and shutter speed. "I'll call this one 'Fallen Woman'. "

"Oh for God's sake," she says, and hurls a handful of mud at the lens.

"My Nikon!" he cries.

She sees his face and begins to run, headlong, deep into the forest. Tangled ivy clutches at her ankles, pulls at her legs. She stumbles on, gasping. She can hear the thudding of his feet, of her heart, of the blood in her ears. She falls and staggers up and hugs the trunk of an oak for support and then she sees the white stag and cannot even scream.

Massive, the colour of soiled cream, he watches her, unblinking. His antlers seem ancient, deadly as the scaffolding that once stood in Place de la République. She cannot breathe. The stag's basilisk eyes are impassive. *Welcome to the royal hunt*, the eyes say. *There is no escape. Thou shalt not pass.*

She seems to faint. A blackness floats before her eyes. She is buffeted by something, by history, by time, by the illicit, by something that is hurting her wrists. There seem to be cords.

"Magnificent, magnificent," Swann breathes. "The royal stag.

I got you both. I'll call it 'The Huntress Bound'." He is taking her violently from behind, the tree bark strafes her face, her belly, her breasts. Her wrists are bound with a leather cord to the trunk. "He's still watching us," Swann says, his voice drunk with arousal. "He knows this scene."

Swann's skin is slick against her back. She can feel his nails on her thighs, drawing blood. Beyond her bound wrists, beyond the bark-strafed skin of her forearms, her eyes meet the eyes of the stag.

11. Woman Getting out of the Bath

When she steps out of the bath, the water is pink with blood.

"Like that," he says, pulling away the towel. "With your hair wet, and one foot still in the water, and the steam rising."

She feels drugged. The shutter flickflickflicks like an eyelash. She is wet as a seal and slippery, her movements tidal.

12. Le Déjeuner sur l'Herbe

An old man leans on a pitchfork and stares at them stupidly. His face is seamed like a quarry. He has no teeth. Behind him, the floor of the stone barn is piled with hay. They can see a few sheep and a horse.

"We could ask him to take a photograph," Odette says.

"We don't need it. We've already got proof. The village sign."

"Both of us together, I mean." She smoothes the linen cloth on the grass near the edge of the pond. From her backpack, she takes out the glasses and the wine.

Swann says: "I'm going to pick apples." A tree heavy with

fruit hangs over the pond and Swann is climbing, the Nikon slung around his neck. "I knew it," he says. "From up here I can see the iron spikes where the stags were hung. It's the hunting lodge. The stone barn was the hunting lodge."

Odette watches the old man who watches Swann. That is surely his apple tree, she thinks. This is his barn. He could be a royal by-blow. He could be Monsieur Bousquet's great-great-grandson, five times removed.

"Can I tempt you?" Swann swings down out of the tree. He offers an apple. When she bites into it, the eye of the Nikon blinks. "*Eve in Eden*," he says, and the high bright sound is in his voice. "Tonight, when the old man goes, we'll sleep on his hay."

"I'm going to ask him to take a photograph."

"He won't have a clue what to do. Look at the way he looks at us. You might as well ask him for the moon."

"He thinks we're trespassing."

"He doesn't. No one owns a village pond or a village well. He's not thinking anything."

"He's scared of us then."

"Inbred," Swann decides. "It's possible no one from outside has been here for three hundred years."

"I'm going to ask him just the same."

"I will take your photograph," Swann promises. "I have six rolls of film. I will take you lying naked in the hay."

"Where Louise de la Vallière got laid."

"Yes. And in the pond by moonlight. *The naked shepherdess sings to the moon*."

"I want one of us together. I want a keepsake. I want the picnic on the grass, just this one peaceful scene."

"You don't need a keepsake in Eden."

"It's no good, Swann. I'm leaving. You must have known. You must surely have realised that."

His face goes still. She sees his knuckles turn white and the wine glass break in his hand.

"You're bleeding," she cries.

He lifts his bloodied palm to her face and strokes her cheek. "You won't be leaving," he says.

13. *That Obscure Object of Desire*

A man and a woman are drinking wine in a sidewalk café.

"Your hair is grayer than last time," Odette says. "It suits you. Men look more distinguished with age." She touches the birthstain under his eye with her fingertip. *"Mon cher volcan."*

Swann takes her hands and kisses them. "There is still a wildness in you," he says, *"ma biche sauvage.* You were like a doe in the forest, always poised to take flight."

"You were so violent, Swann, when we were young. You used to scare me."

"Violent?" He raises startled brows. *"Mais non."*

"I found an old photograph. The picnic with wine and apples in La Forêt le Roi."

He closes his eyes. "A thousand and one nights in the king's hunting lodge," he sighs fondly.

"I was going to bring it, but I couldn't find it in time. It's somewhere in the papers on my desk."

Swann takes a deep slow breath. "I can smell the hay. I beguiled myself for years with that fantasy. It was a considerable work of art."

"We asked that old man to take the picture."

"I had some sort of idea for a show. *A la recherche du village perdu*, something like that. I arranged the hunting lodge and the pond and an apple tree. I could see them clear as a photograph in my head."

"The essence of bucolic tranquillity," she muses. "You would never guess what was just outside the frame."

"The map was real," he says. "The possibility was always there. Camus wrote that the way matters little. What suffices is the will to arrive."

"Do you remember that photograph of you leaning on the village sign?" she asks. "You look pensive. You've found the object of your obsession but it isn't enough. I love that picture. It's the essence of you."

"In my wallet," he says, "I carry the photograph of you in the king's hunting lodge. You look the way you should always look."

"I only look that way in French," Odette says.

NATIVITY

When he passes under the boom, his fingertips turn slippery on the wheel. *No vehicles over six feet.* Jonathan ducks his head, just in case, and listens for a thump, miscalculation being something he has come to expect. He wipes his hands, one at a time, against the car seat, but the grey fabric is clammy too. He leans out to take the ticket. Even in the parking garage, he notes uneasily, as soon as the barrier descends and locks you in, that particular fog settles. Any hospital, any city, the same thing: he has difficulty breathing.

He clicks on his headlights and follows the arrows up, second level, third, still no free spaces, fourth level, he can feel his pulse picking up speed, all these sick and dying people, this fog, he is practically hyperventilating now, he is allergic to visitation hours, to visitations, *Visitation of the Plague, Visitation of the Archangel Gabriel to Mary*, to this fever of unwanted associations, to fifteenth-century woodcuts plastering themselves across his windshield. He turns his wipers on. He has reached fifth level. Sixth. He may not be able to get out of his car. Does that ever happen? he wonders; blackouts, heart attacks, in hospital parking lots? Obviously. He can see attendants in Day-Glo vests checking, all part of the day's work. The attendants hold slim flashlight probes.

They move from car to car. They are looking for bodies slumped low against the wheel. *Potius mori quam foedari*, Jonathan thinks. He wonders what the statistics are.

When he turns off the engine, the fog leaks in through the vents. The smell is always the same, a moist blend of anxiety, disinfectant, roses wilting at bedsides, sweat (the kind one smells on animals in veterinarians' waiting rooms),vital fluids, IV fluids, bed pans, over-perfumed visitors, death.

Maternity wards should be different.

Wards, he thinks. Wardens. Detention. There is no getting away from threat. The concrete pillars undulate slightly, like the pulse in a baby's head, sucking back and then distending themselves. His sense of balance has gone. There is less and less space for the car and he can see that it will not be easy to back out. He will have to work at it. (*Labour's begun, the first phase, and she's been admitted. She especially wants you to be there. Can you drop everything and come down?*) He decides that Atlanta is worse than other cities. (*Apparently there are complications. Something called pre-eclampsia. Do you think you can make it in time?*) He is labouring now, tugging at oxygen, raking it across his ribs. Atlanta is worse because of the congestion, the smog, the violence, the rampant harm.

He does not seem able to move. He leans against the steering wheel and watches a Toyota draw a bead on him, nosing in, docking. He absorbs the soft vinyl jolt of front bumpers bumping. *The eagle has landed.* His mind is like that, a grab bag of not entirely illogical associations. The eagle has landed. The stork circles.

A man gets out of the Toyota. He has roses in one hand, a balloon string in the other. IT'S A BOY! the balloon says, sleekly silver, bobbing above the man's head. The man feels Jonathan watching. He grins and salutes. He is laughing a winning-the-lottery laugh. Rah rah rah, he burbles, or seems to. I've won a son, a son I've won.

Dr Seuss, I presume.

Dr Seuss tugs on his balloon and gives an exaggerated whoop of jubilation. Jonathan is not fooled. The man is terrified.

"Whoa, hey," the man says, rapping on Jonathan's window.

Jonathan considers. This could be as good a summons as any. He opens his door part way, and extends his left leg. He gets both feet on the ground.

"Hey," Dr Seuss says. "Do you know where we get the free tokens?"

"Sorry?"

"Parking tokens. You know. We're supposed to get free ones."

"Are we?"

"Uh-huh. All the new dads. I couldn't find the right desk last night. Mind you, in a bit of a whirl, I'm the first to admit. Know where we have to go?"

"Sorry," Jonathan says. "No idea."

"Shoot." Dr Seuss is frowning a little, assessing him. "You know what? I can tell, just by looking at you, that your stork hasn't made delivery yet. Am I right?"

Jonathan thinks of possible responses, some of them violent. This startles him and piques his interest. He cannot recall ever before having the urge to hit anyone. He is a gentle, scholarly person. At least, that is how he thinks of himself. Other people — his students, for instance, or his son Ben and his daughter Stacey — probably think of him as out of it. He has certainly never had fantasies of violence. Never. But was that honest? Could a classicist truly claim a lack of interest in war, murder, bloody revenge, infanticide, patricide, noble self-immolation, the tearing of bodies limb from limb? *Potius mori quam foedari*, death before dishonor, and yes, at this moment, he would prefer a heart attack, or death by lions, or by man-to-man combat in the parking garage, or by, say, an out-of-control car ramming him against a concrete pillar. At this moment, he definitely feels such sudden escape would be preferable to blacking out in the delivery room in full public view. He slumps back into his car.

Dr Seuss bends over him. "Hey, listen, it's not that bad. It's over before you know it. Mine had ten hours of labour, I'm telling you, I understand why they call it labour, I was wiped, I thought it would never end." He rubs his forehead with the back of his balloon-holding hand. "I stayed right to the end though," he says proudly. He takes a wondering inventory of his own body, amazed by its strength. "Right to the last inning it's touch and go, you're scared the whole damn time, you're thinking there's no way the head and shoulders can get through without ripping her in half, there's no way, and then shazam, you win the pennant, know what I'm saying? *Pennant*? What am I talking about? This is the World Series, this is it, man, there ain't nothing like it. This time tomorrow, you'll know what I'm talking about. Hold these."

He thrusts the roses into Jonathan's hand and fishes in the pocket of his jacket.

"Here, have a cigar. Think of it as a stolen base, and you're there on third just waiting for that one little extra push to get you home free. Compliments of Ernest Hampton Somerset the Third, Ernie for short, in honour of Ernest Hampton Somerset the Fourth, Ernie Junior for short."

Bubbling would be the word, Jonathan thinks. He is bubbling

on, Seussing and sluicing, covering up panic. And Jonathan is unexpectedly swamped by a great rush of mournful tenderness for Ernest Hampton Somerset the Third, whose son has not yet reached the age of disappointment. He stumbles out of his car.

"Your roses," he says awkwardly.

"Oh geez, thanks. Don't know which way is up. I'm flying, I admit it to you, man. High as a kite. Feels like Christmas."

"Merry September," Jonathan says. "Congratulations."

"Here's my card. Every kind of insurance you can think of. Listen, you've got to pull yourself together, it's important for *them*, you know. She's going to be fine, the baby's going to be fine, you're going to be fine, uh … what did you say your name —?"

Another small wave of turbulence rises in Jonathan and recedes. "Jonathan," he says meekly enough.

"You're white as a sheet, Johnnie boy." Ernie takes in the tweed jacket, the horn-rimmed glasses, the greying hair. "Starting over?" he guesses. "Is that why you're so scared?"

Jonathan blinks at him. "Pardon?"

"I mean, you know …" Ernie flounders a little. "Well, I thought maybe second family. Younger wife."

"Oh." Jonathan winces. "No." He is leaning against his car, studying the cigar, trying to think where to put it. "It's my daughter," he says faintly.

"Oh well, for God's sake, that explains it," Ernie says. "Ginny's dad was a wreck. I'm not kidding you. A total wreck. We had to send him packing last night, hours before Ernie Junior took his bow. *Hours* before." He hooks the balloon string around the bunched stems of the roses in order to free his right hand. He pats Jonathan on the shoulder. "Listen, Johnnie, before you can blink, you'll be passing out your own cigars, and signing the kid up for college. That's where I come in, by the way. College tuition fund, the best gift a granddaddy can give. You got my card, give me a call. You're not going to pass out on me, are you?"

"No, no. I'm exhausted, I guess. Long drive."

"Where'd you come from?"

"Boston," Jonathan says.

"Good God." Ernie stares at him, and then walks to the back of the car. "How about that?" he says with wonder. He bends down and runs the knuckles of his balloon hand across the licence plate. He shakes his head. "How come you didn't fly?"

"Bad weather. Fog." Inner or outer? he waits for Ernie to ask. Ernie keeps staring. "The airport was closed," he explains. "So I had to drive to New York, and then I just —" He makes a vague motion with one hand. "I don't know. I just kept going."

A long slow whistle curves out of Ernie's lips like an arc of spit. "How many hours that take you?"

"Um, around fourteen, I think, actual driving." He frowns at his watch. "I stopped somewhere in West Virginia and slept for a few hours. Some ratty motel."

Ernie whistles again and shakes his head. "We all go a bit crazy, I guess. It's kinda like their cravings for pickles or whatever, d'you think?"

Jonathan thinks it was one way to arrive too late.

"Lean on me," Ernie offers. "Here, you hold the balloon. What's your line, by the way?"

Jonathan sighs. He has been blundering into situations of fleeting camaraderie more often lately, with the most improbable people. This bothers him. He fears it means that his haplessness is showing. He never knows how to extricate himself, but he has learned that it is definitely not a good idea to say, in answer to casual exploratory questions, *classicist*, or even *college professor*. It makes people too uneasy.

"I deal in old stuff," he says, replaying one of his children's jokes. He tries for their light dismissive tone. "I recycle it."

"You mean antiques? An antiques dealer?"

"Antiques, antiquities." He feels ridiculous, leaning on Ernie's arm, the two of them shuffling toward the elevator. He cannot bring himself to give offence and break free.

"Lot of money in that, Johnnie, especially in Atlanta. I could tell right off the bat from your jacket, by the way, not to mention your Yankee accent, that you were into something very upmarket."

Non semper ea sunt quae videntur, Jonathan thinks. He feels grotesque. He feels that Ernie has the better grip on life, that Ernie has more substance, more generosity, that Ernie deserves honesty, though he knows perfectly well that the truth will not be of the slightest interest to Ernie. Nevertheless. "*Non semper ea sunt quae videntur*, Ernie. As we say in the trade. Things are not always what they appear to be."

"Very true," Ernie says. "That's very true. Mind if I give you a friendly tip, Johnnie? No offence. But you should leave your car safe at your hotel where they'll have a security patrol. Rent one for driving around in while you're down here. With Georgia tags, know what I mean?"

Jonathan is studying the mylar balloon that still bucks at his own wrist. *Rara avis*, it should say.

"Some people down here have a thing about Massachusetts tags, is what I mean," Ernie says as the elevator doors open at reception. "Listen, you think you'll be okay now? I'm heading up another level."

"Your balloon," Jonathan says.

"Oh, thanks. Give me a call, Johnnie, okay? I work national. Got clients in fifty states."

Jonathan leans on the reception desk and gives his daughter's name. The nurse frowns at him. "You asthmatic?" she asks.

"No," Jonathan says. "It's the —" He gestures at the fog. "Happens to me in hospitals."

The nurse smiles. She runs a fingernail down the ledger on her desk, scanning names. Her fingernails are the colour of bruised plums, and Jonathan wonders how she bathes, how she attends to the body, without gouging furrows in her skin. He tries to imagine her making those rows of tiny braids in her hair, her long nails clicking like knitting needles. Other nurses come and go, ignoring Jonathan, sometimes leaning over the shoulder of the nurse at the desk to add brief notations to her book. The nails of the other nurses, Jonathan is relieved to see, are clipped. Perhaps desk nurses receive a special dispensation. But when they have other duties? He imagines the infant, his grandchild, prinked with blood. Nailed to death, he thinks ghoulishly. He feels light-headed.

"I'm afraid I've arrived too late, nurse," he says. "I think she will have had –"

"I'm not a nurse. I'm the receptionist."

"Oh. I thought ... because of your uniform." He tries again. "I think she will have had the baby by now."

The plum-lacquered index nail stops, scans horizontally, monitors data.

"Nope. Not yet. Let's see, D3. Oh yes, I know her. They brought her down to Delivery before I came on. About six hours ago, I think." She laughs. "Everyone's been teasing her, she was so gung-ho for natural, they always are, the *primos*, for all of about twenty minutes, and she's swearing up and down, no way, no way she's a quitter, she's going to go the whole distance. And then she hears the screaming from Delivery 2, and asks for an epidural on the spot. We laughed so hard you'd have thought we were the ones with contractions." She makes drumming motions with her right hand on the desk and the sound of her nails is like bird feet skittering on glass. "You can say a quick hello, that's all. We've got a lounge down the corridor there, where you can wait after that, if you want. She's being monitored because there are a few complications. It's only relatives now."

"I'm her father," Jonathan says.

The receptionist's mouth opens and her eyes widen. She blinks rapidly, staring at him. "But ..." she says. Jonathan focuses on the O of her lips and waits. "Oh," she says, recovering well. "In that case. It's third door down, on the right. Delivery 3. I, uh, I apologise."

"That's okay."

"Her mother's in there with her."

Jonathan leans on the counter. It hits an air pocket and drops several feet. He breathes slowly. "I'll be fine," he says to the receptionist. "Third door down, on the right. Right?"

She stares at him. "Right."

Delivery 3 is in twilight. The shades are drawn, the light dimmed. At first he sees only the tilted bed, the trolleys, the drips, the equipment, the stirrups, his daughter's face, coffee-pale, and the corona of her hair, black and damp, against the pillow.

He kisses her forehead, pushing aside a mass of curls.

"Dad?" She half opens heavy lids but they fall again.

"Stace," he says.

She makes another effort to open her eyes. A smile flickers and stays. "We've been waiting for you," she says, slurring her words like a drunk. She gropes for his hand.

We.

He peers through the murk of the room and sees an armchair, shadowy against the closed drapes. He sees the form of a woman. His hand jumps like a fish in Stacey's, and Stacey gives a little cry of fright. "Me and the baby," she says, each startled word distinct. "I told the baby not to come till you were here."

The woman in the armchair is not Cathy. He can see more clearly now. He can feel his pupils dilating, pushing against the edges of his eyes. He blinks several times, but the sensation of painful bulging does not go away. Owl-like, he and the woman study each other.

"Hi," she says quietly. "I'm QP's mom." She comes forward and extends her hand. She is a handsome woman, fifty perhaps. Fifty-five? Her face is worn, her hand feels like fine-tooled leather. He notes a wrist band with woven initials: WWJD "I guess you're Stacey's dad," she says.

"Jonathan Wilson. Pleased to meet you."

"Callisto Wade. Your wife's gone to buy Stace a few things. I've been keeping watch."

"Kind of you."

"I'll let you two be. I feel like I know you already, Stacey's talked about you so much."

He is startled. And now, he sees, he cannot ask: Who is QP? Nor can he ask: And what does she say about me? What does she say about her mother, about *us*? He works at words, dragging them up a levee in his mind, but he cannot get a firm purchase.

"No problem at all," Callisto says, and he understands that

some verbal scree, a few pebbles, inane, must have ricocheted up. "I could do with some sleep," she says, "but I'd appreciate a call when things start moving. They gave her something to induce, because of the pre-eclampsia."

"I don't know what that means."

"Means they got to get the baby out pretty quick. Means the hard part should begin in three, maybe four hours. I'll be back for that. This'll be my twenty-third grandchild, God willing, and I get just as excited every time."

"Twenty-third," he murmurs, stunned.

"QPs my baby," she says. "My tenth and last." She sighs. "Though he is like to bring down my grey hairs with sorrow to the grave."

She catches his look.

"The Bible," she says. "Book of Genesis."

"Yes. I thought so."

This interests her. "Whitefolks don't usually know their Bibles as well as us."

"Is it Abraham?"

"Close. Old Jacob, when he thinks he's lost Joseph and Benjamin, both. It's the youngest ones break our hearts."

"Yes." He has not thought of it as a general rule.

She puts a hand on his arm. "They go astray, but they come back." She studies him, considering what to tell. "I'm going to stop by at my church on the way home. Church of the Lord Victorious. I'm going to stop by to pray."

"It's dangerous, this pre-eclampsia thing?"

"You a believer, Mr Wilson?"

"Well," he says.

"All things are possible to them that believe. You see these hands?"

She offers her palms.

"Touch them," she says.

Jonathan glances uneasily at Stacey whose eyes remain closed.

"They don't look much, do they?" Callisto says, turning her hands over and back. "They do hair, is what they do weekdays. Straightening, lightening, braiding, beading, cornrows, dreadlocks, you name it. That's what they do weekdays. But on Sundays, they come to glory. On Sundays, in the Church of the Lord Victorious, they handle snakes."

She waits to gauge the effect of her words.

"Poisonous snakes," she says.

When he says nothing, she lays her cool snake-handling fingers on his wrist.

"All things are possible," she says, "to them that believe."

A nurse comes in and takes Stacey's blood pressure.

Stacey says: "Has something gone wrong? Why have my contractions stopped?"

"They take their own sweet time," the nurse says. "Especially for first births. Not to worry. Dr Steiner's keeping a close eye on you. We have to let him know every little blip and change in your readings. He'll be by again in half an hour." She leaves.

"Dad?" Stacey says.

He gets up from the armchair and comes to her side. This time he manages to say it. "It's so good to see you again, Stace." He kisses her forehead. "It's just so good to see you."

She reaches for his hand. The way she holds it reminds him of a day on the beach north of Boston. She would have been

five or six and they were walking on great ribs of rock, the
frenetic surf between. "Do you remember the beach near the
lighthouse?" he asks.

"That time I fell into the ocean?"

"You were five, I think."

"There was blood all over."

"The rocks *grated* us," he says.

"I had nightmares for ages. I was so scared."

"So was I," he says.

Her eyes close, but she does not let go of his hand. Minutes
pass. He thinks she is asleep and then realises she is watching
him.

"Hey," he smiles.

"I've fucked up again, as usual, Dad."

"Don't think about it. It doesn't matter."

"It does," she says. "But I'm too tired to care."

"We were afraid we'd lost you, Stace. It's been so long."

"Yeah. Two years."

"More than two years. We've been worried sick. We didn't
even know if you were ... you know ..."

"Alive or dead," she says.

"Why didn't you call? Why didn't you at least —"

"I don't know. Too much I didn't want to talk about, I guess."

"At least a postcard."

"Just too much I didn't want you to know."

"Oh Stace."

"Don't go weepy on me, Dad."

"I'm not," he says, embarrassed. "It's the air-conditioning."

"You seen Mom yet?"

"No," he says. "She called me. We talked."

Stacey's eyelids fall shut again. "I'm so tired," she says. "I didn't know it would be such hard work."

Someone pushes at the door and the garish neon of the corridor blares in. Jonathan flinches. A hand and a head appear, not Cathy's. The hand and the head are black. "Oh, sorry," a male voice says. "Wrong room."

Stacey stirs. "Stag?" she asks sleepily. "Is that you?"

Stag's eyes widen. "Stace?" He comes into the room, startled. "How you doin', girl? Thought I got the wrong room."

"You got the right room," Stacey says, turning lively. She sits up. "That is, if it's me you're looking for."

"And who else would I be looking for, girl? How many women you think I know about to pop a baby in Northside Hospital?"

Stacey laughs. "Is that a question we really want to know the answer to, Stag?"

"You watch your mouth, girl. Man," he says admiringly, patting her stomach. "You as blown-up as a whale on steroids. What you cookin' in there?"

"Get lost," she laughs. "Dad, this loser is QP's best friend."

"From when we were this high," Stag says, touching the floor. He locks the index finger of his right hand around the middle finger. "Like this," he says. "Me and QP. Blood brothers. That's what I had to tell the chick outside, by the way. Only relatives, she says. I'm family, I tell her. Blood brother. Had to throw in a little sweet talk as well." He pauses, frowning. He contemplates Jonathan with the air of someone replaying a track in his head. "Stace? —?"

"This's my dad, Stag."

"Your *dad*?"

"You got a problem with that?" Stacey asks, belligerent.

Stag raises both hands, a surrender. "No, ma'am." He falls into a violent mock trembling. "No, ma'am. I ain't got no problem with that."

"Get lost," Stacey says. "You idiot."

"Your dad. Well, how 'bout that?" Stag's smile is full of wonder and white teeth. "Pleased to meet you, suh. Stace never let on her folks was whitefolks."

"Pleased to meet you, Stag. Jonathan Wilson."

"Virgil Haynes, suh. But everyone call me Stag."

"*Virgil*? Your name is Virgil?"

"Yessuh."

Stacey groans. "Don't get him started, Stag. He's about to spout Latin."

Stag is studying her, seeing her differently. "QP know about this?"

"QP know about what?"

"That your folks is whitefolks?"

"Naturally he knows," Stacey says, indignant. "What do you think I am?"

"He never let on. He never give me one little clue. I don't get it, Stace."

"Place your bets, Stag. Genetic miracle or adoption?"

"No, I mean, I don't get it with QP."

"Maybe he's not crazy about it," Stacey says tartly.

Jonathan says, "Would you object to my calling you Virgil?"

"Object?" Stag scratches his head. "No suh, I guess I got no objection, 'cept only time anyone ever call me Virgil is my momma when she is mad at me."

Stacey says, embarrassed, "He gets a big kick out of the name, Stag."

"That so?" Stag asks. "It was my daddy's name, and my grand-daddy's name, and his daddy's before that."

"Drop it," Stacey says. "So what's happening, anyway? Rap with me, man. It's awful boring in here."

"I'll tell you what's happening," Stag sighs. "I just gone and done the most dumb-ass thing of my whole life."

Stacey laughs. "I meant, what *new* stuff is happening?"

"No, I got to tell you this, girl. I got to tell you this. I got to get me some sympathy, because something is pressing heavy on my mind. Man, I got myself lost, big time, coming all the way up here from Decatur."

"Oh, right," Stacey says. "Major voyage."

"Girl, this far north off of 285, you not in Atlanta anymore, you not even in Georgia, you into foreign territory. I miss my exit and next thing I am all the way into Buckhead and I am going around in circles cursing you, girl."

Stacey laughs. "You were driving that souped-up scrap heap around Buckhead? You're lucky you weren't arrested, Stag."

"Well, ended up I had me a good time, not getting myself found by the cops. I saw some mighty pretty houses in Buckhead while I was lost."

"Whitney Houston's got a house in Buckhead," Stacey says.

"Maybe I see it," Stag says. "I don't know. All I know is, I saw me some mighty pretty houses, and I said to myself, Man, I would surely like to get me a house like that. I would surely like to give my woman a house like that for Christmas."

"Which woman would that be, Stag?"

"The love of my life at this present time," Stag says with

dignity. "And here's the thing, Stace, that is pressing so heavy on my mind. I could've got me a house like that, this very day, if it wasn't for what I went and didn't do last week."

"What you didn't do last week."

"Don't mock me, girl. You listen to this, and you'll know not to mock the small inner voice when it speaks, like Callisto says. That snake-handler, she is one powerful woman. And Callisto always tell me: Boy, any time you ignore that small inner voice, you will regret it." He closes his left fist around a bunch of keys. The keys hang on a flat woven ribbon around his neck and he runs the key ring up and down the cord. "Callisto give me this to remind me," he says. "And I am here to tell you that Callisto is right, because last month I got me the idea to play my street number and my apartment number, end to end, in the lottery, and what do you know?"

"What do I know?" Stacey asks.

"I am just two digits off the winning number, I swear to God. So I say to myself: Stag, there is a message here. The inner voice is talking to you, boy. And the inner voice tell me, you're on to something here, Stag. And then it comes to me like Moses striking the rock. *Next time*, it says to me, *you got to play your mobile number*."

"Let me guess," Stacey says. "And now you are just *one* digit away from a million."

"Girl," Stag says. "You do not even begin to understand the scope of this tragedy. I did not play the lottery this month because I was too damn busy with this and that, and because I am dumb-ass stupid, and rejecting of the spiritual life. "

"I can't wait for the moral," Stacey says.

"The moral is this. What do you think is the winning one-million-dollar lottery number this week?"

"Who do I think is the biggest bullshitter south of the Mason-Dixon line?"

"I swear to God, Stace, it is my mobile number. And that is what happen when you do not listen to the inner voice. If I had listen, I could be moving in next door to Whitney Houston." He turns to Jonathan. "Is that a tragedy, suh? Is that a tragedy?"

Jonathan can feel a gust of wild and dreadful laughter, Dionysian, but he swallows it. "That is a tragedy in the classic Aristotelian sense," he says, solemnly. "The most painful kind." He dare not meet Stacey's eyes. He focuses on the bunch of keys and on the woven ribbon around Stag's neck. WWJD, the ribbon says every two inches. He touches the cord with his index finger. "Whose initials?" he asks.

"Callisto give it me," Stag says. "Stands for What Would Jesus Do? And we know what he would've done. He would've listened to his inner voice."

"And played his mobile number!" Stacey is breathless. "Oh Stag, oh Stag, you're going to start my contractions again."

"Woe unto them that laugh at me, girl." Stag pats Stacey on the belly. "I just come by to lay the hand of grace on QP's boy." He splays his ten fingers across her flesh. His span is enormous. "I come for the laying on of hands."

"Get outta here," Stacey says.

"You had better believe I am out and gone before the women's business starts. But first I got to deliver my benediction."

"Idiot."

He lifts Stacey's graceless hospital smock and lays his ear against the great taut globe of her skin. He listens. Then he puts his lips against her belly and murmurs something. He straightens and salutes. "Message from QP to his son. Message delivered."

"Get outta here, you clown."

"I'm gone, girl. Got me a little deal that I got to see to down south in Decatur." He leaves, singing. *He's got the whole wo-orld in his hands ...*

"Virgil!" Jonathan says, bemused. "But Virgil could never have thought him up."

"Only Aristophanes or Plautus, huh?"

"Oh Stace," he says sadly.

"Don't say it," she warns. "Don't even get started."

"Can I ask what you're doing now?"

"I'm having a baby," she says.

"Okay," he sighs. "Can I ask who QP is? Can I ask what QP stands for?"

"QP is the father. His name is Quintavius Paul."

"You're joking."

"I'm not joking."

"It's weird. All these classical names."

"Think about it, Dad," she says tartly. "Think about it."

And he thinks about it. He thinks about all the younger sons sent out to the colonies, about the slaveholders sent down from Oxford with Euripides, Homer, Virgil and Terence in their sea chests.

He asks, subdued, "When do I get to meet QP?"

"I'm tired," she says, her lids turning heavy.

A nurse comes to take readings. Dr Steiner comes. He is short and stocky, and his accent is purely New York. He shakes Jonathan's hand.

"What brings you to Atlanta?" Jonathan asks.

"I could ask you the same, I suppose. I live here. I've lived here for ten years. Life is a surprise to us. How's Boston?" Jonathan raises his eyebrows.

"Your accent. Plus your daughter told me," Steiner says.

"My daughter talked to you about me?"

"About Boston. About Cambridge. You know how it is with us Harvard Square junkies, anything for a chance to reminisce. We go on and on." Steiner shrugs. "Harvard Med. School, I should explain." He looks sideways at Jonathan and says in a low voice, "Give her time. It's my impression she misses her Latin as much as she misses Harvard Square."

Zeno's paradox, Jonathan thinks. I will never get beyond the halfway point of knowing how much I do not know. Nevertheless, he notes a thinning of the fog that fills the room. He feels an easing of his congestion. "Can you tell me what this pre-eclampsia thing means?"

"Most of the time," Steiner says, "it's not threatening. We have to monitor, that's all, to make sure it doesn't turn into eclampsia. That's serious."

"Serious how?"

"Toxic for both of them. Have to get the baby out before that happens. I've given her something to soften the cervix. She's still not fully dilated. If that doesn't happen in the next couple of hours, I'll probably have to do a C-section."

"No," Stacey says, coming alive. "No. I'm going to have my baby the real way."

She makes an effort to sit up, and sinks back.

Dr Steiner pats her hand. "You won't find a gynecologist in Atlanta less inclined to do a C-section than me. That's why we're waiting this out. But if we have to do one, we have to do one. And you have to trust me."

"I trust you," Stacey says.

He pats her hand again. "I'm expecting things to start moving quite soon. Rest up. You're going to need every ounce of energy once that kid decides to move house."

Nurses come and go. Stacey sleeps. Jonathan sits in the dark. It occurs to him, suddenly, that Cathy is avoiding coming back from wherever she went. Could that be possible? Is it possible, for example, that she is as nervous as he is? He levers up the footrest, tilts the armchair back, stretches out. His eyelids droop. He is extraordinarily, exquisitely tired.

Something cold slithers across his ankles. He is aware of it, but cannot open his eyes. He knows what it is. He recognises its stealthy advance, at his calves, at his thighs, at his groin. Anguish. Suppose she really does wait until he leaves? Not that he wants to see her. The room and the engineered twilight are suffocating. He has to have air.

Stacey seems to be sleeping again.

He staggers into the corridor, trying not to make noise.

"Is there somewhere," he asks the receptionist, "where I can get some air? Somewhere I can smoke my pipe?"

"There's a terrace," she says, pointing. "End of that hallway. Go one flight down. Push the exit door."

"Thanks."

When he pushes through the exit door, he sees he is not alone.

"Hi," Cathy says.

He has to lean against the wall. His voice will not come to him. It bobs about like a mylar balloon, out of reach.

"You look tired," she says.

You look good, he would say if his voice should drift within reach. Thinner, but still good. Gaunt suits you.

"I've been here a while," she says. "Working up the courage to go back in."

She sips coffee from a styrofoam cup. It smells burned and bitter. She grimaces.

What are you afraid of, exactly? he thinks of asking.

"It's both of you," she says. "It's everything." She sips and shudders, then sips again. "I'm afraid of having Stacey pissed off with me for looking as though I might, you know ..."

"Go weepy on her."

"Yes."

"Unforgivable sin," he agrees.

She begins tearing little slivers of styrofoam from the rim of the cup.

"How's the west coast?" he asks.

"Warmer. Smoggier. It's okay."

"And how are you? Really."

"I'm fine. And you?"

"I seem to manage."

She turns away and stares out over the city. She sips some more coffee, shudders, and tosses the liquid in a brackish arc toward the skyline. "Too much sadness," she says. "I had to get away from it."

"And now she's made contact. She's okay."

"I think you can die of grief. Literally. I think you can. I've felt as though I'm dying of it."

"It's over now."

"It's like a killing frost. It destroys everything."

"I don't know," Jonathan says. "It seems more like Crazy Glue to me." He wants to touch her. "It's like Vietnam vets. They can only talk to each other." He goes to her, holds her, and she does not yield, does not resist.

"I think I've turned into permafrost," she says. "I won't forgive you if you make me cry."

"Did you know that Callisto handles snakes?"

"What?"

"And QP. Do you know what that stands for?"

"I ask nothing," she says. "I ask no questions at all. I know what Stacey chooses to tell, which is never much."

"It stands for Quintavius Paul. Paul, I strongly suspect, as in Saint Paul, who is credited with starting snake-handling cults. Something in the Pauline Epistles about the faithful being able to handle any deadly thing and it shall not harm them. I'm getting eager to meet QP."

"We won't be meeting him," Cathy says.

"How do you know?"

"Callisto told me. He's doing time, she says."

"Oh sweet Jesus." He leans against the wall. He closes his eyes. We could just float away like balloons, he thinks. At last he says: "She wanted us here. She called. She asked for us."

"We should go back in," Cathy says.

They take turns at the bedside and in the armchair.

Jonathan sleeps and dreams. Rocks grate him, surf harries him, a riptide tears Cathy and Ben and Stacey from his side. The undertow rushes them into the dark. Stacey cries out and Jonathan's heart bursts with effort.

"I'm here," he cries. "I've got you. I've got you. You're safe."

"Dad!" Stacey's voice is shrill. "Shit, Dad! For God's sake, you're hurting me."

"It's okay," Dr Steiner says. "It's okay. Calm down, everyone. Everything's going like clockwork. Now I'd like the two grandmothers to help. One on each side. Take her leg, one each, and hold it like this. Crook your elbow under her knee, hold her ankle with both hands. You're the stirrups."

And Jonathan, dazed, sees that Cathy is there, and Callisto is there, and the big adventure is underway.

"She's going to brace herself against the two of you," Steiner says. "Now Stacey, you push when I say, and everyone count out loud with me, *Push*-two-three-four, *push*-six-seven-eight, *push*-nine-and-ten. Three times, and then rest for ten, and then push again. Count, everyone! Nurse, can you attend to Professor Wilson there? I think he's going to black out."

"Dad!" Stacey calls, reaching for him.

"I'm here," he says. "I'm fine. I won't let you go."

He stands by the head of her bed and holds her hand. Stacey clenches and pushes. Cathy, sweating with exertion, catches his eye. "You okay?" she mouths. He nods. His fingers are crushed. He cannot remember such fraught happiness since the day they all clung to each other in a salt-soaked huddle below the lighthouse.

"— eight, nine, ten, and rest," Dr Steiner says. "— and ten, and push …"

"Here's the head," Callisto cries. "I can see the top of the head."

Cathy's eyes are bright. "You want to see?" she asks Jonathan.

He doesn't. He feels queasy. He prefers to keep placing damp washcloths on Stacey's brow, dipping them in tepid water, wringing them out, applying them again like balm. Cathy puts her hand on his arm. "Sit down for a while," she says.

"I'm fine, I'll be fine." And now he is. He touches Cathy's wet cheek.

"Isn't this something?" she whispers. "Isn't this amazing?"

"And push, two three four," Dr Steiner says.

"I can't," Stacey sobs. "I can't anymore. I'm too tired."

"Almost done," Steiner says. "You're wonderful, you're terrific, you're the world's champion number-one gold-medal pusher. Just the shoulders now, and we're done."

It is quite impossible, Jonathan thinks, terrified. This time he has looked, a quick stricken glance. It is quite impossible for the shoulders to fit through.

And then Stacey gives a final great roar and his grandchild slithers out like a fish.

"It's a girl," Steiner says.

"Where is she?" Stacey calls. "Where's my baby?"

Jonathan sobs like an infant and Cathy holds him, Callisto is hugging them both, they are all laughing and crying and hugging Stacey and the baby. Jonathan kisses everyone. He kisses Cathy on the mouth. Merry September, he says. He is babbling, he knows it. He has no idea what he is babbling about. Somewhere in the melee, he sees that Steiner is rubbing at his eyes with the back of a latex-gloved hand. *Et tu*, Jonathan thinks, staring.

"So?" Steiner says, caught out. "It doesn't matter how many times I do it, it gets to me every time." He is defiant. His tone is aggressive. "It's a great fucking miracle. It's one of the two great mysteries, and I expect it will go on getting to my tear ducts until I slam into the other one."

Cathy says: "We have to call Ben. Ben asked me to call as soon as the baby came."

"What?" Stacey says. "My perfect brother wants to know when my baby arrives?"

"He does, Stace," Cathy says. "He's hoping to talk to you."

"Why didn't you tell me? That's so damn typical, that you didn't tell me."

"I try," Cathy says. "I try never to tell you one damn thing."

"Get outta here," Stacey laughs. "Hand me the phone." She runs a finger over the dark peachfuzz on her daughter's head and says dreamily, "Isn't she beautiful, Mom?"

"She's beautiful," Cathy says. "She's perfect."

"*Ab ovo usque ad mala*," Jonathan tells Steiner. "Which means, translating loosely, from the egg to the balloons. I have to go buy a bunch of those ridiculous helium things and some cigars."

CREDIT REPAIR

The sirens start dropping out of the pines like a mess of crows, but Tirana has already smelled smoke.

"Fire!" she cries, jumping up. When she opens my living room window and leans out, something hot sucks at us and a stack of filing papers rises to meet it. The screen fell out months ago and the pages flutter over the parking lot, their little *sign here* flags a whir of colour.

"Now look what you've done," Carol says sadly. "That's two weeks' work."

"Something's burning," Tirana says.

"It's nothing. It's just fire trucks up on the Interstate," Solana tells Carol.

"There's black smoke."

"Any diversion." Solana folds her arms and narrows her eyes. She could be measuring Tirana: for coveralls, for prison garb, for a coffin. "With clients like her ..."

"But that's the whole point, isn't it?"

In the lee of the Interstate, all points are blurred by the eighteen-wheelers. We can't see them. Thirty years ago, when our world was called forth from industrial waste and red Georgia clay, the developer had a low mountain range ordered in. Earthmovers planted it. It is forty feet high, and curves as naturally as though God himself put it there. Then truckloads of pines and sycamores arrived. All this was before my time, but I've figured it out. In theory, the steep strip of forest buffers us from levels of noise considered harmful. We are below the expressway. We live in its hip pocket. We rent its basement apartments. We can't see it, its roar is muffled, but eight lanes of tractor-trailers, ambulances, police sirens, blowouts and collisions are a syncopated bass thump in our bones and under our feet.

From my window you can see a slash of blacktop below (fifty parking spaces), then Block H opposite, then the hillslope of pines between us and the Interstate. People often stand at their windows and stare into the pines. Sometimes they gaze and inhale assorted substances. Sometimes they just gaze.

Tirana is reading the tips of the sycamores. She is watching the pine tufts for blips of red. "I see them," she calls. "They're on the exit now."

"Tirana knows a bleeding heart sucker when she sees one, Carol, she's a pro. She's got you wrapped around her little finger."

Carol just looks at Solana.

"It's her funeral," Solana says, exasperated. "Her mess. She's got the attention span of a ten-year-old. Why do we bother?"

"You're so harsh, Solana."

"Yes, ma'am," Solana says. "Throw Tirana's folder out," she orders me. "She's disqualified herself."

I look at Carol and she gives me a little smile, puts her finger to her lips, and shakes her head. I like Carol, I like working with her, but she feels guilty for being white. Not me. Already I think Solana was a mistake. When she looks at Tirana, her eyes say: Don't you dare confuse me with one of those.

"They're turning in here," Tirana calls.

Solana dismisses this with a wave of her hand because ninety-eight per cent of the time, here in Eden Gardens, it's a false alarm. But then we hear a sound like fatback spitting on a grill as big as Texas, and even Solana gets up and puts her weight against the sliding doors and goes out onto my screen porch. It is not a real screen porch, but a second-floor balcony big enough for two K-Mart chairs and a plastic table. About three years ago, to qualify for FHA improvement grants, the landlord had nylon mesh stapled to the uprights, but the mesh sags and bellies out like a sail. A four-lane throughway for mosquitoes and flies, Solana says, which is true. Also, it faces south, and the heat punches you as you open the sliding doors, so the porches are reserved exclusively for doggy doo-doo and Hibachi grills. Carol and Tirana join Solana out there, and I close the living-room window that Tirana left open, and then I go out on the screen porch and push the sliding door shut. It is interesting to me that not one of them thinks about my air-conditioning bill. The sliding door shudders and makes a farting noise. It gets stuck with twelve inches still to go. It isn't hung right, and there is rust on its sliding track.

"Can someone help me?" I say, but no one hears.

The trucks are careening into our little blacktopped saucer of paradise now, trailing long red streamers of sound. In every unit, people are running out to their balconies. Kids are climbing on dumpsters or rollerblading along the footpaths between the blocks. One fire truck is stuck between Block G and Block H and turns its hose on a unit where someone's barbecue is merely scorching steak.

"What the fuck —!" screams the barbecue man, punching a

hole through his screen. He is wearing nothing but his jockey shorts, and the blast of water gets him full in the gut. He is on the third floor, which is as high as our projects go because we are low-rise garden units, and he sort of floats at the edge of his balcony, waving his arms, as though he might swim down the rope of water to the truck.

"Serves him right," Solana says.

Carol looks at her. "Oh, Solana."

"*Oh, Solana,*" mimics Solana. "You sound like my mother. Don't try that long-suffering mama tone with me."

Tirana turns to look at them. "That's funny," she says.

"It's not funny," Solana says. "It's illegal."

Tirana blinks. "If you talk white and Carol talks black?"

"It is illegal to light a grill on the balconies."

"But we gotta," Tirana says. "Where else do we got? Everybody do it."

Everyone does. The smoke detectors go off twice a week, sometimes more. The firemen are supposed to report false alarms, and then the landlord is supposed to pay the city a fine, and then there are supposed to be fire inspections, but the landlord slips the firemen a summer bonus, and most of the firemen aren't about to report because their own kids live in the projects, if not in these particular ones then in others that look just the same, and anyway, this is July. The children are entitled, the city owes us. There is no public swimming pool within ten miles of this place, and no grass either. The only green things are the pines and sad sycamores on the man-made slopes of I-20 and the odd shag blanket of kudzu. So the children follow the fire trucks in a swarm, cartwheeling, making whoops of sound by wumping their hands against their mouths, waiting for the moment when the blast of the hose will fly them right into Christmas.

"Who on fire?" Tirana calls down to a kid in the parking lot. "Block F," the kid calls back up. "I dunno who. Someone told me Jimmy the Pyro's place."

"I know'd it." Tirana turns to us. "That welfare-to-work shit just one more exploitation by the Man."

"Oh my," Solana says, placing her hand on her heart.

"Jamika go to work every day like they make her," Tirana says, "and look what happen."

"We don't know whose unit's on fire," I point out. We are still all crowding on my tiny balcony, trying to see.

Tirana crosses all her fingers and does something strange with her arms and chants down to the parking lot: "*Jamika-bird, Jamika-bird, fly back home, Your house is on fire and your children alone.*"

"Here we go again," Solana says.

"Fuck you, Solana." Tirana seems to be crying. "No social worker gonna make *me* leave my kids all day, make me flip Burger-King patties, make me leave —"

"And where were your little ones when you went out clubbing last night?"

"With Denise, Miz Bitch. Me and Denise swap, but we talking 'bout one hour, two hours here, maybe three, not all-day work."

"All-night work is more like it. Setting the local tomcats on fire."

"You wouldn't know fire if smoke was coming out o' your ass," Tirana says. She mimes the act of striking a match and tosses the quick imaginary flame across the room. "Why don't you leave us alone?" she asks Solana.

"You have no idea how great the temptation is."

"Jamika's Jimmy damn crazy 'bout playing with matches. And why he do that now? Because he sending up smoke signals for his mama, that's why."

"I do hope it's not Jamika's," Carol says.

Jamika is our star exhibit, our shining hope.

Now there are flames as high as the sycamore trees. The air is full of black smoke.

"Can someone help me?" I say, pushing my shoulder against the jammed-open door. "I don't want this place to stink of smoke for a month."

"Hey, you!" Tirana calls at a boy on a skateboard. "Who burning?"

"Block F," the boy calls back. "Seventeen."

"Told you!" Tirana says.

Carol turns pale. Jamika is in 17B. "Dear God," she says. She presses both hands to her mouth.

Tirana looks at her, curious. "Ain't that something," she asks Solana, "when white folks turn white?"

"Regis and Jo-Jo and the baby!" Carol says, squeezing through the stuck door.

"The firemen will take care of it," I call after her, but she is gone.

"Fucking Saint Carol," Solana says.

Tirana is hot on Carol's trail. "I'm gonna go watch," she calls over her shoulder. "I'll be back, okay? I still need all them forms and shit."

Solana is so angry, she would scorch the balcony uprights if she touched.

This is the way it works. Carol is the social worker, Solana is

Legal Aid (she has only been with us three months), I organise. I do the paperwork. They don't live in the projects; I do. They have degrees and framed certificates. I have no particular quali- fications, other than being an expert on how to fuck up a life, which gives me a special kind of usefulness in this setting. Breathing Space is what we call our operation and it runs out of my apartment (my donation). I also run a couple of businesses on the side. My business ventures are not unrelated to the general scope of our enterprise. One business is called Ways and Means (*Bad credit history? No problem. Talk to us about Ways and Means*) which is an essential service in this neck of the woods; the other is Credit Repair, for those who seek a new beginning and are willing to take a slower uphill path.

"These are your options," I explain to Tirana, "once Solana gets you off."

"*If*," Solana says. "I'll have my work cut out. Possession of stolen vehicle, driving without a licence, failure to report —"

"How was I s'posed to know it was stolen?" Tirana asks.

"Maybe because of the California plates? Why would someone who lives in Eden Gardens be driving an out-of-state car?"

"Because his friend was visiting, that's what he said. I just *borrowed* it."

"That might hold water," Solana says, "if your friend the golden-hearted lender hadn't vanished into thin air."

"I hadda get Dessie to the hospital, didn't I? What else could I do?"

Solana raises her eyebrows and gives me a look. "You see?" Her tone implies: *might as well try to explain colour to someone born blind.*

"You see?" Tirana says to me, meaning: *when your kid has a*

fever of 103 and you don't have a car or a phone, what's the point of
trying to explain to someone like Solana?

"Anyway," I say, "if Solana can get you off, and if Carol can
get you an 'extenuating circumstances' waiver so you can keep
your rent subsidy and your training job, we could start a clean-up
operation on your credit."

"I could charge stuff again?"

"Well, I wouldn't advise that. But you'll be able to get the
power turned back on."

"Carol said you'd do that anyway."

"We will co-sign for you with the utility company until you're
credit-worthy again. The way it works, Tirana, there's a gazillion
rules that merchants and collection agencies are required to follow
before they report you to a credit bureau, but they break the
rules all the time. Sometimes it's unintentional, because they've
never checked the regulations, sometimes it's just because they
are impatient or boiling mad. Either way, we get them on the
fine print. I get a copy of your credit history, I challenge the
items one by one, the bureau has to take them off your record."

"Then I gotta pay all that stuff I owe?"

"No, you don't. The slate is wiped clean."

"Cool."

"You'll be free to start a brand new trail of unpaid bills,"
Solana says, acidly.

"This takes a while," I explain. "There's a lot of paperwork.
I need your birth certificate, your Social, I'll give you a list."

"How long's it gonna take?"

"Six months, maybe more, depending on the circumstances
for each item."

"Six months! I got to get my phone back before that. I got to think of my kids."

"Well, there are ways to get a phone without credit. We can work on both fronts at once. I can have you hooked up in three days, not with Bell South, needless to say, but you'll have a number, and people can reach you there. To call out, you have to dial a whole bunch of other numbers first. You also have to pay the basic fee in advance each month, and you have to use a pre-paid card for long distance calls."

"How much I gotta give you?"

"$25 when your next welfare cheque comes."

"Carol will give it to me."

"Where *is* Carol?" Solana wants to know.

"She's at the hospital," I say. "She says it's bad."

"Regis maybe gonna die," Tirana says.

"Carol wants us to join her when we can."

"Let's shut up shop and go then," Solana says. "If I don't get out of this place, I'll go crazy."

"Could you guys drop me and the kids off at Wal-Mart on the way?" Tirana asks.

"Sure," I say.

"No," Solana says. "We could not."

We drive past the black hole in Block F — the charred shell of 17A, 17B and 17C; Jamika's apartment and the ones above her and below — and out of the parking lot. The entire place smells like an ashtray. "You know," I say, "her kid may or may not have been playing with matches, but the wiring in these places is sub-standard. They're all fire-traps. In case you wanted grounds for a suit."

Solana skews herself sideways in the passenger seat and studies me.

"The problem is," I say, "that if you won, the city would order the landlord to re-wire, re-plumb, re-roof, and God knows what else that is decades overdue. The city will say: if this work order is not carried out, et cetera, Eden Gardens will be condemned. And the landlord will say: condemn the dump, you're welcome, because a tax write-off is pure candy to him. *Ta-ra!* And you'll close off one more lousy chance of lousy housing for folks on the bottom rung."

Solana says nothing. She goes on contemplating the right side of my face. It's not my good side. You want a magnifying glass? I feel like asking. After two miles of non-stop staring, I wind down my window and turn the air-conditioner off.

"Hell, it's hot!" she says. "Why'd you do that?"

"Is my profile up for audit or something?"

"I'm trying to figure you out."

"Don't waste your energy. It's not required."

"Why are you living in a dump like that?"

"Is this the long census form, or the short?"

"You a full-time bad girl? Is that your career?"

"It's something I'm good at," I say, caught off guard. "Which has diddly-squat to do with anything."

"Let me guess, white girl. College degree from Randolph Macon or some such deb hatchery. Affluent Republican parents, daddy in the oil patch or in guns. Sheer pleasure to give them this much grief."

"Way off base," I say. "So far out in left field, you're in the wrong ballpark."

"Was it you or Carol started Breathing Space?"

"What's it to you?"

"You two hired me. I could quit. I've got an interest."

"It was my idea, as it happens."

"That's what I thought. And that's what doesn't add up. You're not a bleeding-heart do-gooder like her."

"Sucking up will get you nowhere."

"You're prime-cut bitch, to be blunt. Cynical, pragmatic, and no illusions whatsoever about Tirana."

"Watch your mouth," I say mildly.

"You know how to run a business on federal grants, you're probably skimming some off the top, you're probably downright bent in a small-time-crook kind of way, but you're a cockeyed idealist all the same."

"Just like you."

"Not just like me," Solana says. "Not just like me at all. You couldn't be more wrong."

"Wrong about you being bent? Or wrong about you being a cockeyed idealist?"

I know I was wrong about hiring her, but I'm not going to tell her that yet. I brake for a red light and the radio from the pick-up in the next lane hits us like a tsunami. I give the driver a dirty look, then I notice the decals on his wing window and I concentrate on the road straight ahead. One decal says *Charlton Heston is MY president*, the other one's a confederate flag. The guy leans on his horn. He's on the CREDIT REPAIR side of my van.

"Hey, you!" he calls, jerking his thumb at my sign. "That really work?"

"Sure thing," I say.

"What's the catch?"

"No catch."

"Gotta be. What's in it for you? How'd'ja get paid?"

"There's a fee. You can pay in instalments."

"I'll bet. I'll bet I can. You got yourself a client, baby."

The light changes. "Call my number," I say, as we move off.

"Oh, I got your number, baby. You better believe it."

All I need. Solana is smouldering. "Odds are good he won't call," I say, but she's on a different track.

"It's anger drives *me*," she says. "Not idealism."

"Yeah. Well. I do anger too, for the same reasons. Easier than sadness or despair."

"Oh please," Solana says. "Don't make me puke."

"Third degree burns," Carol tells us in a low voice.

"Will he pull through?"

"They think it's doubtful."

It's Regis, the three-year-old, and I have to look away. Jamika is sitting at the bedside, opposite the machines and the intravenous drip. The child is inside a kind of bubble, so she cannot touch him, but she is resting her hand and her cheek on his clear acrylic sky. She has the air of being inside an invisible bubble of her own. She has the air of someone who has always known the worst will happen and has been laying in supplies. "Mama's here, Regis honey," she murmurs. "Mama's here." She says it over and over again. From time to time, she puts her lips against the bubble's skin.

"Shock," Solana whispers.

"She's under sedation." Carol's lips move, but we have to watch them to hear. "He's lost most of his skin. There's nothing left for grafts."

We can't look at the child and we can't look at each other.

"Where are the others?" I ask Carol in a low voice. "Jimmy and the little ones?"

"Tirana's got them, didn't she tell you? She was here all morning. She offered to look after them as long as Jamika needs."

"Jesus Christ!" Solana says. "And you let her?" Her voice comes at us low and intense, almost soundless, like a bullet from a gun with a silencer.

Jamika looks at us the way a sleepwalker blinks at an obstruction. "Tirana's been wonderful," she says.

"Can I drive?" Solana asks.

I can't pretend I'm not surprised. "Sure," I say. "If you want. I hadn't picked you for a '93 Ford minivan type."

"You know nothing about my type."

She guns the engine. I raise my eyebrows at her, but she's oblivious. "This is an elderly car," I remind her, but she is fixed on some urgent target in her head. I've never seen my speedometer needle move so fast. We've passed take-off and gone straight to the van's wheel-wobble range. "Solana, for God's sake, you want us to fall apart on the Interstate?"

"I have to burn something," she says.

"Yeah, well." My mind skitters away from the plastic bubble and the small skinless body. "Better get used to it, though. Hey, slow down, slow down." She's changing lanes like someone on speed and I'm pressing brakes on the floor-mat on my side. "Breathing Space is what we try to give them, but Crisis Central's more like it."

"I don't think you get it." She accelerates. Her foot is emphatic. "I'm talking about Tirana. I'm talking about Carol. I'm talking about shooting yourself in the foot. I'm talking about this whole endless merry-go-round of willed haplessness. It makes me so furious, I could —"

"Kill us?"

She weaves out of the fast lane, overtakes on the right at somewhere above eighty, weaves left again.

"High chance of success at this moment," I say. I'm calculating my chances of leaning over and taking the wheel. I can practically hear the chemicals shloshing around in her veins: anger, exasperation, smashed idealism, despair. It's a white-lightning mix. Her blood makes the sound that skyrockets make just before they fizz into coloured moons.

"Any last wishes?" I shout.

"What?"

"Any final messages?" I'm feeling dangerously light-headed myself. "Last will and testament? Last rites?" I'm screaming at her now. I'm thinking about my kids who are with their father this week. "Any regrets? Anyone you wish you'd fucked or fucked over but never did, you raving maniac?"

She glances at me, and my face must sober her up. "Oh shit," she breathes. "Oh shit, oh shit." Her hands start trembling on the wheel.

"You," I gasp. I'm slapping her: face, arms, anywhere. "Mother of all mistakes. Because Carol thought you'd be perfect, what a laugh."

"Oh shit, I'm sorry. I'm a time bomb. I'm losing it." Her hands are trembling so violently that the old rattle in the dash — the one I've had fixed — kicks in.

"Should've trusted my instinct" — slap, flat of hand on cheek, shoulder shove — "I knew you couldn't cut it. Useless law-school bimbo."

"What the — Stop it!" she yells at me. "Stop it! Crazy white bitch, you want to kill us?"

We're almost down to normal just-over-the-speed-limit speed. I take a breath that goes down to my ankles. Another crisis come and gone, you get the knack of it. She scoots across four lanes at an angle of sixty degrees and I can feel everything south of my waist turn to mush, but then we've made it. A guy on our left leans on his horn and gives the finger and I give it right back, but then I tap my forehead and point to Solana and make a gesture of what-the-hell-can-I-do? with my hands. He grins and shakes his head and I grin back. Solana's oblivious. She's got the shakes.

"Hey," I say gently. "It's okay. It happens. There's a Shoney's at this exit. Let's have some fries and a coke, then I'll drive us home."

In the parking lot, she slumps across the wheel. "Jesus," she says. "I really lost it. I'm sorry."

"Forget it."

"I think I'm going to be sick."

When she gets back from the bathroom, I've got our order. Over fries, I say: "You're not cut out for this. It's no big deal. We go through two lawyers a year."

"I'm not quitting."

"Then you'd better learn to think in a different way, or you'll never last. A completely different way. You have to approach each day like Sisyphus rolling his rock uphill or Hercules —"

"Where *did* you go to school?"

"Not Randolph Macon."

"Where?"

"University of South Carolina, the Honors College, if you must know. To get back to the subject, you have to think of this like Hercules emptying the ocean with a shell. It's not that you're getting anywhere. You're not ever going to get anywhere. It's just something you do each day because you can't not."

"Bullshit to that." Solana crunches hard on an ice cube. "You're trying to believe I'm suffering from missionary burnout. I'm not. I don't have a single do-good cell in my body."

"Oh right. You're just in Legal Aid for the money. Using a Yale law degree to claw your way up to the Public Defender's office, a well-known shortcut to wealth and prestige."

"I'm in it for the rage. There is no possible way you could understand."

"Oh no? I know what a rage high feels like. Who're you hooked on hating, girl?"

For a second, I think smoke might come out of her ears. I think she might stab me with a fork. Then she says: "My father. My tail-chasing work-allergic alcoholic bum of a father. My mother always took him back and gave him money and covered up for him and prayed for him and worked two shifts to put us through college and wore herself right into the grave at fifty-three." She breathes a few fire breaths. "What about you, white girl? Who's pushing your stops?"

"My perfect sister," I say. "The hot-shot lawyer." I look Solana dead in the eyes. "You remind me of her. Everything she touches stinks of success."

We smoulder at each other for a minute or so, and then she says: "We could arm wrestle for the Rage Cup if you like."

"What?" I start to laugh. And then she starts. And then we

can't stop. We're holding our sides, rolling about, knocking flatware off the table, until the waitress comes to ask what the problem is and all the other diners are staring and we still can't stop and then the manager comes and asks us to leave.

We're in the parking lot facing Tirana's unit, bracing ourselves to go in.

"You want a cigarette?" I ask.

"Quit years ago," Solana says. "But I think I will."

"It's pot, actually. Hand rolled."

"Then I definitely will."

We just sit for a while, inhaling, breathing out, inhaling.

"So you're a scholarship kid too," Solana says.

"Yep."

"And your father?"

"Construction. Small time. Odd jobs. Fences, decks, building screen porches, that kind of thing."

"Honors College. So how'd you get from an Honors College degree to this dump?"

"Dropped out in my senior year, for a start. One of my many unfinished projects." I inhale slowly and hold the sweet smoke in my lungs for a while. "I don't know. It sort of creeps up on you," I say. "It's not like you decide on it as a career. You just get into the habit of expecting to fail or mess up, and after a while you simply find you know how to be a loser. You're good at it. You know the ropes, if you see what I mean. It's something you can count on."

Solana says: "I can feel anger coming on again, just listening to you."

"But that's it, you see. That's why the two kinds just separate out, winners and losers, like oil and water. That's why I choose to live here and not where you do."

"Look, the reason people like my father and Tirana never change is there's always someone to bail them out. They *know* it. They know a good thing when they see it. They need the rug pulled out from under. They need a kick in the butt."

I inhale and let the pot float around behind my eyebrows for a while. "It should work like that," I say. "But it doesn't. I don't know why." I breathe out slowly. I think of the pot as white coming in, blue going out. When it eddies up from my lungs to my brain, it's an in-between colour, milky opal. "What happens is you realise that life in loser-land is not so bad. It's actually kind of warm and fuzzy, and you have this fondness for other losers. You know they've got the same little broken spring inside them as you have. It's not that they dug out this pit for themselves. It's just that they found themselves in it, and they know it's hopeless to try to get out."

"I can feel a rage high coming on."

"Feel free. Other side of the coin."

"What? Bullshit."

"You going to tell me you never panic about having your father's loser virus in your blood? I bet you wake in a sweat some nights."

"You're out of your mind."

"Ever dream you've turned into your father?"

"Look," Solana says. "You make a decision. You decide it's either drown in his cesspool or climb out. You decide you will not be your mother. You decide you will not throw lifelines to idiots who can hardly wait to dive back in."

"So how come you're here and not in some glass tower doing corporate law?"

"I told you. Rage. I'm not here to pull losers out. I'm here to punish them."

"That's an interesting angle." I can feel the mellowness coming in, a lovely slow tide. I close my eyes. "When I was a kid, we used to spend summers at this nowhere beach in South Carolina. Helen, that's my sister —"

"The hot-shot lawyer."

"Right. She's two years older than I am. Funny thing is, I was the daring one. I was the leader then. She was always getting sick and missing school, she was a very timid child."

"So she got more attention."

"I guess. I don't think I minded. I think I adored her really. I mean, the whole family did. She was much prettier than me and much much smarter, and my mom and dad always said: *Helen's going to put her mark on the world.* She won a scholarship to a private school and after that the family embarrassed her. At school, she'd say Dad was in business, in real estate, *a developer,* she said. At home, she was a bundle of nerves. I *worried* about her."

"Got it," Solana says. "It makes sense now. You're mama's type. Branded as caretaker for life."

"We were out in a row boat. We weren't out very far." Helen's so close I could touch her. I'm ten, she's twelve. There is one oar in the bottom of the boat and Helen still has her sandals on. I dive in and tread water. I dare Helen to jump in too. I tell her it's shallow. I tell her I'm touching bottom, but I'm not.

I try to explain for Solana. "I don't know why I did it. I think I thought that if she *had* to swim, she would. She'd learn how.

She'd learn to protect herself." I light up again. My hands are sweating now. I remember the blue around Helen's lips when they pumped her lungs. I remember getting her hair in my mouth.

"Can I borrow your cell phone?" I ask Solana.

I dial a number. "Hi," I say brightly to an answering machine. "Just wanted to know how you're doing. It's been a while." I nearly don't say it, then I do. "I miss you, Helen. Give us a call when you've got a minute, okay?"

"There's no comparison between you and losers like my father," Solana says. "You *did* save her. And you *do* fend for yourself. Hell, I've watched you for three months. You're a fake loser. You could be superwoman if you want."

"She used to make the most elaborate sandcastles you've ever seen." I remember the cat's eyes for windows, the mussel shells for doors. "When she was eight and I was six, she used to read me stories at night. She used to hide a flashlight under her pillow and we'd wait till Mom and Dad had gone downstairs and then I'd crawl into bed with her."

"Will she call you back?"

"*The Little Mermaid* was my favourite."

"Will she call you?"

"She might," I say. "Eventually." I inhale slowly. "She'll tell me I'm my own worst enemy. I make her feel the way you feel about your father."

And then I tell her: "I didn't actually call her. I dialled my own number and left a message on my answering machine."

There is a long orange electrical cord snaking across the hallway and disappearing under Tirana's door. Solana trips on it.

"God," she says. "I thought *your* building was the pits. What's that stench?"

"Sewer back-up. A lot of the toilets don't work." I look at her curiously. "You must have lived in projects somewhere. Back before college and Yale law school. Where're you from?"

"Atlanta," she says. "This is my home town. We *never* lived in housing projects. My mother would rather have died."

"Well now you know. For Eden Gardens, my block is upper middle class. Block C's pretty bad," I acknowledge, eyeing the squalor. "But it's not the worst."

I knock on Tirana's door.

"What's this frigging cord for?" Solana says.

"A neighbour's feeding her power." I bang on the door again. "That's the way people manage. Losers look out for one another, that's why I like them."

"Don't make me puke."

I put my ear against the door and hear the TV. Cartoons. I thump with my fist. Everything's quiet except for Spiderman's voice. "Tirana," I call. "It's me. It's just me and Solana."

There's a fumble of sound and the door opens a crack. The chain is on, and Evie's sweet and dirty little face peeps through. She's standing on a chair.

"Hi, Evie," I say.

She puts a finger to her lips. "Mama says don't wake the baby," she whispers.

"Okay," I whisper back. "Can we come in?"

"Okay," Evie says. She unchains the door and climbs down off her chair and lets us in. The TV set is running off the orange extension cord. There's not much else in the room: a formica table, two plastic chairs, a carpet remnant on the floor and a yellow vinyl beanbag on top of it. There is no air-conditioning. The windows are open and the children are wearing nothing but underpants, but it doesn't help. The room feels like a furnace and stinks of body sweat.

"Jesus," Solana says under her breath.

Everyone is snuggled in the beanbag. I think of bees clustering on pollen. Tirana's the sunflower, and on her stomach, curled like a petal, Jamika's baby sleeps. Jimmy the Pyro and Jo-Jo and Evie and CJ and Dessie all seem attached. You can hear all those baby bees purr. In the background the TV drones, but no one pays it any mind.

"Mama's telling us a story," CJ says.

"If you want lemonade," Tirana offers, "it's in Denise's across the hall. Or there's beer. Evie can get it for you. My fridge don't work."

"Don't worry," I say. "Just came by to see if you needed help."

"Mama," Dessie says, pulling at her sleeve. "Don't stop. Tell what the mirror said."

"Mirror, mirror, on the wall," Tirana begins.

No, they all clamour. You told that already. Tell what the mirror said, tell what the white queenlady did.

Tirana's eyes glitter. "You want to know what that ol' mirror said?"

Yes, yes, they breathe, eyes shining.

"You gonna be very quiet and listen up?"

Shhh, they all chorus, fingers to lips.

"'Cause that mirror got a voice as soft as cream," Tirana warns.

Shhh, the children say.

"Listen up then," Tirana whispers, and they squirm in close.

"The mirror say: you got a big shock coming, white queenlady.

Yes, ma'am. 'Cause I got news for you, I got a announcement to make. You not the hottest babe in Block C. Not no more."

Mirror, mirror, you tell ME, the children chant on a rising curve of excitement. *Who the hottest lady in Block C?*

"If you wake the baby," Tirana warns, "the mirror won't tell."

Mirror, mirror, you tell ME, the children repeat, whispering but insistent. *Who the hottest lady in Block C?*

"Now here is what the mirror found," Tirana says. "Black Velvet be the hottest chick around."

The children scream with laughter and clap their hands. *Jazz be nimble, Jazz be quick, Black Velvet be the hottest chick*, they chant. They tumble together, licking pollen and rubbing legs. Jimmy the Pyro tickles CJ and CJ shrieks with pleasure. The baby cries.

"Now look what you gone and done," Tirana says.

The children smother the baby with kisses. *Tell what the white queenlady did to Black Velvet*, they beg. But the baby is fretful now.

"If someone take the baby," Tirana says. "If someone get the baby's bottle from Denise's."

"I'll do it," Solana says.

"Denise will show you."

Solana holds the baby against her shoulder and rubs her cheek against the peach fuzz of its head. She won't catch my eye.

Tell about Black Velvet, the children beg.

Solana closes the door.

"The white queenlady, she call takeout," Tirana says. "Express home delivery. And what she ask for? What she order now?"

A poisonapple! the children respond.

"And why she do that?" Tirana wants to know.

Because she want Black Velvet to die!

I wait, half listening, for Solana to come back but she doesn't. Ten minutes, fifteen. Tirana doesn't seem worried, but I am.

In the hallway, I find her. She's sitting on the floor with her back against the wall. She has the baby in her arms. The baby sucks furiously on the bottle, her eyes wide, her gaze on the face above hers. Solana doesn't even notice me. She's looking into the baby's eyes, singing softly.

"*Your daddy's rich,*" she croons, "*and your mama's good-looking. So hush little ba-by —*"

Then she sees me and stops dead.

We stare at each other.

"Don't you say one fucking word," she warns.

SOUTH OF LOSS

In July, the auto shop is hot as a furnace. *Zach's Oven* is what they should put on the sign, Billy says. *Get your car baked here.* Heat billows out and down from the sheet-iron roof. Fumes of gasoline rise. The shop, a made-over barn, slumps beside rural route 6, half way between the South Carolina coast and nowhere. It is not exactly on the antebellum heritage list, but it does do oil-change-and-lubes for the carriage trade. (*For the weekend Gone-with-the-Wind types and the gentlemen farmers*, Billy says.) Several grand neo-plantations are close by—all bed-and-breakfast listings with verandas and white wicker rockers—and they keep Zach's Auto Repair in business, but only just.

Billy spits on the blacktop in front of the shop and his spit sizzles and disappears before his eyes. "How come we don't move to the off-ramp by I-77?" he wants to know. "How come, Zach?" He suggests this at least once a day. "Like that Exxon place. Get the interstate breakdowns. Get the weekend traffic. Get rich."

"Get air-conditioning," Joshua says.

"Get down to Charleston every night."

"Get the hell out of nowhere."

"Nowhere is exactly what my great-great-greats were looking for," Zach tells his boys, unruffled. Boys. He thinks of them all that way, black and white, young and old, the ones whose fathers worked for his father and the ones whose grandfathers did: Joshua, Quintus, Robert E. Lee McGonigal, age 72, known to the wide world as Robbity or Robbity Reb, and Billy, nephew of Robbity Reb.

Billy rolls his eyes. "Nowhere is surely what they found."

"Secret is," Zach says, "that you start with where you're at. Take Izzy Rubenstein, my don't-know-how-many-greats grandfather. He started out fixing carriage wheels and wooden axles."

"Bullshee-ee-it," Quintus says. He raises his eyebrows at Josh. "We know how Mister Izzy started out."

"Started out giving orders," Josh says.

"Started out ordering *my* great-grandaddy and *your'n*," Quintus says, "to work up a sweat."

Zach holds a dipstick up to the light. "So *Rubenstein and Sons, Wheelwrights* still owes you, Quintus," he says. "You got that new alternator in or are you waiting for me to kick your ass?"

"It's not the alternator," Quintus says. "It's the battery."

"Can't be the battery. Miz Annabelle's car? I put that one in just six months ago."

"Reconditioned, Mister Zach, sah," Quintus reminds him, with an exquisite edge to his tone. "Terminals corroded something wicked."

"You got some baking soda?"

"I got baking soda. I'm already cleaning them, Mister Zach."

"If it's the alternator," Robbity calls from under a Chevy, "we got no spares for that model. Have to send to Columbia or Charleston."

Billy cannot resist. "An auto shop in the boonies makes as much sense as a shop in the desert selling bait."

"Maybe so," Zach says. "Maybe so. I'm not twisting anyone's

arm. You're all free to leave, and no hard feelings. But this is where the first Izzy pitched his tent around 1690, and this is where Zach's Auto Repair is going to stay."

"Until bankruptcy doth come," calls Robbity from under the Chevy.

"The promised land was what Izzy thought," Zach says, "and I'm not messing with family tradition. Of course," he adds, "I don't claim Izzy was greeted with open arms, but nobody drove him out either, so here we still are."

On the high and holy days Izzy had to go down to the synagogue in Charleston as every Rubenstein since has had to do. The Rubensteins have also had to go to Charleston for their wives, and this custom, like the family business, has been less than an unqualified success. A decade ago, Zach's own wife went to New York for a wedding and has never come back. Zach's son has moved to Israel, and his daughter to who knows where, but Zach does not budge. "The place whereon I fix your Ford pickup or your tractor," he says, "is holy ground. At least to me."

Quintus, born and raised in St Jude, is inclined to agree, "even though," he likes to remind, "your great-granddaddy owned mine, Mister Zach."

"I can feel it coming, Quintus. You want another Friday off."

"Mister Zach," Quintus says, offended. "I ain't asked you for a thing, but I do got the wedding of a cousin coming up."

"The wedding of a cousin."

"Down on the coast," Quintus says.

"Ten degrees cooler than here," Josh points out helpfully to Zach from under a car. "Tourists passing through all year round. Good place for an auto shop."

"I know that Josh, but I'm stubborn."

"You are stubborn, Mister Zach," Josh agrees, because not only is Zach's shop five miles too far from the interstate for collision action, it is also one hour too far from the ocean for even a stray cool breeze.

Each year Zach makes promises.

"Next year, boys," he says. "I'll get air conditioning put in."

"That drums I'm hearin'?" asks Robbity, head against the concrete floor, hand cupped to ear. Sweat courses down the grease-lined ravines of his face. "Do I hear General Electric marchin' in, as long foretold by the prophet Zachariah?"

"Judgment Day gonna get here first," Joshua says.

"Definitely by next summer, boys," Zach promises. "No question. If all our customers pay their bills."

"And pigs might fly," Billy says.

"Shee-ee-it," Robbity says, "I would settle for a ceiling fan with one more speed than slow." Robbity, who is a mean hand with mufflers and brake lines, is grandson on both sides to men who fought with General Lee.

"The whole shop floor," Zach promises. "Not just the front office. I've had estimates. I've had the Carrier people out."

No one believes him.

He leans in over the engine of a red Toyota: dirty spark plugs, leaking radiator cells, frayed fan belt, everything held together with string and cussedness. Zach cleans the plugs with a wire brush. Heat buffets him, coming off the blackened innards of the car like sharp punches between his eyes. He could do with lubrication and an oil change himself. He can't handle July in the shop the way he used to. He mops at his face with a carbon-smeared grease-streaked rag.

Robbity laughs. "Look like a nigger," he says. "Hey Josh, hey

Quint, look at Zach. Don't he look like a nigger to you?"

"Look like a nigger yourself, Robbity."

"You insinuatin', Joshua boy? You insinuatin' something?"

"You seen yourself?" Josh retorts. "Ever time you go down under that Chevy?"

"Could be axle grease," Quintus says. "Could be who-knows-what in his family tree, eh Josh?"

"Hey, looks we getting him all steamed up," Josh says.

"Got a souped-up muffler on him, it look like."

"You keep your dirty mind off my muffler, Quintus boy."

"Hush your mouths!" Billy calls in sharp warning. "There's a lady."

Zach looks up, they all look up, and there she is in the wide opening where the street gapes in, outlined in the garish yellow-white of mid-afternoon. The sun is so fierce that Zach can see right through her, he can see right through to her bones. Her hair is on fire.

Zach holds his breath because she is not quite so thin as last time. "Miriam," he says, walking blindly into the street, arms out-stretched, but it is not his daughter transfigured.

This woman is older. Much older.

This woman is old.

"Alma Nicholson," she says warily, made uneasy by Zach's extended arms. She looks disheveled and gestures over her shoulder. "My car broke down ... about six miles back, I think. I had to walk."

And then she faints, and Zach catches her as she falls. "*Mon fils, mon fils,*" he hears her murmuring.

Perhaps it is Alma's foreignness that makes his heart flip over twice like a well-oiled gear shaft. Perhaps it is the exotic scent of grief.

. . .

"It should be near here, I think," Alma tells Zach. They are out in his tow truck, looking for her car. Puzzled, she adds: "But I didn't pass that gas station. I didn't pass *anything.*"

"We must have missed it," Zach says. "Or else someone has already towed you in."

"I thought I was on 601, but I might have taken a wrong turn. I know the last town I came through was Fort Motte."

"Fort Motte! You must have been on 419." Zach does a U-turn and heads back toward the junction with a rural route so narrow, so closely hugged by pines, that it could easily be mistaken for the driveway to a farm. "Fort Motte," Zach says, shaking his head in amazement. "You walked more than ten miles."

"It did seem a long way," she says.

"And ninety in the shade."

"At first, it seemed a long way. Then I didn't notice. I sort of floated. Your shop was under a rainbow."

"You were dehydrated. Hallucinating. No one should be walking in this heat."

"It was rather pleasant," she says. "After a while. I saw people I haven't seen for a long time."

Zach studies her, frowning. "I shouldn't have let you leave the doctor's office. You should still be lying down."

"No, no," she says. "I have to find my car. I have to be back at work on Monday morning. Look, there it is." But as they get closer, she says: "Oh. No. It isn't mine. I don't know why I thought it was mine, it isn't even the same colour." A mile later they pass an old Ford Fairlane on the side of the road. The car is empty and bears an orange sticker on the window. Its hubcaps, tyres and exterior mirrors have been removed. "There seem to be a lot of abandoned cars," Alma says.

"Pretty typical for Calhoun County," he tells her. "Keeps me in business."

"I passed two when I walked into town, but I don't think those were the ones."

"Where were you headed?"

"Charleston. It's my weekend off."

"Where'd you start out from?"

"Columbia. That's where I live."

Zach raises his eyebrows. "You were certainly going the long way round to Charleston," he says.

"I know. I don't like the interstate. I try to avoid it. I love the little back roads. They remind me of France."

"France. So that's where you're from."

"Since so long ago," she says, "that France is like an hallucination. In France, I was a young girl."

"Your name isn't French."

"No. Well. I married an American name."

"That's a funny way to put it," Zach says.

"I married an American soldier a long time ago. I didn't keep the soldier, I just kept the name."

"You still have family over there?"

"My son is there. There's my car!"

"The blue Peugeot?"

"It's very old," she says, "but it never gives trouble."

"My son is in Israel," he says.

"Will you be able to fix it very quickly?" she wants to know.

"First I have to tow it in and find out what's wrong. If it needs parts, you're out of luck. I don't have Peugeot parts lying around."

"I hope it won't need parts," she says.

"What went wrong?"

"I don't know. It wasn't giving any trouble. I stopped because I wanted to walk in the pine forest, and when I came back, it wouldn't start. It was completely dead."

"Battery."

"But I got a new battery last year."

"Then it's probably the alternator. Or maybe you just need a jump-start," he says. "Maybe you drained it with too much air-conditioning, radio, you know, too much at once for too long in this hot weather."

"I did have the radio on."

"Let's see what happens."

He pulls the tow truck up to her car, nose to nose, and gets the jumper cables out. He clamps the metal jaws to the battery terminals, positive to positive, negative to ground. He tells her when to turn the ignition, when to accelerate. Her Peugeot hiccups into life.

"So simple," she says, smiling with relief.

"You'd better follow me back to the shop," he says, "where I can look the engine over. Don't want you breaking down between here and Charleston in the dark."

"Oh," she says. "I suppose you're right." She frowns a little. "But I really want to be in Charleston in time for dinner."

"You're meeting someone?" he asks.

"No."

"You'd better follow me."

Back at the shop, only Robbity is still poking about in the privates of the Chevy Cavalier. "When you didn't come back from the doctor's," he tells Zach, "Quint and Josh and Billy figured you'd closed down for the day, especially it being Friday. On their way to shoot pool in Orangeburg by now."

"You sticking around a while?" Zach asks. "Might need your help on this car."

"What else would I be doing?" Robbity says.

Zach asks to see Alma Nicholson's driver's license. "Have to keep records," he says, "of every time I take the tow truck out."

"Yes, of course. I understand."

From her license, he learns that she is sixty-three years old. She looks about fifty. He memorises her Columbia address. He casts about for a reason to lift her into the cabin of his truck again. She has hair like faded copper that she wears in a loose knot on her neck. Against the late afternoon light, it wisps about her face like marsh lightning. Her bones are thin and frail as bird bones.

"St Jude," he says stupidly, staring at her, "is the purple martin capital of the world. It's one of those freakish things. Every summer at dusk. No one knows why."

"Yes," she says, a little puzzled. "I know. I saw them once, driving back from Charleston. It was amazing. Like leaves in a tornado."

"Hundreds of thousands of them," he says.

"Yes. Their wings made a noise like paper rustling."

"I'm fifty-eight," he tells her.

"Oh," she says, pushing her eyebrows together. She tries to translate.

Zach bends his head under the hood of the blue Peugeot. A host of martins twitters and twists down inside there somewhere. He feels disoriented and deafened. The martins bank and turn in his mind like a purple squadron. They make him giddy. "You have the potential for major trouble here," he says, speaking into the intestines of the car. His voice reverberates and booms in his ears. "I wouldn't recommend driving on to Charleston in this."

"Oh dear," she says. "What's wrong with it?"

"Robert E!" Zach calls.

"What?" comes Robbity's voice from under the Chevy.

"I think we might have a cracked head here."

"That the lady you towed in?"

"I didn't tow her, I jump-started her, but I think we got potential problems here. What I want is for you to check everything out and do what's necessary."

"Right now?"

"Right now. I'm going to take Miz Nicholson on to Charleston."

"But no," Alma protests. "How will I get back for my car?"

"Sounded like you got hotel reservations in Charleston."

"Yes, but I could cancel."

"And you want to get back to Columbia Sunday."

"Sunday afternoon," she says. "I have to work Monday morning."

"Can't drive it anywhere right now. But we can have it ready by Sunday. I'll come to Charleston to pick you up."

"That is incredibly kind of you," Alma says. "But I really can't let you do that."

"No trouble at all," Zach assures her. "Got to go to Charleston for parts in any case, so no trouble at all."

"If you're sure," she says doubtfully.

"My son is in Israel," Zach says. In Magnolia's, in spite of the breeze off Charleston Harbor, he feels uneasy. He would have preferred the Lobster Shack.

"Yes," Alma says. "So you said. Do you miss him?"

"Yes and no," he says. "He doesn't approve of me, so it's, you know ... He's become very orthodox."

"He makes you sad."

"He won't eat with me. I'm not kosher." He corrects himself. "Not kosher enough."

"Children grow up and become stranger than strangers," she says quietly. She is turning the stem of her wine glass round and round in her fingers. "It happens a lot. It happens more than anyone knows."

"I'm a disappointment to him," Zach says.

"You have your work," she says. "You love your work."

"I do," he says, surprised.

She smiles. "It shows."

"How does it show?"

"Well ..." She turns up the palms of her hands, like someone who is placing her last chip on a roulette table. "You'll know for sure I'm crazy if I tell you, but you have ... *colours* ... coming off you when you do things with cars."

Zach can feel electricity zipping along the surface of his skin. He can feel pins and needles in the groin. He leans forward across the table, close enough to notice that she smells of cinnamon. "I do go a bit crazy with cars," he says. "I love the smell of gasoline, motor oil, I guess you could say I get high on them in a way. And fixing broken things, making them tick like clockwork, that gives me a high. Whenever I'm really down, I work on rebuilding an engine. I just stop thinking about anything else when I'm doing that."

"That's a lot," she says.

"I've got three wrecks sitting on their axles behind my house. I could show you, if you like."

"Doing something that makes you forget who you are. That's as good as it gets."

He gropes for his linen napkin on the floor. He pleats and unpleats it. "Your American soldier was a Southerner, I suppose."

She raises her eyebrows. "No, he was a Yankee. We lived in Maine."

"But now he's down here?"

"He lives on the west coast now. At least, I think he still does. He moves around a lot. He only stayed here a few months."

"So what kept you in the Deep South?"

She studies a palmetto tree through the window. The palm fronds move languidly, scraping the wall with a papery sound. "I'm from the south of France originally," she says, without looking at him. "I like a warm climate."

"That isn't why," Zach says.

She looks at him then. "No," she says. "That isn't why."

"My daughter lives somewhere in Charleston," he says. "I think. Maybe a block or two from here, for all I know."

For a long time, they do not move, do not eat, do not even sip wine. Their eyes, hesitant, sometimes meet, sometimes study the tablecloth.

"I think she's still alive," he says. "I hope so. Her name's Miriam."

Alma reaches across the table and rests the palm of her hand lightly on the back of his.

"She is starving herself," he says. "No one seems to be able to stop her. She looks like a refugee, skin and bones. Sometimes I drive around Charleston for hours, looking for her."

"And when you see her?"

"I haven't seen her for over a year."

"When you are completely alone," Alma says very quietly, "and when there is something about which you cannot bear to speak, you need strangers. You need to live among strangers."

"That is why you stayed in the south."

"That is why I stayed in the south. When you are very foreign, people leave you alone."

"I've lived in St Jude all my life," Zach says. "But I'm still a foreigner. And no one there knows about Miriam."

A waiter appears at their table, concerned. "Is everything all right with the food?" he wants to know.

"It's perfect," Alma says. "I'm just not hungry, I'm afraid."

"Me either," Zach says.

On a bench on the esplanade, looking across the harbor toward Fort Sumter, Alma says: "I saw my son this afternoon."

"The one who lives in France?"

"I saw my mother too, though she died a long time ago. And I saw a girl I used to walk to school with when I was ten. They took it in turns to walk beside me. We spoke in French."

"And your son?"

"He was walking on the other side of the road, from the opposite direction, with his wife and children, my grandchildren. At first, I wasn't quite sure, because the pines cast such a deep shadow. I haven't seen them for a long time, but it *was* my son, I could tell from the way he walked, and I was so happy. I called out and waved and I started to run towards them."

She leaves the bench and walks over to the sea wall. She leans on the railing. The wind whips her hair about her face. She seems so frail that Zach is afraid she might be blown out to sea. He fears that her wrists, which hold tightly to the railing, might snap.

"Alma," he says. He wants to offer himself. He stands behind her, his body against hers, and he grips the railing with both hands, sheltering her in the rampart of his arms.

"I thought they saw me, because they all stopped and looked at each other. But when I ran across the road, they disappeared."

Zach can feel the tide rising.

"Then I saw the rainbow and your shop," she says. She turns around inside his arms. She touches his cheek.

"Each year, on Miriam's birthday," Zach begins to say, but the words turn into great juddering sobs and the wind carries them off with the gulls.

At the Shelter in Columbia, when the women ask Alma where she is from –and the new ones always ask, the first day, the second day, they always ask – Alma will pause at oven or sink and say, "Nowhere, really," and then she will dust her hands on her apron and offer hot fresh bread or soup. For the children, there are always cookies, still soft and warm. She smells of cinnamon.

No, but really, the women say. Where's your funny accent from?

"Bits and pieces from everywhere and nowhere," she says.

You mean *Not from South Carolina*, the women say. Her foreignness reassures them for a reason that Alma understands. She can detect an ease in their breathing, though only for two beats, three, a minute at most. Their vigilance is extraordinary.

"I can't bear it sometimes," she confesses to Zach. "How little it takes to set them off. And how little it takes to make them weep with gratitude."

She has tried to describe to him the scraps they live on, the thinness of their hopes. This gets to him too. "Let me help," he says. "Let me fix their cars."

"It wouldn't work," Alma says. "They're so scared of men, especially the children."

"But they'd get used to me. They'd feel safe. That's important," he says.

"We can't let a man near the shelter, that's our strictest rule. When we accept them, we make a contract with them. If any friend, any family member visits, even their mothers, their fathers, the location of the Shelter must not be revealed. We drop them off at a MacDonald's a mile away. The visitor meets them there. If they break that contract, they're out."

Even so, Alma tells him, they have a constant problem with the stalkers. They have to move to a new location once a year.

"Let me help with some of the heavy work," Zach begs. "The laundry. Can't I help you with that?"

She has told him that night after night, in the laundry room, she and the housekeeper never say a word to each other. They feed the sodden bedding into Maytags, they add powder and bleach, they add fabric softener, perfumed, to mute the rank ammoniac smell. It is a silent routine. The sheets stink of sharp cries in the night.

"Half of them go back to the batterers," Alma says, "because they aren't able to imagine anything else. The laundry's nothing compared to that. That's the part I find hardest to bear."

"Why don't they move out of state?"

"Because they can't imagine living anywhere else. Their world of possibility is so small."

Now and then, the women speak of large expeditions beyond the state line. "I went to Savannah once," Zarita says. "I had an aunty there and she kept me one summer when I was six." And Delilah tells her, "My daddy took me to Charlotte one time." But when Alma presses them, the memories are either distant and fabulous or troubling. In general the concept of *Not South Carolina* is opaque though possible, as God is possible. As another sort of life might be possible — but for other people, not for them.

"If I could save one child," Alma says. "If I could save Zarita's little girl, Luanna."

"We could take her to Charleston. We could take her out to Fort Sumter on the ferry."

"She screams when her mother leaves the room. All the children do."

"Can't we take them both? Luanna and her mother?"

"We could try," Alma says. She brightens and smiles. "Yes, let's try."

"White trash," Robbity Lee McGonigal whispers to Billy. "If ever I saw it."

"This is Zarita," Zach says. "And this is her little girl, Luanna. And this is Robert E. Lee ... and Quintus ... and Joshua ... and Billy the Cub."

Zarita blows smoke rings into the air. Her hand trembles. "Nice to meet ya, fellas," she says.

Luanna clings to her mother and watches them all, wide-eyed. She is very solemn.

Quintus pulls a peppermint candy cane from the pocket of his shirt. He squats down on his haunches and offers it to Luanna. "I've got a little girl," he says, "just about your age. I bet you're five."

Luanna edges back behind her mother's stretch pants. Her eyes never leave the candy cane.

"You like peppermint?" Quintus asks.

Very solemn, she nods her head, but when Quintus holds it out to her, she does not move.

"Maybe Luanna would like it later," Alma says. "I'll look after it for you, shall I, Luanna? Thanks, Quintus."

"Pleasure, ma'am," Quintus says.

"We're taking the big Pontiac," Zach says. "Look after the shop, Robbity. We'll be back tonight."

After they leave, Billy says to the shop at large: "Zarita. *Shish!* Figures. I know her type. You think Zach's gone nuts? You think he's poking her?"

"Shut your mouth," Quintus says.

"Zach is looking for trouble," Billy assures them.

Not until after the picnic lunch, when they take Luanna and Zarita for a ride in a horse and carriage, does Luanna smile. The horse clip-clops along the esplanade, the harbor on one side, the grand old Charleston houses on the other. Luanna sits on her mother's lap, and her mother's arms are tightly around the child's waist. The wind buffets them and a gull, coasting on the air-slip in the wake of the carriage, seems to float alongside. Luanna flinches and leans back into her mother, but when the gull suddenly lofts itself upwards on a great sweep of wing, Luanna gasps with surprise and delight. Spontaneously, she spreads her arms and banks her body into the wind.

Later, in Battery Park, she runs into a cluster of gulls, arms extended. She raises and lowers her wings, giving herself to thermal updrafts, swaying like an acrobat on planes of air, caught up in a rapture of the body. She believes she can fly. Her laughter is high and excited.

Zach takes a photograph.

"It's a start," Alma says to him over the wind, her eyes shining. "She knows another life is possible now."

"Hey, Zach," Billy calls. "The blue Peugeot's here."

It's almost dusk, and as soon as he sees Alma frail against the light in the great open end of the shop, Zach knows something is terribly wrong.

"What?" he says, running to meet her. "What's happened?"

Her face looks drawn and haggard. "Zarita's gone back to her boyfriend," she says. "She's taken Luanna."

"Shit," Zach says. He balls up his chamois cloth and hurls it against his truck.

"I just wanted to stop in and tell you. I'm driving down to the coast. I need to walk up and down the Battery in the wind for a couple of hours."

"I'll come with you," Zach says.

"No," she says. "I need to scream and sob and shout curse words. It'll be better if I'm all by myself. You don't want to see me really deranged."

"You think you're the only one needs to scream and sob? Let's go."

But less than a mile from the shop, before they get to the Interstate, the purple martins come. Zach pulls off the road as a cloud, dark indigo, swoops over the windshield like a cape. The cape makes three passes and banks to the left and returns. High up, from over the Interstate, another formation unswirls itself like a bolt of dark cloth and falls toward them.

Alma opens the door of the truck and slides down to the long roadside grass.

She lifts her arms and leans on the air. She takes one dance step, then another.

Above her, the purple martins wheel and twist in response, thousands of wings with the mind of a single dance partner, brilliant and daring. The last light goes, dropping like spent shot behind the Interstate, and the dark humming funnel of birds, spinning and swaying, lifts itself, hovers, lifts, and is sucked up into the night.

"They've gone," Alma says, staring up. "But I can still hear them."

Later, after they have cruised the back streets of Charleston looking for Miriam, after they have leaned on the sea wall and held each other and wept, Zach gives Alma a keepsake: a photograph of Luanna in flight.

NIGHT TRAIN

Philippa gropes for the sound coming out of the dark. Where is she? The sound is too bright, too hurtling. She is on a night train, that much is clear, there is rush and a grapeshot of rain against the windows. The speed at which she is travelling is so great that her body has come unfastened and slipped off her shoulders like a loose jacket caught in a slipstream. She clutches at it convulsively.

I've got it, Brian says. It's okay, don't panic, I've got it.

I can't breathe, she gasps. Where are we? Where are we rushing?

Into the tunnel, he says. It's the wind effect, the centripetal force. Relax. You get used to it.

The motion of the carriage, the side-to-side rocking peculiar to trains, pitches her about in the upper bunk. The movement is more lullaby than violent. Sometimes she can feel the top of the ladder against her back, sometimes her face touches the panelled oak wall, dark-stained and lacquered, to which the bed is attached. The varnish punches straight to her lungs like cleaning-fluid vapour, and then she remembers: a Queensland train, unmistakable. Fragments reassemble themselves: the station, the farewells, city lights falling off into the dark, Brisbane left behind like lost luggage.

Brian, typically, did not make it in time.

Is it the train whistle, that sound? It could be ocean. It could be surf between sphinctered rocks. The Sunlander is rushing north up the curved coast, she remembers everything now, the Pacific lapping at the lines on one side, the little towns and sugarcane fields on the other. Probably, possibly, by this time, they have passed through Nambour, through Gympie perhaps, maybe Bundaberg. To the north, there is not a living soul she knows. To the north, beyond another thousand miles of cane and dark, her first teaching position waits, and she thinks of it as a lush plant, like pomegranate, fruited with students and gaudy new experience.

"I'll call," Brian had promised, "if I don't get to the station in time."

"I know you won't get there in time." She had leaned on his front gate, clicking it shut between them. "You won't even try. You're annoyed because I'm leaving first, which means I can't be there to see you off to Melbourne."

"Your choice," he said.

"But the difference is, if your train left first, I *would* be there to wave goodbye."

Brian kept brushing something off his arms. "Brisbane's like a cobweb," he said. "I can't wait to get it off me. The last thing I want is sticky goodbyes."

"You're frightened."

Brian pulled at something invisible on his face and scraped his hands against the fence. The wooden pickets, sun-blistered, needed a fresh coat of paint. Philippa had never noticed this before. Where she touched, the wood was soft and pulpy, and flakes of white came away. She ran her fingers across the four smashed palings where Brian's bike had once come violently to rest. His leg had been reset; the fence had not. The frangipani tree, somewhat damaged at the time, had long since repaired itself and now hung over them like a misshapen umbrella. Between its lowest branch and the fence a funnelweb spider had hung its delicate deadly cone. Brian reached up and pulled at one of the tree's odd, blunt, blossom-crowded fingers. The thickish stalk did not give and he twisted it savagely.

"Ouch," Philippa said.

She wanted it to be two months ago, when they were still arguing and riding the buses out to the university. She wanted the time to be years back: high school, primary school, childhood.

The frangipani stalk cracked and dripped milky sap down Brian's arm. "Damn," he said, and swiped his stubby flower-crusted wand through the guy wires of the funnelweb. Expertly, he flicked the spider into the street. "Look," he said with disgust, displaying a shroud of cobweb spindled around the stalk. He stripped it and crushed a handful of flowers in his hand. He shredded petals with his thumbnail, one by one.

"How can you do that?" Philippa asked. The fragrance was extraordinary. Brian let the confetti pieces flutter: chopped satin, a rip of perfume. Philippa felt bruised. "It's like a sermon," she said mournfully.

"Please."

"Dearly Beloved, we have come to the parting of the ways. From next week there will be two thousand miles of parallel steel lines between us, and parallel lives never meet."

"Oh for God's sake, Philippa."

"Wait! Don't go in. I'll stop. I promise. Are you okay?"

"No," Brian said. "I feel sick."

"It's because the world as we know it is ending."

"It's because of the cobwebs in my head." Brian raked his fingers through his hair. He drummed the palms of his hands against his skull. "Stuff keeps coming back. I keep remembering this kid in fifth grade."

"Can I come in?"

"No."

She opened his gate, and they sat on the mango trunk in the lee of the ferny heave of rootball. Six cyclones back, the tree had been knocked askew and had gone on growing laterally. "I've just noticed," Philippa said, "how untidy Queensland gardens are. We've raised untidiness in vegetation to the level of high baroque."

"It's a mess," Brian said, "since Dad died."

"It's a rampant luxuriant mess, always galloping back into rainforest. It's magnificent. You don't think about these things, you don't notice them, until you're going away."

"This kid," Brian said. "He always rode his brother's bike to school. His older brother's, it was really too big for him. It was held together with wire and electrical tape, a heap of rust."

"In Melbourne, everything is manicured," she said. "You'll hate it. You'll be crossing two state borders, three railway gauges. When you change to Victorian gauge, you have to get out at Albury in the middle of the night, did you know? The Victorian trains are *enormous*."

"There was something about this kid. He never smelled good for one thing, and then his wreck of a bike. And he had bruises everywhere, his face, his arms, his legs. He was the kind of kid that automatically gets picked on. Teachers, other kids, everyone."

"You know, you could be in Melbourne before I get to Cairns. I'll probably be stuck on the tracks at Tully."

"But the worst thing, for him I mean, he only had one testicle.

On swimming days, the other kids were merciless. I used to sweat for him."

"The Sunlander's been stuck for three days already, and if Darcy hits, two cyclones just one week apart—"

"His pants were too big, they were his brother's too, everything was his brother's. Nothing belonged to him, ever, not even standard birth equipment. The rumour was that his father and his brother both beat him. Bruiser, we called him. One-ball Bruiser."

"Bruiser? That kid who used to hitch on the tailgates of trucks?"

"I did it myself a few times. Made fun of him."

"Wasn't he killed?"

"An outcast from Day One. You know, people get designated that way. Kids get designated, they get marked, and once that happens, it's only a matter of time."

Philippa stared at the windows of Brian's house. "What is that sound?" she asked.

"His mother. She called me the night of the funeral."

"No. I mean that sound in your house. Is that a dog? Did you get a dog?"

"She was sobbing. She said she wanted to thank me for being Bruiser's best friend. Albert, she called him. *Albert said you were his best friend.*"

Philippa stared at the windows, apprehensive. She closed her eyes. The sound dropped to a whimper then disappeared. "Didn't you hear that?" she asked.

"She couldn't stop crying. And now I can't even remember his last name." Brian jumped up and paced the length of the slanted trunk, back and forth, agitated. "Can you?"

Philippa listened, but the sound of past names had grown faint.

She felt queasy. "I never really knew him. I just remember the accident because it was in the newspapers. When he got pulled under the truck."

"*Albert would have wanted me to tell you*," Brian said, pacing, pacing. "That's what she said. I was terrified. I'd never even met her. But she knew, she recognised me at the funeral. If you're marked, you give off signals."

"Brian," Philippa said quietly. "The only signals you give off are the blips of a high-speed mind in overdrive. Why don't you sit down?"

"I've been designated." Brian looked at his hands, where the words lay, studying them.

"Sometimes," Philippa said, "you're a designated pain in the arse, I have to admit it."

"Is my mind in overdrive? Do you really think that?" He clasped and unclasped his hands. He brushed cobweb off them and rubbed them in the grass. "It's true my dreams are speeding up."

Philippa counted the broken palings. She saw Brian again, twelve years old: the wild freewheeling swoop down Newmarket Road, the turn into Green Street, the thrill, the legs splayed wide, the crash. No brakes. Brian was still laughing when they reached him. To Philippa, later, he had confessed: *It was worth it.*

"Sometimes I'm on a train," Brian said, "and it's rushing into a tunnel and I can't find the phone in the dark. Sometimes I'm in the locker room when it rings, and I'm laughing at Bruiser when I answer."

"Brian, everyone's done it. Been a coward some time. Don't torment yourself."

"They used to flick their towels at his balls. His ball. They'd laugh, he'd laugh. Sometimes I laughed. I always felt sick when I did. The worst thing was, he knew that. He would give me this sad little smile. He understood. He forgave me. I'd go outside and I'd want to hang myself, like Judas. I used to vomit in those bushes outside the school."

What is that dreadful noise? Phillipa wants to know. What is that shriek? Is it Darcy? Is it the cyclone barrelling down?

It's the tunnel, Brian says. We're going into the tunnel now.

Philippa sits bolt upright in the dark. Brian! she calls, panicked.

I'm sorry, he says. I can't help it. Whenever I hear a phone ringing at night, I black out.

Philippa gropes for the sound.

"Hello?" she says. "What? Who *is* this?"

Philippa wakes. Against her window, the feathery plumes of ripe sugarcane toss and shiver. The moon is not white here, but blood orange, the effect of volcanic ash somewhere off to the east, somewhere out in the thrashing Pacific. She has papers to mark, lessons to prepare, it is still pitch dark, and already the school bell is ringing.

"Hello?" she says, her voice thick with muddle and sleep. "Who? My God, Brian! Where are you?"

"Have you heard the news?"

"What time is it?"

"I don't know. Night time. I can't sleep when I get home from the lab, so I watch the news. I saw it live. President Kennedy's been shot!"

Philippa blinks and fumbles for the bedside lamp. She knocks something over. "Damn," she says. "Brian, where are you?"

"Melbourne," he says impatiently. "Where do you think I am?

They keep replaying bits. Now they're talking to people who were lining the motorcade route, who saw it happen."

There. She finds the lamp, the switch. And the clock. "Brian, it's 3 a.m."

"That's all you have to say? The American president has been shot in Dallas — it's still yesterday there — and all you have to say to me is: *Brian, it's 3 a.m?*"

"Let me think," Philippa says. "No, it's not all I have to say. I have to say you are as oblivious and obnoxious as ever. You promised you'd call, you bastard, if you didn't get to the station when I left."

"I'm calling."

"Ten months later! I got your number from your mother, and I've called and called, and you never answer, you pig-headed pig."

"Because I unplug my phone when I'm working. If I'm interrupted, a whole project could be lost. Listen, a marksman got him with a high-powered rifle, but I don't believe for a second it's a one-man job, do you? The CIA's behind this."

"Why don't you call the White House and offer your expert advice?" But his news seeps under the foreground haze of sleep and suddenly floods her. "My God," she says. "The *president?* Shot? Do you mean …?"

"Yes."

"Shot dead?"

"Killed. Assassinated. In Dallas."

"Oh my God."

"They've found the sniper's nest. But there are witnesses who heard other shots from other directions. My bet is the CIA."

"Oh Brian, there you go again. The whole world is ganging up against the innocent."

"Against certain designated people, yes. Kennedy was marked."

"It's probably some crackpot. From what I read, Texas is full of crazies on the far right."

"You get matrixes," Brian explains, excited. "Fertile mother-pockets where crystals of hate can form and multiply exponentially and link up with each other to make violent superstrings. Texas would be a matrix. I see parallels with the work I'm doing on proteins. You get these multiplying speeded-up reactions. There are certain protein crystals, the ones I'm working on, that only exist two-dimensionally, you can only examine them in suspension, in solution, so you have to —"

Philippa hears something bearing down from the tunnel of the past, she can feel the disturbing movement of air ahead of it.

"Brian, Brian, slow down. Are you okay?"

"I have to go, Philippa, I'm sorry. I just got an idea, I have to go after it. I'll call you later from the lab."

"How do you manage it?" Philippa wants to know. "Do you calibrate time zones with malice? How come it's always after midnight at my end?"

"It's you," Brian says. "You keep moving further into yesterday. You're on the wrong side of the Pacific. It's daytime here."

"What I notice, whether I'm in Boston or London or Toronto or Paris, you always manage to wake me up. You do it on purpose."

"I am utterly consistent," he protests. "I call when I'm feeling low."

"Or high," she reminds. "You call when you're manic."

"If you mean that I call when there's some intense intellectual issue that needs discussion, I plead guilty. You should be honoured that I always choose you."

"Purely habit on your part," Philippa says. "And the fact that I put up with it because it's the only way to stay in touch with you, you bastard. Where are you calling from this time?"

"Japan."

"Japan!"

"Osaka. This'll be ongoing, for half of each year."

"Is it a research company?"

"Research partner. We're teaming up. He's at the university here, but he'll spend half the year in Melbourne. We just got a huge grant."

"So this is a high."

"Well ..." he says doubtfully. "To some extent. Partly. The living conditions are hell, though. People live in *cupboards* here. And the noise level's worse than New York."

"So you wake me in the middle of the night."

"You understand, of course, that time is a completely artificial construct. It's quite arbitrary."

"I saw this film," Philippa says, "about Glenn Gould."

"I've got his Goldberg Variations with me. Wouldn't travel without. I'm living in a fifth-floor pigeonhole beside a freeway overpass and the noise is unbearable, but Bach at full volume helps."

"It's called *Thirty-three Short Films about Glenn Gould.*"

"I know. I've seen it."

"He used to drive around Toronto all night and call his friends from payphone boxes. He'd talk for hours. He could only connect with other human beings by phone."

"I know. I've seen the film about six times."

"Made me think of you."

"What? There's no comparison. He was a genius, but he was really screwed up. I have a whole other life when I'm not on the phone."

Philippa laughs. "Do you?"

"What do you mean, do I? When I'm working, when I'm in my lab, I'm alive two hundred per cent. There's nothing like it."

"Can I hear sirens?"

"I remember once, when I was a kid, losing control of my bike on a steep hill. Well, on Newmarket Road, as a matter of fact. You probably don't remember. It was fantastic, the speed, the rush. I knew I was going to crash, but it was worth it. My work's like that."

"Brian, am I imagining it, or can I hear sirens?"

"What? Oh, all the time. Freeway traffic. It drives me crazy. I've had to invent my own white-noise machine. And this is university housing for full professors with grant money. Imagine the living conditions of the junior faculty and graduate students."

"How many firetrucks are there?"

"They're ambulances. Looks like a whole convoy from here."

"Sounds terrifying. Like a scream choir from hell."

"There's a writer for you: emotive and imprecise. No objective or neutral observation. Nothing of the decent reticence of the scientist. It could be said of you, Philippa, that no matter what your senses take in, all you see and hear are words."

"As opposed to numbers and equations. Brian, listen, speaking of hair-raising sounds, there's something I've always wanted to ask. When we were kids —"

"Kids? Philippa, you should realise that childhood is something I work hard at not remembering," Brian says.

"I don't know if this is something I imagined or not."

"Who *would* know?"

"But it's important. Sometimes at your house I used to hear, I think I used to hear, someone, or something, in pain. Wailing, moaning, I don't know how to describe it."

Osaka ambulances streak across Philippa's room, her lamp flashes blue blue blue, her walls weep. She hears a fence splinter. She counts flashbeats, heartbeats, white vans. They are years and years long.

"Brian?"

"Yeah." He sighs heavily. "It was my father. War nightmares."

"You never seemed to hear anything, you never seemed to know a thing about it."

"My goal has always been to know everything," Brian says passionately. "*Everything.* Preferably before anyone else."

"I heard it again, just once, years later. The most awful sound. It was the day before we both left Brisbane. You acted as though you couldn't hear a thing."

"I heard it," Brian says. "I always hear it. But *you* couldn't have, Philippa. Not then. That was a few years after my father had died."

Philippa curls down into her bed and hugs the receiver. Her room is careening through the dark. Brian, she whispers, or tries to. Where are we? She clutches the headboard, her fingers white, but the slipstream is fierce. I can't catch my breath, she says. I'm afraid I can't hang on. I've got vertigo. Where are we rushing?

It's the tunnel, Brian says. There's no way out.

★ ★

"Philippa?"

"Hhnnh."

"Philippa? I can't hear you. Are you there?"

"Hnh."

"Are you awake?"

"No. I don't think so."

"There's something I've been wanting to ask you. For years. I've been wanting to ask you for years."

"Mmm?"

"The high-speed thing. Sometimes I'm scared my mind's over-heating. If the brakes fail ... you know, if anything should happen, would you do something for me?"

Philippa's eyelids are weighted down. She concentrates, concentrates, tries to lift them. "Do what?" she mumbles.

"Be the curator of all my stuff."

"Huh? Sure, okay. What stuff?"

"Everything. I'm leaving everything to you. Research, prizes, nightmares, everything. I want someone who'll cherish it. Make it make sense, that's all I ask. Otherwise it's unbearable."

"Philippa?"

"Oh God, Brian, what time is it? I have to fly out in the morning to give a paper and I haven't finished writing it yet."

"Is it too late?"

"It's horribly early. I've been working all night. Where are you?"

"Melbourne."

"Can I call you back in three days?"

"You know you can't call me," Brian says, agitated.

"Right. I know I can't call you. You keep your phone unplugged, except for calling out."

"My work," Brian explains.

"Right. Your work. Let me struggle to be circumspect and just say one little thing: this is uncalled for, Brian. I have the greatest respect for your work. Have some for mine. I'm not up for interruption tonight."

"Philippa, *wait*! I'm in a pay phone box. I've been driving round for hours."

"So keep driving. Call someone else." She hangs up. She stares at the phone. She picks it up again, frantic. "Brian?" She hears dial tone, train wheels, the hollow rush of wind in a tunnel. "Brian," she pleads into the dial tone. "Keep your phone plugged in tomorrow. I'll call."

How many times, Philippa wonders, can an unplugged phone's ringer ring before the ringer wears out? Once, masochistic and curious, she counts one hundred chimes, a shrill tocsin, the tolling of guilt. Ask not for whom the telephone rings, she says into the receiver. She keeps listening. If a butterfly moving its wings in Brazil can cause storms in Maine ... She is comforted, slightly, by the sense of connection. In Melbourne, fibre-optic cable vibrates in his walls.

She calls his secretary at the university and leaves a message. *Brian, you may call at any hour.*

She lies awake listening for the phone.

She dials his number again and talks to the ringing in Melbourne. *I'm trying to tell this, Brian. I'm curating your life. I'm trying to cherish each detail and make it make sense.*

She calls his department again. "I think he's in Japan," the secretary says. "We never know. He's got teaching leave because of the grant, so we never see him. We have email connection, but in his case, you can't count on a response."

Philippa sends distress flares by email. *Brian: Where are you? I miss you. On my honour, you may call whenever you want. Love, Philippa.*

A week later, she tries again. *Brian: A curator needs cooperation. I'm trying to preserve everything, all the way back, but dread is interfering. It's affecting what I recall. It's affecting the order, it's affecting what I set down. If you called, I could tell it differently.*

She posts cyber bulletins daily. Often, late in the night, she speaks to his phone jacks in Melbourne. She leaves messages in the air of his room.

There are no answers.

When the ringing comes out of the dark, Philippa knocks over the lamp.

"Listen," Brian says, "I've got good news. I've remembered Bruiser's last name."

"Oh Brian, thank God." Gusts of laughter, like the riffs at the edge of a cyclone, buffet Philippa. She finds she is crying. "If you ever do that again," she says, "I'll kill you, mate."

"Do what?"

"Go silent for over two years."

"For over two years?" Brian repeats the words slowly, inter-rogatively. He might be reciting Latin, translating to himself as he speaks. "Was it?"

"Where have you been?"

"I've been tracking down data. When there's a gap in the

mourning chain," he explains, "it's like a black hole. It sucks everything into it. If someone has never been adequately mourned, my father, for example, or Bruiser — Albert Brewster, that was his name — that creates an event horizon, are you with me? It's a question of absolute density. Once the event horizon has been crossed, game's over. Everything's pulled into that hole and crunched up."

Philippa's lungs feel tight. "Something terrible's the matter," she says. "I can tell from your voice."

Brian laughs. The sound frightens Philippa.

"I crashed," Brian says. "I've been in for repairs."

"You've been ill again."

"One word for it. I've been living inside a funnelweb, eye to eye with the spider himself. But I got out again. I've been patched up. I'm okay."

"Can you talk about it?"

"I don't think I told you my second wife left me. Maybe that was it. And the children. She got custody."

"Oh Brian. I'm so sorry."

"And then, I don't know, things speeded up too much. The brakes failed."

"I don't know what to say. How are you now? How are you *really*?"

"I've lost ground," he says, anguished. "That's the unbearable part. I've lost too much ground. Lost my research partner, lost my place on the team. I don't know if I can ever catch up."

"At least you're here. At least you're still with us. It's all that matters."

"How can you say that? It's not all that matters. My research is the only thing that matters. But I'm picking up speed again, thank God. The thing about being at the edge of a breakthrough, Philippa, is you wake with an idea and it's pure adrenalin. It's like the scent of fox to a hound. You're off after it come hell or high water."

Philippa gropes for the sound coming out of the dark. Where is she? The sound is too bright, too hurtling. She is on a night train, that much is clear, there is rush and a grapeshot of rain against the windows. The speed at which she is travelling is so great that her body has come unfastened and slipped off her shoulders like a loose jacket caught in a slipstream. She clutches at it convulsively.

I've got it, Brian says. It's okay, don't panic, I've got it.

I can't breathe, she gasps. Where are we rushing?

Into the tunnel, he says. There's no way out.

Philippa sits bolt upright in the dark, her hands frantic to shut off the sound. Brian! she calls, panicked.

I'm sorry, he says. I couldn't stop.

"Brian?" she says. "Brian? What? Who *is* this?"

"Philippa," a voice says. "My name's Yvonne. We met once, years and years ago. I'm Brian's wife. Well, his former wife. His former second wife."

"What's happened?" Philippa asks faintly.

"It's bad news, I'm afraid." The voice reverberates, unclear, like announcements at airports. Philippa is floundering. She catches only the peaks of words. *Coma ... barricaded himself in his own study at home a week before he was found ... miracle ... touch and go, but a very slim chance he may pull through.* "I'm at his bedside in intensive care now," Yvonne says. "He wants to talk to you. He can't speak, but he's conscious, and he knows I've got you on the line. Will you talk to him?"

Philippa nods.

What she hears: exertion; a rush of noisy breathing like a broken bicycle swooping down a hill. What she sees: the funnelweb spider's eye.

Philippa can't speak. *Brian*, she pleads, but she is sobbing. *Don't go. Please don't go.*

She can hear Brian's voice straining to escape from its leash, frothing like a tied-up hound at the scent of fox.

"Brian," she says tenderly. "It's okay. I've got everything. I will cherish it. I'll try to make it make sense. Safe voyage, mate."

She waits until his train pulls out of the station and slips into dark.

Sometimes, when it is after midnight there, Philippa dials the number of Brian's lab at the University of Melbourne. No one ever answers. They've retired your number, she tells him.

She says: I can't write your death. Not yet. The details are too terrible. But I keep your life in a jewel-box lined with silk.

It's a mess, he says. Always has been.

A rampant luxuriant mess, she counters. I don't want to tidy it up. It's dear to me the way it is. But I'm working on gaps in the mourning chain. You were right about that.

I was right about everything, he says. Always. Before anyone else.

You were always impossible, she sighs. And extreme. Your death was extremely untidy.

I'm sorry about that, he says. The brakes failed. That's all I remember. I remember going into the tunnel, and after that ...

Sometimes — quite often, in fact — Philippa wakes in the middle of the night. She hears a telephone but when she answers the caller has already hung up. She lies awake, waiting.

LITANY FOR THE HOMELAND

A supernova is on its way, it is even now shopping through the galaxies of which there are millions upon millions, its arrival in our neighbourhood — so astronomers tell us — is long overdue, it is casually browsing in the Milky Way, entirely neutral, without malice or forethought of any kind, and it could drop in on us.

On earth, our homeland.

On *Terra Australis*, on Queensland, on Brisbane, on Newmarket Road, Newmarket, on the wooden house with its high ant-capped stilts and on the mango tree and on the spot below the frangipanis where I first made intimate contact with the heavenly hosts. This was a miracle. I was looking through my father's telescope and gobbling light years like water.

Under the frangipani tree at the age of seven, lost, homesick for Melbourne which had so recently been mislaid, bemused by the fact that I could clearly see the craters on the moon but not the beloved grandparents left behind, homesick under the frangipani and the Queensland sky, I collided with immensity, outer and inner, and with the great riddle of our foothold on the whirligig of space.

A supernova is on its way and it could drop in on us.

We take it personally.

Among the galaxies, we are not city folk. Earth itself, *this goodly frame ... this most excellent canopy, the air, look you, this brave o'erhanging firmament, this majestical roof fretted with golden fire*, why, it has been demoted since Copernicus and Kepler to the outer bush-league suburbs of the cosmos, our sun itself just a boondocks firecracker, our whole solar system some 30,000 light years from the core of the universe. We are galactic hillbillies. *Beyond the black stump* is our address. The refulgent snuffing out of our entire planet, homeland of billions, would be nothing more than a third-rate piss-ordinary common little matchflare of a nova just one galaxy over, and we know it. Yet we place ourselves front and centre. Still the galaxies wheel around the hub of our own buzzing heads. This is home, we presume to say with touching and ridiculous hubris, sticking a pin into a spinning ball in the margin of the margins of the void.

In margins and in longings: this is where all homelands begin.

Once upon a time a mapmaker doodled in the edges of his maps, and wished a place into being and dreamed up "The Arguments for the Existence of Terra Australis, 1764": *Having shewn that there is a seeming necessity for a Southern Continent to maintain a conformity in the two hemispheres, it rests to shew, from the nature of the winds in the South Pacifick Ocean, that there must be a Continent on the South.*

And so there was.

Captain Cook, with sextant and compass, bumped into it and traced its bumps onto paper.

Yet homeland exists before and after maps. The Great Unknown South Land, wished onto the blank spaces of cartographers' knowledge, was already home to Sam Woolagoodjah's people:

The first ones, those days,
shifted from place to place,
In dreamtime before the floods came.

We, the visitors, all of us, those who came in 1788 and those who came later and those who came last year, we the visitors acknowledge the presence of the first ones brooding over and under and before and after all our maps, those first ones who are still with us in the land, all of us together in the margins of the Milky Way, all of us passing through, both latecomers and first ones, those Wandjinas, *bird Wandjinas, crab Wandjinas ... She the rock python. He the kangaroo,* all those ancient ones on whose flesh and river-veins we latecomers have so recently presumed to tread, to set up camp, to speak of home.

Have mercy upon us for we have been crude and arrogant guests and have given much offence.

Have mercy upon us.

Now you see nothing is made up,
Each father has been told what happened:
How Wandjina Namaaraalee made it all
How he sent the flood
How he said no.

First ones and visitors, we shift from place to place, we build homes, we construct a homeland, we deconstruct it, we make and unmake, we wander from past to future *for here we have no continuing city but we seek one to come,* we wait together for the bush fires, the floods, the wars, the supernova, the millennium, the Second Coming, for Wandjina Namaaraalee to send again the great deluge that will sweep us back to the Dreaming where the first ones are, *world without end, amen.*

★   ★

And it came to pass in those days, the days of childhood under the mango and the frangipani trees, that a wild boy beckoned from the back fence to the girl with the telescope. The fence was soft and rotten and choked with passionfruit and crucifix orchids, and the boy pushed his head and shoulders between the palings and crooked his index finger. He had glittering eyes.

Beyond the fence was paddock. In the middle, where footballers trampled Saturdays and Sundays into dust, the paddock clung to its legal but provisional state; its thick margins had already slid back under bush. Unnameable acts, thrilling, dangerous, illicit, were said to take place under cover of tea-tree scrub, even during daytime, even during soccer games, even Sundays. Secrets bred there like rabbits. When the girl with the telescope put her ear against the fence palings, she could sometimes hear a murmur of voices and low throaty laughter, and the rustle of all that was forbidden. The bush pressed up against the fence, forever threatening to cross the line, forever sucking the backyard out between the palings.

"Come into the paddocks," the boy enticed. "Come and play with me."

"I'm not allowed." The girl with the telescope recognised the boy. She knew him from school. He was utterly disreputable, he was caned every single day, *but he doesn't feel a thing* ran the playground legend, because the boy always grinned, jaunty, when he came back from the headmaster's office. It was said that he tamed flying foxes and kept them as pets, it was said that he could fly, it was said that he could travel underground and pass through walls and that he had a magic protector, a guardian angel maybe, or maybe a devil, who held an invisible shield between his backside and the cane. He was bad. All the teachers and all the girls said he was bad. His name was Paddy McGee.

Paddy-with-his-head-between-the-palings laughed. It was a low, wicked, irresistible sound. His glittering eyes pulled at the girl. "What's yer name?" he demanded.

The girl searched for a name. "Stella," she said at last, because she had the stars at her fingertips and she had been studying maps of the sky and she was someone else now, not the girl she had been in Ballarat where her grandfather had pointed out the planets and named them, and not the girl she had been in Melbourne, and she certainly didn't want to be the girl she was at her new Brisbane school. She was reinventing herself.

"No it's not," the boy said. "You're new. Where're ya from?"

"I'm Stella," she said stubbornly. "I'm from the moon. You wanna look?"

The boy smiled his dangerous smile and she smiled back (she knew she had crossed a line), and he wriggled through the fence and joined her under the frangipani tree and she held the telescope for him. He was filthy, he gave off a musky bush smell, and where his hand touched her arm it burned her in a damp feverish way.

"Can't see anything," he said.

She turned the focusing ring with trembling fingers. "You will," she promised. "You have to get it focused right. Tell me when."

"Holy Jeez!" he said. "Struth!" Every word could attract a bolt of lightning from God, yet he lived, he breathed, he laughed his wicked and jaunty laugh, he was a miracle of fearlessness.

"What can you see?" she asked.

"Craters and stuff, holy Jeez!" He laughed in a breathless

excited way and turned on her his glittering burning eyes. "Hey," he said. "You're okay for a sheila. You got guts."

At school, he meant. The taunting, he meant, and the other stuff, the bullying. She didn't think she had guts at all, she was terrified.

"I go for guts," Paddy McGee announced, placing the telescope down in the thick unmowed grass. "I came lookin' for ya. I followed ya home."

She knew this meant she was marked, just as he was. She knew this meant he recognised the mark on her, and that it was somehow visible to everyone at school.

Through the open neck of his shirt, she could see the dirty silk cord around his neck and the gold chain and the delicate little gold cross. "What's that?" she asked, touching the cord with an index finger.

"It's me scapular." He took hold of her wrist and licked her finger with his tongue. "Come into the paddock," he said. "There's some good trees to climb. You wanna catch tadpoles with me at Breakfast Creek?"

"Yeah," she said, "I reckon." And recklessly, heedlessly, she went. She climbed through the fence with the boy who was half-wild and only half-tamed, and crossed into no-man's-land, and that was where she sensed she belonged.

Something there is that doesn't love a boundary line. In the medieval *Books of Hours*, people step out of goldleaf miniatures and into the margins and sometimes right off the page. Falcons and hounds and pheasants and antlered deer, marginal to the Holy Offices for the day, outside the pale of theology, persist in nosing their way in from the white edges of the page to the text. And in response, as though lured by the exuberant outsiders, words put forth glowing tendrils, curlicues of *Dominus*, fronds of P and W and T which finger their way past the borders, past the rapture of martyred saints, into the white parchment margins where they swell and turn into gryphons, dragons, creatures of glowing crimson and lapis lazuli that are neither fish nor fowl, text nor subtext, not fully on this page and not quite on the next.

These are my kin. They are always beckoning me to the mysterious space behind the word, between the pages, beyond the pale and the fence palings and the text and the sanctioned structures. Their eyes glitter. Listen, they murmur seductively: rules are for transgressing, borders for crossing. They whisper: no little man from Customs and Immigration stands at the doors of memory or imagination demanding to see your passport. No arts bureaucrat or ComLit satrap can stamp *OzLit*, *CanLit*, *FemLit*, *MigrantLit*, or *Displaced Person* on your visa. Censors and critics alike overlook the margins. In the margins one is ignored, but one is free.

That is where homeland is.

In that shifting space, kinfolk know one another by secret signs; and wherever kinfolk meet, homeland soil coalesces about their feet in the mysterious way that coral cays, like seabirds pausing in flight, anchor themselves to the Barrier Reef.

Down by Breakfast Creek where the warm water sucks at mangrove roots, Paddy McGee shows the houseboat where he lives. It doesn't look like a house, and it doesn't look like a boat. Stella is round-eyed with disbelief and an excitement she cannot quite name. To live in a creek, to live in something that can move away, to live, in a sense, *nowhere*, it suggests that seemingly immutable laws can be called into question.

"But you can't *live* in a creek," she says, tugged at by the rules, by what is known and what is allowed.

"Why not?"

And she looks down a mirrored corridor of *why nots?* infinitely multiplying themselves and leading to who knew what possibilities.

"Because." She says it lamely, not really resisting, more than willing to be swept into a world where houses swim. "What's your address, then?"

"Breakfast Creek."

Paddy McGee, Breakfast Creek, Brisbane. Stella Maris, Crater Lane, The Moon. She smiles to herself, and Paddy McGee laughs, complicit.

Sometimes (so he says) his Mum and Dad are there (though Stella never sees them), sometimes not. His Dad is mostly at the pub or the races, he says; his Mum is a barmaid at the Newmarket Pub. Most days he comes to school, but often not. On the days when he doesn't go to school, she knows he will be waiting for her at the back fence, beckoning, and she will wriggle out between the palings into the forbidden world of bush and creek.

"Oh," she says vaguely when asked, "I was up in the mango tree reading a book." She is famous, both at home and at school, for disappearing and for reading books.

Paddy McGee never reads books, but he knows more than anyone she has ever met. He knows the saps of trees and their differing uses, he knows where tadpoles breed, he knows which ants bite and which don't, he knows how to read the telltale flying-fox tracks in banana clumps.

At school, he knows nothing.

At school, Paddy McGee and the girl live on different planets and it would be quite impossible for them to speak or to acknowledge each other in any way. They are absolute strangers at school, they never even look at each other. Nevertheless she is always conscious of him. Once, in the playground mêlée (she does not hear or feel these things any more, she goes away to another place inside her head, and it is said of her, as it is said of Paddy McGee, that she is made of wood, that you can kick her and she won't feel a thing, and in fact this has become true; there's a trick she has learned), during one of these times when things are happening and she is somewhere else, inattentive, she does become aware of Paddy tossing punches around and screaming *Leave her alone, you bloody bullies, leave her alone!*

He is caned for this violent behaviour.

On another occasion, for reasons unclear, one of the teachers, a rough giant of a man named Mr Brady, thrashes Paddy McGee to within an inch of his life, and the hushed class watches in fascinated terror as blood oozes from the purple welts on Paddy's legs. The classroom building is high up, on stilts above the cool under-the-school where the children eat lunch, and Mr Brady, convulsed by some inner cyclone of rage, finally throws the cane across the room (its cuts inadequate to his fury), and picks Paddy McGee up by the shoulders ... Paddy McGee being small and wiry, though *tough as bootleather,* teachers say. Mr Brady shakes Paddy McGee as though he were a stray tomcat and he holds him out the casement window.

"I'll teach you, you insolent filthy little mick," thunders Mr Brady.

A number of the girls in the class are crying with fright. Stella herself has moved right into Paddy McGee's body, she can feel

Mr Brady's claws eating into his flesh, she can feel the sickening air below his dangling feet, she can feel the warm trickle when he wets his pants. Perhaps the still eye of his own storm reaches Mr Brady, or perhaps he hears the nervous shuffling of feet and the murmurs and the crying of girls. Quite suddenly he stops. He goes slack, as though the storm has exhausted him. He drags Paddy McGee back through the window and dumps him on the floor like a sack of sugarcane cuttings and orders gruffly, "Get back to your seat."

It is the only time in recorded history that Paddy McGee is unable to flash his jaunty smile at the class, but he most certainly does not cry and he does not speak. In spite of the wet stain on his khaki shorts, he fixes his glittering eyes on Mr Brady and he stands as tall as his purple-striped legs and drenched pants will permit. The class is as one person, scarcely breathing. It seems to the class that something curious is happening now, that one end of an invisible seesaw is going down and the other end, the Paddy McGee end, is going up. A whiteness has appeared around Mr Brady's lips. No one moves, no one breathes. Then Paddy McGee turns and walks from the classroom, head high. He never comes back.

That afternoon he does not appear at the back fence, but when Stella slips through the palings and through the bush and across the paddock, she finds him down by the creek. They sit side by side, saying nothing.

At last Paddy McGee says, "You wanna be my blood sister?"

"Yes," she says.

And with his pocketknife, he makes a small cut in the vein at his wrist, and then in hers, and he places his wrist against hers, flesh to flesh, blood to blood.

She never sees him again. He vanishes. Day after day, she waits for him to come to the back fence, she roams the creek, but the houseboat has gone without a trace. Weeks go by. She begins to fear she dreamed up both the houseboat and Paddy McGee, but then Mr Brady makes a terse announcement. "Good riddance," he says. "Bad blood."

And she is comforted. She is comforted by the fact that Mr Brady *had* to say his name, and by the precious drop of Paddy McGee's bad blood in her veins.

Who decides what is margin and what is text? Who decides where the borders of the homeland run? Absences and silences are potent. It is the eloquent margins which frame the official history of the land. As for geography, there are divisions and boundary lines that fissure any state more deeply than the moat it digs around its nationhood.

In every country there are gaping holes. People fall through them and disappear. Yet on every side there are also doors to a wider place, a covert geography under sleep where all the waters meet.

From time to time, when I am least expecting it, in the most unlikely countries, I run into Paddy McGee. He wears unpredictable names but I always recognise him by his eyes and by the mark of the outcast on his forehead. Like some ancient but ageless mariner, he keeps seeking me out to finish his tale, he keeps setting his compass for my shores. And whenever I see him, I find I have the mud of a Queensland creekbed under my feet.

In Boston his name was Franklin D. He was one of my students at MIT, though he was a good bit older than the others. He wore jungle-camouflage combat fatigues with the Marines insignia removed. I never saw him in anything else, nor did I ever see him without his rollerblades on. They seemed attached to his feet like calluses and he moved on them with dazzling speed and grace and dexterity, his feats eyecatching and incredible. He could skate up flights of stairs and down them. He moved along the endless corridors of MIT, especially the famous Infinity Corridor, head and shoulders above crowding students and professors, weaving, braking and pirouetting, swooping along like some exotic jungle creature, part human, part bird. Certainly flamboyant. He skated down subway entrances, into trains, onto buses, into bars, and into class. I think the desire to be untrammelled had blazed its own evolutionary detour and caused his legs to sprout wheels. He was doing a Physics degree on the Veterans' bill. He was black.

In my office, we were discussing the profoundly disturbing stories he had submitted: tales of gang rape as weekend sport, casual deaths, violent excitements.

"I don't know how to grade these," I told him. "I can hardly bear to read them. They frighten me."

It was as though I had turned a key, as though all his life he had been waiting for someone to acknowledge: your life is frightening.

"I'll tell you two stories," he said.

His first death: he was six years old, a basketball-obsessed kid in Harlem playing on a charred lot between stripped cars when he saw two teenage boys knife an old man for his cash. The man struggled. "Forget it, Gran'pa," the boys said, and slashed him several times across the chest. Grandpa's chest unfurled itself slowly toward the child Franklin D. like a fresh steak, and Grandpa looked at his own ribs in mild surprise and raised his gnarled hands vaguely to hold himself in before he curled forward like the steak of his chest and died on the sidewalk. This happened in slow motion, Franklin D. said. It took an extraordinarily long time for Grandpa to hit the ground. Franklin D. felt nothing at all, he said. Nothing at all. Except that suddenly he had to run inside to the bathroom and vomit.

A story about the Marines: when he turned eighteen, Franklin D. signed up because it was a job, the only one he could get. He was promised good pay, a uniform, status, women, the chance to become a finely tooled killing machine, an adventure to remember. He remembered, constantly, another Marine in the same company. What this other Marine used to do for a hobby on afternoons off, was to catch a squirrel or a chipmunk and skin it alive so delicately, so tenderly, with such a sharp and masterly knife, that the animal still lived and trembled in the palm of the craftsman's hand after it was totally skinned. Then the Marine would let it go.

"A thing people don't understand about the Marines," Franklin D. said, "is that once you've signed up, you realise in the very first week you want out, but you've got six years like a Mack truck in front of you. I've known guys," he said, "break their own legs to get out of combat drill. The problem with being in the Marines," he said, "is figuring out how to become a human being again when you get out. When you get out," he said, "the only people you can talk to are war vets and other ex-Marines. You're not army, you don't know how to think civilian, you're *nowhere.*

"But what do you do with all the stuff in *here*?" he demanded, knocking on his forehead. "You need a garbage truck to cart it away. If I could write stories and send them to you ..." he said. He held his head in his hands as though the clamour inside was deafening. "If I could let it *out*," he said. "If I could send you letters."

In northern Manitoba, Paddy McGee had a Cree name, and he surfaced in a ramshackle van at a tiny airport, 54°N. (I was on a reading tour of prairie outposts, heading north to the tundra.) The drive into town was long enough for two entire life histories to be exchanged, though it seemed to me that the bridge which divides strangers from kin had been crossed (in the mysterious way in which such things happen) before we got out of the airport parking lot.

It was January, deep in a bitter northern winter, about 30 degrees below zero, as I recall. The van's heater wasn't working too well, and when we spoke, our words made little white clouds in the night.

"Have you always lived here?" I asked. "Were you born here?"

As though I were Aladdin and had suddenly touched the magic spot on a lamp, he turned to me with an air of immense and barely controllable excitement. "It's there now," he said, cryptic, intense. "It's there again, where I was born. I can show you. Would you like to see?"

His eyes glittered in the bitter black air, and so, knowing that whatever this entailed was momentous, I simply said yes. He made a U-turn. Snow barrens stretched as far as the eye could see. Since we'd left the airport, not a single car had passed us either way. We two might have been alone in the universe, under the immense night sky and the stars.

The young Cree Indian (he was about twenty, I think) was lit by some inner radiance. Until this abrupt decision we had talked non-stop, but now silence enfolded us. So great was his excitement, so intense the light within, that an aura shimmered around his body and the van seemed to me full of golden fog. We swung off the road and drove over bumpy packed snow. He was steering either by stars or by instinct. By a grove of scrubby dwarf conifers, he braked sharply and we got out and stood by the shore of a frozen lake, and then he stepped a little way out on the ice and pointed.

"Out there," he said, transfigured by moon and snow and rapture.

It was the week of his birthday. His mother and grandmother had been ice fishing on the night of his birth, camped out on the lake, fishing shack tethered to the ice, unstable, when his mother's pains came upon her, suddenly, early. They were strong women, his mother and grandmother. By the light of tallow candle, on the frozen wafer that ties December to May, inside the smoke-warm shack, his grandmother delivered him into the world. In the morning she pulled the sled containing her daughter and grandson to shore.

The young Cree held his arms out to the moon and the sky and the frozen lake, embracing his history, paying reverence to life itself and to two strong women and to that birthplace which only existed for a few months each year.

He turned to me but could not speak.

I could not speak.

I was overwhelmed by the magnitude of the honour conferred on me.

In that shining moment, stamping my frozen feet on packed

snow, the stars so clear and close they could be touched, I swear I smelled the frangipani tree and Breakfast Creek.

The world spins in the margins of space, Australians float in the edges of the world, Queenslanders live in the rind of Australia, I have always drawn breath in the cracks of Queensland.

Queensland itself is fluid in shape and size, it ebbs and flows and refuses to be anchored in space, it billows out like a net that can settle without warning, anywhere, anytime. It is always larger than would appear on the map. There is no escaping it.

Here where I write, where a brilliant cobalt scar of river has just slashed the white surface of March, where the St Lawrence is still mostly skating rink but part flow, I have smelled and touched Queensland. I have woken, disoriented, to see orchids in snowdrifts. Along the bare knotted trunks of maples and hickory trees, epiphytes and creepers have run rampant. I have smelled rainforest.

Homeland is where the senses steer by instinct when the reins are let go. It is always accessible in that small space between sleeping and waking.

Down at the bottom of my yard, the St Lawrence sucks away at the base of our limestone cliffs, it plucks and thaws, plucks and thaws, subtracting from Canada here, depositing American silt there. New York State smudges the horizon. I live at the desiccating edge of things, on the dividing line between two countries, nowhere, everywhere, in the margins.

Wherever I am, I live in Queensland. I know to what brown country and to what wet rainforests my homing thoughts will fly in the moment between living and dying, when *desire shall fail, for man goeth to his long home*, and woman too, there where the evening star goes down, and where the first ones and the latecomers make temporary camp together under the violent stars.

Shining on its short stalk, the Evening Star, always there at the clay pan, at the place of the Dugong … The Evening Star goes down across the camp, among the white gum trees … It sinks there into the place of the white gum trees, at Milingimbi.

Amen.

THE END-OF-THE-LINE
END-OF-THE-WORLD DISCO

Flutie reckons it's an even chance the world will end before the shearing cuts out, and therefore they shouldn't wait, they should have the party tonight. Sure, a train is coming from Brisbane, volunteers are coming, sandbags and sandbaggers, a train's on the way, but will it arrive in time? Already vultures hover, a sure sign. When Mike leans out the pub window, their shadows blacken him and his hurricane hair whips across his face. "Hey, vultures!" he calls. He hoists his beer and gives them the finger, gives it to the helicopter pilots, to the Sydney producers, to the cameramen dangling from slings, to the whole bang lot of them. "Hey, vultures! Stuff that up your TVs and poke it!" Grinning, grinning. "Gonna be on 'The 7.30 Report' tonight, mates," he laughs, as he winds himself back inside.

"River's reached Warrabunga already." Flutie pushes the phone back across the bar. "She's coming down like a seven-foot wall, Paddy Shay says. How about another one, love?"

"Cooper's, is it?" Gladys asks, as though she hasn't been serving him beer in the Millennium Hotel every day and night for six months, as though in the last ten minutes she's forgotten every relevant detail about him.

"Drive a man to drink, Gladdie." Flutie is baffled, exasperated, because she really is waiting for an answer. She really is not certain, in spite of the small regiment of empty Cooper's stubbies at his elbow. Or maybe she can't quite believe that a man in these parts would ask for anything but Four-X, and maybe she needs confirmation each time. Or maybe, as Mike maintains, she's just *slow*; but Flutie doesn't think that's the reason. She's still standing there with her watery blue eyes looking at him but not quite seeing him, blinking and waiting.

Waiting.

"Yeah," he says, awkward. "Cooper's."

Mike rolls up his eyes, taps his forehead, grins at Flutie, but Flutie frowns. It drives him crazy, the way he feels protective of Gladys, and he's damned if he knows why, because she's no spring chicken, she's not a looker, she's skinny as a bloody fencepost, almost no tits at all. He thinks — for a reason he can't fathom out — that it's got something to do with the tired way she rubs the back of her hand across her eyes, and with that strand of faded hair which is always falling out of the loose bun she twists it into, always falling down behind her ear into a hollow of her shoulder-blade, and he always wants to brush it off her neck, tuck it into the elastic band, and let the pad of his thumb rest very lightly in the hollow below the bone. Jesus. He must be going soft in the head. It's almost frightening, that hollow, it's deep as a bloody egg cup. He wants to put his tongue in it.

She's staring at the spigot in her right hand, the spigot on the Four-X keg, having run him off a pot of draught without thinking. "Oh fuck," she says mildly. "Sorry." She reaches for a clean glass. "Cooper's, wasn't it?"

"Wake up, Australia," Mike says. "You'll miss the end of the world if you don't watch out."

"Why don't you bloody leave her alone?"

"What?"

"You heard me."

"Jesus, mate. Keep yer shirt on." There's a gleam in Mike's eyes though. Flutie with the hots, well well.

Flutie scowls, embarrassed. He knocks back the Cooper's to clear a space, start fresh. "Anyway," he says, "Paddy Shay climbed up to his roof last thing, saw the water coming. He's got the wife and kids in the ute, gonna run for it, should be here by dark. That's if he makes it. Another day, he reckons, and goodbye Charleville."

Goodbye Charleville, good riddance, Gladys thinks. She leans against the glass doors of the refrigerator and closes her eyes and sees the swollen black snake of the river nosing south. A little higher than her head, preserved as curio, is the last flood souvenir, a decade old but still a clear corroded rust-brown line, threading its way across the white enamel wall behind the stubbies: the high-water mark.

Last time, the high-water level stayed exactly there for six whole weeks. Nothing moved. Not so much as a damn cockatoo moved upon the face of the waters, and all flesh died, both of fowl and of cattle that moved upon the Queensland earth anywhere west of the Warrego. And the flood was forty days and forty nights upon the earth — so Mike says, and so Flutie says, and they can prove it from the *Courier-Mail*, though the figures were disputed in the Sydney papers — and every living thing upon the ground was destroyed, both man and cattle and crops and creeping things (except for the bloody mosquitoes and flies, it goes without saying). And only Noah O'Rourke the publican remained alive, and that they were with him in the ark of the Millennium Hotel, a regular zoo. And for forty days and forty nights the waters prevailed. Those are the nine last words on the subject from Flutie and Mike, who tell only the gospel truth.

Then Queensland unplugged her drains, glug glug. Ssschloop. There was a swift season of sucking back. The regulars haven't stopped talking about the "afterwards" party yet — there will always, damn it, *always* be an afterwards, Gladys thinks wearily. Oh, the regulars can trot out befores and afters from 1880 on, but the last afterwards party is particularly vivid. It was more or less yesterday, that resurrection party, that wild fishing-for-stub-bies-in-the-mud party, that jamboree, wangaree, rainbow time. Wheee! what a way to come home.

"This hotel," Mike will tell every visitor who leans across the bar, "the river took 'er clear down to Cunnamulla in 1990, and then she came floating home on the backwash." Hallelujah, is the standard response, and don't let the pint pot stand there. "What we got," Mike explains, "is life everlasting. What we got is the Hotel Indestructible, we gonna outlive the millennium itself in this here pub."

Gladys presses back against the slick flood-surviving glass of the Millennium Hotel's stock of beer, feels the blessed frigidaire-coolness through her cotton shift, feels it sweet as a lover against her sweaty buttocks and thighs, feels herself go heavy between the legs. The wet blunt snout of the river is past Warrabunga. Here, baby, she murmurs, moving her hips.

Wavelets slap against the mirrored wall of the disco and the dance floor is two inches awash but in any case the musicians are on an island dais. Confidence is high. Some tried to flee — in cars, on horseback — but there was nowhere to go, with all the rivers running in packs and the creeks gone brumby. Water water everywhere, it's a bloody stampede.

The mirror tiles are pocked with black holes. A glittering rind of alum peels from the damp edges and leaves streaks that might be read as a map of the watercourses that are rising in convocation. Revellers arrive and arrive. Under the watchful eye of the helicopter, trucks and utes and horses and drays are still fanning out and then fanning in again like ants, for the disco lures them and where else can they go? This is the place of refuge, the end of the line.

This is the day and the hour.

The great inland sea, vouchsafed in vision to the prophet-explorers, has come into its own, so everyone's giving up. One by one, they are turning back for the Millennium. For a while, the regulars could watch themselves on TV in the upstairs lounge. There's Paddy Shay's ute, they could say. See? With that box thing he built on the back. He's turning back, keep a Four-X good and cold for 'im, Gladdie."

But now the power has gone.

The power went hours ago.

Gladys has strung up the hurricane lanterns, and volunteers have been working in shifts to see the beer safely stowed in iceboxes on the wide upper verandahs. It's party time. No worries, mate. As for the sandbags and sandbaggers, the train was last seen, glugging at the windows, going slowly under somewhere west of Muckadilla. No question, this is the safest place to be. The beer is safe, and high time too, with the years spilling over the Warrego embankment, the years welling up and over like the zeros in an old Holden odometer, the century shifting, the party in full swing.

Oh when the saints ... plays the motley band (one trumpet, one bass, three guitars, four harmonicas tuned to four different pitches, one Jew's harp, real drums, saucepan drums, about twenty people playing the spoons) ... *go marchin' in* ... The cymbals, two rubbish-bin lids, are banged with gusto by Noah O'Rourke himself.

"Marching? We're gonna *float* across the New South Wales border," sings Mike. "We're gonna float to kingdom come. We're gonna float into the next century, mates."

Oh when the saints, booms the bar-room chorus, *go floating in* ...

"Amen," says Flutie. He watches Gladys coming downstairs with more beer. "Put that bloody tray down," he calls. "It's every man for himself now, let 'em nick up and get it for themselves." He can feel a sort of bright madness in his voice, he can see it dancing above the heads of every last one of them, tongues of fire, disaster excitement. He takes the stairs two at a time, whisks the tray from Gladys, puts it on the landing, and grabs Gladys round the waist. "Come a-waltzing with *me*, Gladdie darling."

He knows there's no way in the world she can resist him. He can feel the revving like a dynamo, the cyclone of final possibilities gallumphing down from the Gulf of Carpentaria, an irresistible force that sweeps her down the last steps, past the bar, into the swampy space around the musicians. For just a half-second he feels her body stiffen, then she moves against him and with him. They're both barefoot, everyone's barefoot, and they stomp and splash like children at a wading-pool party. Big Bill, the Maori shearer playing guitar, leans from the dais and booms the words in their ears. *Oh when the saints* ...

Go barging in, Gladys sings back, and Flutie hears again that edge of wild and dangerous pleasure.

In the mirror, he sees musicians turning into dancers, dancers leaping on stage to have a go on drums or at the spoons. If the water doesn't weaken the foundations, he thinks, the stomping and clapping will. Any minute, the hotel could slip its moorings.

Oh when the saints ... Flutie sing-shouts into the hollow in Gladys's shoulderblade.

"How come," she gasps, breathless, slapping up a fan of water with the balls of her feet, "they call you Flutie?"

"It's my baritone, my incredible bloody beautiful voice."

"Come off it."

"Hey," he says aggrieved. "Listen. You're talking to a winner of a Bundaberg eisteddfod. The nuns made me perform as a boy soprano, a fate worse than death. When me voice was breaking, I swung a punch at every kid who called me Flutie, but I never managed to beat off the name." He puts his tongue into the dip of her shoulder. "You've been here five months. Six maybe? You run away from a husband, or what?"

In the mirror, he sees her throw back her head and laugh. Her bun has come loose and all her faded red hair flies free. She cannot stop laughing. Flutie thinks they might all drown in her laughter.

Now the ground floor has been surrendered, the revelry transposed up several notches. Although it's far too hot and humid for sleeping, couples are disappearing into the rooms off the verandah. Flutie's looking for Gladys. Pacing the old verandah boards, he can hear the fizz and spit of concentrated life, it's like walking the deck beside a row of pressure cookers just before they blow. It's sensible, he thinks, telling death to fuck off. Where's Gladys?

At the verandah railing, interest in the swooping flotsam is intense. Will the milk can pass the bucking sheet of corrugated roof-iron? Will that green thing (is it the top of someone's ute?) beat the fencepost down to Corones? Will the black water kiss the verandah in one hour, two, three, tonight, tomorrow night, or never? Bets are formally laid.

"Vultures!" Mike shouts, and yes, the whirlybirds are back but what are they dangling? Not cameramen. No. It's a fat sausage-string of rubber dinghies.

They know something we don't, Flutie thinks. The water's still rising. In slow astonishment, because he has always, deep down, believed himself immortal, he says to no one: "You know, we just mightn't make it."

"Hey, Flutie!" It's Big Bill, the Maori shearer, strumming his guitar at the railing. Flutie has traded punches with Big Bill on the issue of wide combs or narrow combs for shearing. He can't believe his own life. "This is it, Flutie," the Maori says.

"We gonna make it, d'you think?"

"Dunno, Flutie. This is it, the Big Water." He plucks at the strings of his guitar. *Oh when the saints ...* "Hey, Flutie," he grins. "You remember that fight at Reardon's shed?"

A funnel of laughter descends on Flutie like a willy-willy and sucks him inside. "The combs ..." he tries to say. "We bet you Kiwis would never ..." But his voice goes spiralling upwards, round and round, faster, faster, beyond the reach of his breath and into the high whooping grace-notes of absurdity. And Big Bill enters the funnel with him, they are dizzy with glee.

"Jesus," Big Bill bleats, in pain with mirth. "You silly fuckers bet us ... You fuckers claimed that New Zealand wool ... You dumb fuckers lost your fucking *pants*."

Through the fog of vertigo and laughter, Flutie sees Gladys fishing for dinghies with a pole. He sets his compass and strikes out for her shore.

Gladys thinks that at last has come a day with real *juice* to it, a day she can sink her teeth into. God, how come the bloody water's so cold when they're all sweating like pigs from the heat? She's got it now, she's hooked one of the dinghies. She'll have to share, damn it.

What she'd really like to do is stand in the dinghy and spread her arms and descend on New South Wales like one of the Furies, singing at the top of her lungs. Dimly she senses there'd be a letdown somewhere. There always is.

"Gladys," Flutie says, encircling her from behind with his arms. "Tell me why you came here. Because there's no time left, you know. You confess and I'll confess. I wanna know the lot."

"Jesus, Flutie." She can't believe men, she really can't. Boss cocky to the very last second.

"Where'd you come from?" he persists. "Brisbane? Sydney?"

Because he can smell a city girl, yes, that's partly what's been grabbing him, that dazed state of the city slicker in the bush, that *Where am I? What am I doing here?* bemusement, he's a sucker for that.

"Brisbane," she says. "If you must know."

What will she tell him? She ticks off items in her mind: married twenty-seven years, three kids all grown up and married, Mum dying of cancer in Toowoomba; and while she sits at Mum's bedside, her old man buggers off with the neighbour's daughter. End of story.

How boring, how *embarrassing* a life is, once it slides down inside the tacky skin of words. Cheap skin, sharkskin, vulgar. Who could bear to say them? They had to be shoved away somewhere, in a suitcase under a bed. Goodbye words, good riddance; because what you felt afterwards, after the disorientation, when your clumsy tongue got free of dead explanations, was an immense and intoxicating freedom. You felt like singing your new self without any words at all.

You felt like a snake discarding the skins of past lives, sleek, unimpeded.

"When Mum died," she says absently, smiling, "I hopped on a train and bought a ticket for the end of the line."

"Amen," says Flutie.

"I didn't bring any luggage," she says. "No luggage at all."

"Amen," he says again. It doesn't matter if she tells him anything or not, they're both end-of-the-liners. Compatible histories is something he can taste, and he moves his tongue into the warm currents of her mouth.

When there's a space, she says mildly: "I don't mind fucking you, Flutie, but I'm never going back."

To a man, she means. To routine. To luggage. To intolerable ordinary life.

Then he realises, *of course*, it's her sheer indifference, her un-reachability, that's been driving him crazy.

"Hey," he says sharply. "Hey, your dinghy!" — because floating rubble, like a tank on the move, is ramming the rubber boat against the railing, ramming the lattice, ramming the shipwrecked verandah, oh Jesus, are they in the water or swamped on the deck? Chaos. He swallows an ocean. Verandah posts approach, an anchor holds, he is wrapped around something vertical and he can see her scudding out of reach, body-riding the dinghy like a surf-board queen.

"Gladysssss ...!" He dingo-howls across the water.

She waves, or so he wishes to believe. Yes, she waves.

Gladys waves. But what she is seeing is the swooping green of the mango tree in Brisbane. The leaf canopy parts for her and she keeps flying. She is on that wild delicious arc of the swing, soaring up, up, and out from the broken rope. A sound barrier breaks. There are shouts, but they reach her only faintly through the pure rush of bliss, they are a distant and wordy murmuring of bees in mangoes.

We *begged* you not to swing so high ... We told you the rope was frayed, we warned, we warned, we promised we'd fix it but you just can't wait, you can't ever wait, you foolish stubborn little girl ... you wilful impetuous ... *Buzz buzz* to reckless ears.

"I don't care! I don't care!" she shouts. She has flown beyond the farthest branch of the mango tree, she is higher than the clothes line, euphoria bears her upward, she is free as a bird. Any second now the broken legs waiting on the lawn will come rushing to meet her, but she doesn't care. This is worth it.

She waves. But all that comes back to Flutie is her laughter, the wild clear rapturous sound of a child on the last Big Dipper.

ACKNOWLEDGMENTS

Seven of these fourteen stories appeared in *Collected Stories: 1970–1995* (University of Queensland Press, 1995), which includes Hospital's first two collections (*Dislocations* and *Isobars*) plus the seven stories marked below with an asterisk.

Details of original publication of stories (sometimes in slightly different form):

*   "The Ocean of Brisbane" in *Outrider*, vol. X, 1993, no. 1 (Australia)

*   "North of Nowhere" in *Nimrod*, 1993 (USA)

    – Also included in *Best Short Stories in English, 1994*, edited by Giles Gordon & David Hughes (London: Heinemann, 1994; NY: Norton, 1994)

    – Also in France as "Au Nord de Nulle Part", trans. by Marie-Odile Fortier-Masek, in *Revue Le Serpent à Plumes*, #28, été 1995

*   "For Mr Voss or Occupant" in *More Crimes for a Summer Christmas*, edited by Stephen Knight (Sydney: Allen & Unwin, 1991)

*   "Unperformed Experiments Have No Results" in *Eureka Street*, vol. 3, no. 10, 1992 (Australia)

    – Also included in *Best Short Stories in English, 1992*, edited by Giles Gordon & David Hughes (London: Heinemann, 1992; NY: Norton, 1993)

    – Also included in *The Best of Best Short Stories 1986–1995*, edited by Giles Gordon & David Hughes (London: Heinemann, 1995)

    – Also in France as "Ces Expériences qu'on n'a jamais faites", trans. Marie-Odile Fortier-Masek, in *Revue Le Serpent à Plumes*, #23, printemps 1994

*   "Our Own Little Kakadu" in *Ormond Papers*, 1994 (Melbourne, Australia)

"Cape Tribulation" in *Westerly*, vol. 42, no. 4, 1997, pp. 16–25 (Australia)

"Flight" published in French, as a novella, under title of "L'envolée" trans. by Mimi Perrin. [Commissioned for a select literary series called "Le Miroir Etoilé"] (Paris: Editions Solal, 1995)

Subsequently published in English in *Cheatin' Heart: Women's Secret Stories*, edited by Kim Longinotto and Joanna Rosenthall (London: Serpent's Tail, 1998)

"Frames and Wonders" in *Literary Review* (USA), fall 2001 (Nominated for a Pushcart Prize)

"Nativity" in *Nimrod*, vol. 44, no. 2, summer 2001, pp. 155–71 (a finalist for the Katherine Ann Porter prize in fiction)

"Credit Repair" in *Hecate*, vol. 28, no. 1, July 2002

"Night Train" in *Antipodes*, summer 2000 (U of Texas, Austin)

*   "Litany for the Homeland" in *Homeland*, edited by G. Papaellinas (Sydney: Allen & Unwin, 1991)

*   "The End-of-the-Line End-of-the-World Disco" in *Millennium*, edited by Helen Daniel (Penguin, 1992)

–   Also included in *Best Short Stories in English, 1992*, edited by Giles Gordon & David Hughes (London: Heinemann, 1992, NY: Norton, 1994)

–   Also in France as "Club Terminus au Bout du Monde" trans. by Marie-Odile Fortier-Masek, in *Revue Le Serpent à Plumes*, #30, printemps 1996